SILVER
STALLION

ALSO BY THE AUTHOR

White Badge

SILVER
STALLION

A Novel of Korea

AHN JUNGHYO

First published in Seoul in 1986
Translated from the Korean by the author.

Copyright © 1990 by Ahn Junghyo.
All rights reserved under International
and Pan-American Copyright Conventions.
Published in the United States by
Soho Press, Inc.
853 Broadway
New York, NY 10003

Library of Congress Cataloging-in-publication Data
Ahn Junghyo, 1941-
Silver Stallion/Ahn Junghyo.
p.   cm.
ISBN-10: 1-56947-003-0; ISBN-13: 978-1-56947-003-9
1. Korean War, —1950-1953—Fiction.   I. Title.
PR9520.9.A78S5   1990
823—dc20   8939219
CIP

Printed in the United States of America

TO DR. GEORGE SIDNEY

CONTENTS

Part I

THE VILLAGE

ONE

Old Hwang flung open the gate to usher the new day into his house. The sun had not come up yet and late stars glimmered faintly in the dawn-tinged eastern sky. He could tell by their positions that this was the fourth hour. He always woke up before the roosters; he was an old man and did not need much sleep.

He took a bush-clover broom from the rice barn and started sweeping the courtyard. By the time he reached the stepping stones outside the gate, white streaks of smoke rose gently from the low earthen chimneys of the huts in the fields. The women inside were cooking the breakfast rice. Farmers trickled out of their homes one after another, each slinging a shovel or a long-handled hoe over his shoulder, to do some work before the first meal. This was the tranquil landscape the old man had watched from his gate at this early hour on summer days all his life.

Then Old Hwang glanced over at the huge columns of dark smoke rising from the town. He frowned. High in the air above Phoenix Hill black clouds of smoke hung suspended like great chunks of frozen vapor. The air raid over the town had lasted for about two hours yesterday afternoon and the buildings near the railroad station were still burning.

The farmers of Kumsan village had never considered that the war had anything to do with them. Until as recently as yesterday morning, in fact, they had hardly believed that a war was actually going on. Some of the villagers had seen Communists guarding buildings draped with red flags when they went to town to sell radishes or straw ropes. Nobody dared to go near the People's Army soldiers armed with the strange Russian rifles. But the presence of those soldiers in town was the only visible evidence of war for the villagers, although it had been three months since this war had broken out. Some townspeople said the Communist Army had come to liberate the South and unify the divided nation; others that the Reds were nothing but bloody murderers who were determined to wipe out the southern half of the nation. Confused by these conflicting rumors, the villagers listened and nodded or shook their heads half-heartedly: "Whatever you say, whatever you say."

Old Hwang spat twice to ward off evil fortune in general and went back to the rice barn, muttering, to replace the broom. The old man was vaguely apprehensive. What was happening at the town might eventually affect his village, too, but he could not believe it.

As he was drawing water at the garden well to wash himself, a sparrow twittered tentatively in the lone magnolia standing outside the earthen wall. He cleaned his teeth with salt and gargled loudly by the chest-high wall, watching the floating fog slowly recede across the rice paddies toward the river. He washed his face and sprinkled the used water in the narrow flower bed by the gate. Then he glanced again at the sky over town. Now he could see the smoke more clearly. It looked much dirtier now that the grayness of dawn had vanished from the sky.

The old man shook his head, narrowing his eyes in displeasure. If something were to go wrong with Kumsan or the other nearby villages, he would be primarily responsible because he was the county chief. A generation ago, his father had been appointed chief both by the farmers in the county and the Japanese authorities in the town, although there had never been any official election. Nobody questioned the authority of the Hwangs, the wealthiest and most educated family in the West County for the last eight generations. If a perplexing dispute arose among the farmers on this side of the two rivers, they naturally came to consult the Hwangs, to obtain their wisdom and hear their judgment. Due to their high status, the Hwangs would be the first target if the Communists took control of the West County. The merchants in town said "listed persons," those who had held public offices before the war, including policemen and village chiefs, had been arrested and even executed by the Communist cadres. Hwang had heard many incredible tales of massacre, but those tales made no sense to him and he refused to believe them. Such propaganda was liable to circulate in times of war.

The old man heard the rooster give his hoarse morning crow beyond the stable. He went over to the pen. Hens cackled noisily and expectantly on their perch, flapping their wings, as he opened the rickety plank door of the wire cage. The chickens fluttered out of the door, passed around his legs, and flocked to look for stray grains of rice. The brash, multicolored rooster pranced audaciously a little distance behind his hens. The old man chuckled at the pretentious gait of the rooster, aloof and detached like a grave patriarch; he always liked the proud ones, men and animals alike.

He entered the dusky hen house, which was fishy smelling from chicken droppings, picked up an egg from the straw-padded nest, and smiled. The egg was still warm against his palm and the smooth pleasant warmth of the eggshell reminded him of his grandson's testicles, that always felt soft and reassuring to his touch. The egg made him feel much more confident and he decided to believe that the war would not affect his world after all.

When the Japanese had invaded, tens of generations ago, the Southern Pirates paid no attention to this remote village; it had no riches to loot. The Mongol horde plundered the country several decades later, but the Northern Barbarians did not notice this secluded region. Five centuries later, Japan colonized the country for thirty-six long years, but no Japanese, not even a single soldier or policeman, had ever shown up at Kumsan village. During this period of colonial rule, collection of tax and "war-supporting materials" such as spoons and washbasins and all sorts of metal objects was undertaken in the West County by Korean petty officials dispatched from town.

The national liberation five years ago had not brought changes either. They were supposed to have been officially liberated from the Japanese Imperialists, but nothing actually happened. There was not a single incident of confrontation between the rich and the poor, the landowners and the peasants: The farmers lived on, without politics. They farmed the little land they had and produced what they needed for survival. Most were born in the West County, lived there and died there. Outsiders rarely moved into this unpromising land. At Kumsan village, time had simply stopped.

For most West County farmers, the town of Chunchon was the only outside world they ever saw. They never bothered to find out what might exist beyond it. These out-of-the-way farmers were not much impressed by the news that an American general with the queer name of *Megado*, commanding thousands and thousands of the United Nations Forces, had landed at Inchon to liberate the South Korean people. The villagers thought nothing would be changed if they were liberated once more by the famous American general.

Old Hwang did not believe it mattered too much even if his county remained unliberated. There were many things the old man could not understand about war.

Old Hwang chased the last chicken on the perch out of the pen and collected the eggs from the nests. He took the wicker basket hanging on the hook nailed into the clay wall and put the eggs, one by one, carefully into it. He brought the heavy basket to the kitchen, where his daughter-in-law, sitting on the rolled rush mattress, was burning pine branches and dry oak leaves in the oven hole under the cauldron to cook the rice, cradling her eleven-month-old son on her lap with her free hand. As white steam began to hiss out through the chink under the lid of the cauldron, she scattered the burning branches in the oven and covered the fire with ash. She removed the heavy wooden lid to see how well the rice was done. The rice was cooked just right and she replaced the lid; she had to wait half an hour longer for the compressed steam inside the cauldron to turn the grains palatably gelatinous. In the meantime, she had to prepare several side dishes. For breakfast today, she planned to serve parsley pickles, soybean paste soup and sweet potato cubes in sauce.

Old Hwang stopped by the kitchen door which was smudged by old smoke stains. He cleared his throat so his daughter-in-law would be aware of his approach. She quickly examined herself to see that she was properly dressed before bowing to him with her eyes lowered.

"Did you have a good sleep last night, Father?" She gave him the morning greeting.

"I did, I did," he said, offering the egg basket to her. "You have twelve of them this morning. How many are you going to sell today?"

She laid her son on the pile of pine branches and came up to the door from the sunken cooking area to take the basket. "We won't have anything left to sell today, Father," she said. "Kangho's mother promised to bring me a pair of cotton trousers for the child from the town. I already gave her ten eggs for the pants and she will come again this afternoon to collect another ten."

"Fine, that's fine." The old man cleared his throat once more to tell her that their conversation was over, and left.

Young Hwang was stretching himself luxuriantly by the stable when his father coughed behind him. He turned back with an embarrassed smile. "Have you slept comfortably, Father?" he said.

"Yes, my son. Going out to the field?"

"Yes, Father. I want to finish weeding the sesame patch before sunrise," the son said, removing the crossbar of the stable door. "I will take care of the broken dike after breakfast."

"You won't need that animal for weeding the sesame patch, will you?" the old man said as Young Hwang herded the ox out of the stable.

"Oh. Changsu's father wants to borrow it this morning to remove the stump of a dead tree in his back yard," the son said. "I told him you wouldn't mind."

"I don't mind," the old man said. "Just tell him to bring us some jujubes when he harvests them. We'll need many kinds of fruits for the autumn memorial service for the ancestors."

"I will, Father." The son rolled up the sleeves of his mud-caked shirt to his elbows and drove the ox out of the gate, ordering the beast, "*Iryo, iryo!* This way!"

Old Hwang watched his son and the ox hasten down the bank of the stream which ran down the middle of Kumsan village. He was proud of his only son and regretted that he did not have ten more sons like him because his first wife had died only two months after Sokku's birth from too much flux, and his second wife had been barren.

He sighed.

Once more he glanced over at the dark smoke still rising from the town. This was a morning like any other, but he sensed an overshadowing gloom. Ever since the air raid, he had not been able to shake off the fear that today might not be like so many yesterdays had been.

———•———

Laughing and chattering, five boys and a dog strode and hopped along the narrow winding path in the woods on General's Hill. In the east the sun was just coming up to bleach the sky white with late summer heat; brilliant sun rays filled the air over the patterned rice paddies and quiet river as the last thin layer of floating fog burned off. The glimmering ripples of the river sparkled like powdered glass.

In the north, the Soyang River skirted the foot of Phoenix Hill and meandered down the sandy plain like a giant turquoise serpent to define the eastern edge of West County. The North Han River branched out from the main body of the Soyang River a little upstream from the Kumsan ferry and then the two streams joined again forming a long cucumber-shaped island. Then the river disappeared into the V-shaped Kangchon valley. Phoenix Hill looked like a volcano now with dark smoke from the bombed buildings slowly rising high above its peak, but the boys were too engrossed in their expedition to notice anything beyond the dew drops shimmering like crystal beads at the tips of the pine needles along the mountain path.

The boys were cheerful because the sun was bright and the mountain air was crisp and, above all, because they were on a special expedition this morning to search for the Secret Cave. This was not the first time that the Kumsan boys had come to this hill two miles away from their village to search for the legendary cave. They searched this hill several times every year but so far had never succeeded in discovering the mythical cavern underneath a huge white rock where a great general had been born twenty generations ago. Almost all the farmers of Kumsan, Hyonam, Kamwa, Charcoal and Castle villages had come here in hopes of finding the cave at one time or another in their childhood when they had been young enough to believe in fairy tales about egg goblins and tobacco-smoking tigers. But nobody in the West County had located the secret cave yet. The Kumsan boys were determined to be the first; Kumsan was the village located nearest to General's Hill and the boys believed that the hill, along with the legend, naturally belonged to them.

The legend said that long long ago in the ancient days of the Chosun Dynasty, savage Mongols invaded the country, burned all the beautiful palaces and Buddhist temples, killed the valiant Korean warriors in droves in one fierce battle after another, and destroyed all the great cities as they marched on the capital city of Songak. At this time of impending crisis for the kingdom, the benevolent mountain spirits sent a seven-foot-tall general to this world to save the distressed king and his doomed people. This general was not born as an infant but as a fully-grown man with a three-foot-long beard cascading down his chest. His birth cry was so thunderous, the legend said, that more than ten mountains around the town collapsed while heaven and earth trembled alike in fear at the terrific bellow. At the very moment when the general flew out of the pale bleached rock, a thunderbolt shattered the frozen air into a thousand pieces and a silvery stallion with a dazzling crystal mane leaped out from the lush eastern gulch of Phoenix Hill. The silver horse galloped across the sky, over patches of rainbow-colored clouds, toward the awaiting general, who soared up into the air to mount his steed. After a deafening war cry, they galloped to the royal city to defeat the Mongols and rescue the besieged king. At each stroke of his tremendous weapon, three thousand enemy fighters fell dead before the general, like falling leaves before the autumn wind. It took only one afternoon for him to save the whole nation with his mighty sword.

For West County boys, the most fascinating part of this legend was that the white rock and the entrance to the cave were instantly covered by bushes and vanished from sight when the general left for Songak. The farmers were told by their parents, generation after generation, that the cave entrance would open again if the nation faced another major crisis that required the return of its savior, the general on the silver stallion. He did not return when the Japanese invaded and enslaved the Koreans for four decades. Perhaps that was not a big enough crisis, or the general might have been taking a very long nap at that time. Now there was a big war going on all over the country. Surely this was the time for the general's return. Maybe the cave entrance had already opened some-where in the gulch, so the general could ride out to attack the enemy.

The Kumsan boys had set out with high hopes that morning because a week earlier a woodcutter from Castle village said he had found a deep pit hidden under entangled tendrils and dense foliage in a steep ravine near Eagle Rock. It might be the entrance to the legendary cave. The woodcutter said he had also seen a part of the white flat boulder beneath the heavily intertwining leaves and branches in the pit. The Castle village boys were planning to go with the woodcutter to explore the pit soon. The Kumsan boys wanted to be the first to find the cave.

A short procession of five boys and a dog climbed the ridge and picked their way along the narrow, winding path. The dog was considered a member of the gang because it always accompanied Mansik, the boy who lived at the Chestnut House.

The sun was blazing yellow high in the sky when the five exhausted boys and the dog began to plod down the western ridge of General's Hill along the weedy pathway. They rounded a wide, dark brown boulder partly covered with moss and creepers, burrowed into tall weeds, and then appeared again at the other side of an acacia bush. Chandol, the tallest and strongest boy among them, was in the lead while Mansik and his dog trailed in the rear.

"We've been walking through the woods for four hours now, but where is the cave?" complained Kijun irritably. The stocky, short boy obviously found it very difficult to climb up and down the ridges as fast as the other boys did, and then push his way through the intermingling arrowroot tendrils and mulberry bushes that thrived on the crags among the pines. "My legs are so tired. Let's take a rest."

"You want to rest every five minutes," said Chandol impatiently, pushing an oak branch aside and stooping to pass under a low-hanging knotty pine bough. "If you can't walk fast enough, you'd better go home."

"I don't want to go home alone," said Kijun, still petulant but somewhat intimidated. "Let's all go home. It's almost noon and we'd better go and have lunch." But he immediately realized that he had put his foot in his mouth. Among the five boys, only Kangho and Kijun were sure to have lunch if they went back home; the other boys often skipped a meal because their families could not afford the noon rice every day. He quickly added, "The cave is not in this gulch. I know for sure that it's not here. We'd better go home instead of wasting any more time."

"It must be here somewhere," Chandol persisted. "You heard what the Castle villagers said."

"I don't give a hoot. Have you forgotten what we went through because of their lie last year? We searched the woods for nine days, remember, nine days, because somebody from Castle village said he had seen a boar's den in the mountain behind Hyonam village. But we didn't even catch a weasel. And my father almost killed me one night when I was late."

"I said you could go home if you want to."

"I don't want to go home *alone*."

"Then shut up and keep walking, Toad."

Kijun, who had earned the nickname of "Toad" because of his squat build and bulging eyes, grumbled, but in a very restrained whisper so that Chandol would not hear him. Chandol was the undisputed leader of the Kumsan boys, and Kijun could not afford to get on his nerves, for he wanted and needed to be in Chandol's favor all the time. Kijun tried to stay by the captain of the village boys' gang as long as he could, afraid that otherwise Mansik or Kangho would be selected as his second-in-command, if Chandol were to name one. He knew that if he went home now, alone, they would scoff at him, belittle him, and call him a fat ugly toad. But he was infuriated by the prospect of crawling up and stumbling down hills and ridges all afternoon with these dumb kids who were not bright enough to know by now that the cave had never been here in the first place and the Castle village boys had made fools out of them. Exasperated, the stocky boy whipped a wilted fir branch with the stick he carried for beating the grass to scare away hidden snakes. Dead brown needles popped off the branch and landed gently on the undergrowth. A startled quail flapped out of a nearby grove and flew away to vanish down the slope beyond a millet patch.

Mansik trailed a few paces behind Kijun, playing with his bowlegged white puppy. Behind Mansik were Kangho, a lanky, quiet boy who rarely argued with anybody about anything, and Bong, a child with long hair who had to do chores for each of them because he was the youngest of them all. Three weeks ago Bong had finally turned six, qualifying him to participate in the adventures of the older boys.

Mansik had also begun to doubt that they would be able to find the general's cave in this gulch. Not today, anyway. They had searched thoroughly but found no trace of the concealed pit or the white rock. "Maybe somebody buried it," he mumbled to himself.

"What did you say?" asked Chandol, glaring at Mansik over his shoulder. Chandol had been annoyed already by Kijun's challenge. "You said something to me, Mansik?"

"Never mind. I was talking to myself."

"About what?"

"Well, you know, the cave."

"What about it?"

Mansik did not answer. He was not sure if it was all right for him to be honest.

"What about it?" urged Chandol, stopping.

The other boys also stopped because the path was very narrow and Chandol was in the lead.

Mansik realized he did not have much choice. He said, "I wonder if the cave entrance is really here. We've searched every inch of this gulch. We couldn't have missed it. Perhaps somebody buried it."

"Why would anybody want to do such a foolish thing?" said Chandol with a sneer. "Do you want to go home, too? Sure, you can go, if you really want to. Toad'll be glad to have your company."

Mansik decided it would be wise for him to shut up. He had a lot more to lose than to gain by aggravating the angry boy who was their leader.

As Mansik did not reply, Chandol gave him another hard reproachful glare and then turned back. The five boys and the dog trudged down the narrow winding path in silence.

There was no breeze to cool the sultry air as the five boys and the dog rested beside a tobacco patch. Kijun breathed heavily through his mouth, his eyelids drooping from exhaustion. Chandol took off his sweat-soaked shirt and fanned his face with a broad tobacco leaf. Leaning against a pine stump, Mansik absent-mindedly gazed at a black butterfly with a torn wing fluttering feebly, entangled by a cobweb netted in the bramble bush on the other side of the trail. Kangho was lying on the grass beside him, sweating profusely. The fluffy dog stretched at its full length on the rocky path a little distance away from the boys.

Nothing seemed to move around them and the boys did not want to move either. Then, suddenly, the dog bristled and started to bark fretfully. Bong, who had been picking wild damson fruit further down the trail, froze. As his frightened eyes searched, he screamed, "A snake! I hear it but I can't see it. There's a snake here! Come and help me!" The dog barked frantically at the sky, jumping this way and that.

The other boys also heard the hissing sound. But it was not a snake. The sound came from the sky, somewhere beyond the mountains in the south. It sounded something like a whistle. The shrill tinny sound grew more and more distinct, coming closer and closer, fast, very fast, and the dog barked, and the sound came so fast and close that Mansik thought it must explode any moment, and it did explode. A deafening noise shattered the still silence of the mountains as if the whole earth had split into a million pieces, and Mansik momentarily thought, here it comes, the general is coming back on his silver stallion.

The five boys saw four shiny objects in a diamond formation screech into the open sky from beyond the southern peaks. The thundering birds blasted across the sky over their heads, their metallic white wings shining in the sun, and then swished away towards the town.

"Hit the dirt!" Chandol shouted, throwing himself flat within a bush-clover grove. "Take cover!" he yelled again, crawling on his belly deeper into the grove. "They're airplanes!"

Now the boys understood what was going on. They scattered, yelling and blubbering in fear, to hide themselves from the fiery flying machines.

Four more airplanes, and then another four, spurted out from beyond the southern peaks and whizzed off to the town, trailing white tracks of vapor behind them.

Mansik grabbed Fluffy and hurled himself into a sunken furrow in the tobacco patch; Kijun rolled into a thorny bramble bush, whining in a terrified voice; Kangho remained lying flat on the trail, covering his head with his hands; Bong, whimpering, crawled back down the trail the way they had come like a stunned fish swimming the wrong way, its sense of direction lost.

When the airplanes vanished, silence suddenly returned. In the eerie quiet, the bewildered boys scrambled to their feet one by one. They heard the faint rumble of distant explosions—*whum*—*whum*—*whum*—beyond General's Hill.

"Do you hear that? Do you hear that?" Kijun gasped, rolling his terror-stricken wide eyes. "It's an air raid. They're bombing again. Maybe they're bombing Kumsan."

"Why should they bomb our village?" asked Kangho, his eyes flashing. He did not seem to be too sure of his own words. "Nobody is fighting any war at our village, you know."

"They must be bombing the town again," Chandol said wisely, dusting his pants. "There're Reds in town and it's *them* that the planes are after."

"We'd better go home now," said Mansik, putting his dog down. Nobody objected to Mansik's suggestion.

The bombing continued even at night. The villagers of Kumsan and Hyonam flocked to the riverbank early in the evening, many of them skipping supper, to watch scarlet and black pillars of flame and smoke belch up from the town. Several searchlights streaking up from the provincial capital building at the foot of Phoenix Hill swept the night sky, crisscross, to ferret out the invisible planes that droned and whizzed around in the dark space, spitting out fire again and again. Orange flames gushed up anew from the darkened town following each explosion blast, while the ground artillery burped and shrieked in a frenzy.

"How can they see the buildings in the dark from high up there?" said Yom, the stumpy ferryman, sitting in front of his cabin astride the plank bench for waiting passengers. "I guess someone is giving signals to them with a torch from the ground."

"What will we do if they drop the bombs at our village by mistake?" said Han, the mill owner, sitting next to the boatman on the bench, resting his chin on the long handle of his hoe.

"But all the bombs do fall in the town," the boatman said with apparent admiration. "Maybe the bombs have some sort of eyes that can see in the dark."

"I've never heard of bombs that have eyes," the miller said.

"Anyway this war will be over in a few days," said Kijun's uncle, standing under the willow tree beside the bench with his hands folded on his chest. "Nobody can survive such a bombing very long."

Flames flashed up suddenly near the railroad station, subsided for a moment as if to take a breath, and then spurted in all directions with renewed ferocity, reddening the sky. "There it goes again," said the boatman, rising, and some twenty Kumsan villagers, who had gathered around the ferry, silently watched.

The villagers who had been to the town that morning said the police station and many other big buildings occupied by the People's Army, as well as half the stalls at Central Market, had been completely destroyed. And dead bodies were scattered everywhere on the downtown streets. There was urgency in their voices as the farmers discussed what they had seen or heard about the bombardment, because now they knew the same thing might happen to them.

When the bombing started the previous evening, Kijun's uncle had been playing flower cards with three carpenters at the town brewery. At first, he said, they heard that strange hissing sound, the eerie distant *shu-shu* whistle, and then an earthquake-like noise at a deafeningly close range, and everybody in the room instinctively threw themselves to the floor. "It kept coming and coming, explosions, in all directions. Wham! Wham! WHAM!" he went on. "We could not stay in the house any longer because the ceiling fell down on us, with broken tiles and dust and everything. So we ran out to the street. Many houses were engulfed by smoke and clouds of dust, and people were running away, helter-skelter, stumbling and screaming. They were running, running, running with their children in their arms, shrieking and whimpering and calling, their hair all in tangles and their clothes torn to flying shreds. They did not know where they were going, where they should go, or what they were supposed to do. They ran back and forth going nowhere. And I saw a woman whose arm had been just blown off," he said. "Blood was gushing out of the ragged stump of what was left of her arm. She was digging in a pile of dirt on the curb, sobbing, 'Where's my arm? Where's my arm?'"

The villagers did not believe everything Kijun's uncle said because he was such a blowhard, but those who found it absolutely necessary to go to town that day planned to leave as soon as possible so that they would not have to risk the dangers of a nocturnal air raid.

The Kumsan farmers were the most nervous among the West County villagers about the continual bombing and what might happen next, because their village was located nearest to town. When the villagers discussed what they had watched from the riverbank or heard in the town, their voices grew shaky from anxiety. Some believers in folk religion said nothing would remain of this earth but piles of dirt and ashes if so many planes kept coming and pouring down so many bombs; they worried that the world was about to end in flames and explosions, before the creation of a new universe, fulfilling the ancient prophecy.

"We have to do something before the war crosses the river and destroys us," Kangho's father, the miller, said to Young Hwang, watching the burning town from the ferry. "We have to stop such a terrible thing from happening."

"But what can we do?" said Kijun's uncle. "Shoot down the planes with slingshots?"

Young Hwang said nothing, for he was not supposed to have any answers. Only his father, the county chief, was authorized to have opinions and make important decisions about serious matters involving the whole community. When they faced a big problem like this, it was always Old Hwang who gave them helpful instructions and valuable advice, and the farmers always respected and followed the old man's judgments. But the county chief did not seem to have any ideas as to how to stop fire pouring down from the sky either. Without any guidance, the only thing the villagers could think of was to hide underground. After the air raids continued the second night the Kumsan villagers began to dig bomb shelters in or around their houses. Then they thronged the riverbank at dusk once again to watch the burning town.

When the planes did not come in the daytime nor at night on the third day, the farmers found themselves strangely restless. The lull only increased their anxiety because it might be nothing but a momentary reprieve before a more astonishing event—something totally destructive, fatal. The villagers felt inexplicably relieved when the bombing was resumed.

The five boys and Fluffy met in the afternoon under the tall aspen tree on the hillock behind the ferry and sat down on the grass to watch the town burning again. The planes swooped, flipping their shiny wings, to strafe or drop bombs, and then soared again like hunting kites after snatching their prey, through the patches of white flak smoke. To the boys, the flying machines looked like tiny specks acrobatically scuttling around among kernels of popcorn floating in the air.

"I didn't know there were so many airplanes in the world," said Chandol with a stupefied expression, pressing his cheek to the aspen bark. "Maybe more than fifty planes have bombed the town in the last several days."

"Seems *they're* really coming," said Kangho, his hand patting Mansik's dog but his eyes attentively following the planes.

"Who is coming?" Mansik asked.

"The United Nations Army, of course, who else?" Chandol said with a slight sneer. "Haven't you heard anything about General Megado and his U.N. warriors coming to liberate us?

"You must have heard *something* about the army of many countries, Mansik. People talk about them all the time."

"Soldiers from sixteen countries are coming to save us, they say," Kangho explained.

"Really?" said Kijun, who had been standing on his knees to look over the tops of the potato plants at the town. Then he added, disbelieving, "I didn't know there were so many countries in the world. What countries are they, anyway?"

"America, Pillipin, Toiki, Belgi . . ." Kangho said. "I don't know all the names."

"*Belgi*? That's a very funny name," said Bong, who had been squatting like a partridge a little distance off from the other older boys. "*Belgi* means fleas, doesn't it? Are they sending flea soldiers to liberate us?"

"But that's the name," Kangho said, somewhat dubious himself. "And all those foreign soldiers have *bengko*, they say."

"*Bengko?* What's *bengko*?" Bong asked again.

"*Bengko* means 'big nose,'" Chandol explained. "*Bengko* are foreign soldiers with their noses this big." He pressed his right cheek to his shoulder and stretched out his arm at its full length to imitate an elephant's trunk.

"That big?" said Bong, frightened. "How can people have such big noses?"

"I don't know because I've never seen them," said Chandol. "But there's no doubt they do have huge noses, because that's what all the town folks say."

"Did you hear it yourself?" Bong asked.

"No. But Jun's uncle did. Right, Toad?"

"Yes, that's what my uncle told me," Kijun said.

"They must be a mighty army, anyway. The U.N. Forces, I mean," Mansik said. "Look at all those planes. The Reds certainly don't have a chance against them."

"The town will be very crowded when all sixteen countries of them arrive," said Bong, blinking his eyes, puzzled.

"I guess the Reds will start running away soon," Mansik said, wetting his dry lips with his tongue tip.

Then, frowning with sudden fear, Chandol said, "If all of them run away to the north and the war ends today or tomorrow, we may never have a chance to see a Red."

As if on cue, the four boys stared tensely at Chandol. They knew what their captain meant. Ever since the first days of the war, the boys had been wondering what kind of persons the People's Army soldiers were; they had never seen a Red because they had not been permitted to go to the town after their school had closed down. The villagers said red flags flew on the roofs and at the gates of all important buildings in the town and the Communist soldiers armed with Chinese rifles and Russian submachine guns drove around in splendid automobiles magnificently decorated with vines and leaves. Chandol had been hoping that some day they could go to town and watch all the exciting war stuff going on there. And now the National Army was coming back with all the armies in the world to drive away the Reds! There would be a great battle on Phoenix Hill or somewhere by the river between the Reds and the *bengko* army, no doubt. Chandol was determined to see that fight.

Two airplanes zipped down to the river upstream, red smoke and fire mushroomed up near the Soyang Bridge. The boys could hear a distant boom a moment later. Chandol, biting his lips, narrowed his eyes to scan the remote world beyond the rivers.

"We must go there," Chandol murmured as if to himself. "We must. If we don't go there now, we will never see a war."

"My parents won't let me go to the town. But I really want to see the Reds," Kijun said, obviously frightened but trying to convince the others that he was the second bravest boy of them all. "Don't you want to see what the real Reds are like, Bong?"

Bong winced. "Not really," he said. "They must look like a sorcerer's monster. Red all over, you know."

"My father says they aren't actually any redder than we are," Kangho said, swatting a fly on his sweaty neck with his palm. "My father saw several of them when he went to town."

"Why do they call them Reds, then?" Mansik asked.

"No one knows," Kijun said. "Maybe sometimes their skin turns red or something."

"We have to see what the Reds are really like," said Chandol. "We have to go there before it's too late."

TWO

The first breath of autumn had begun to blow over the West County. Ollye, Mansik's mother, felt the early morning chill against her skin as she came out of her room; the sun had not risen yet. A silky veil of mist crawled under the willows along the stream traversing Kumsan village. She listened for a moment to see if Mansik and Nanhi, his little sister, were still asleep in the other room and then stepped down to the yard. Fluffy hopped from behind the chimney and followed her to the kitchen, wagging his tail. She built a fire in the oven hole with dry twigs and leaves. While the breakfast rice was boiling, she went to the back yard and cleaned the hoe and the bamboo rake she had used the previous afternoon on the weeds which thrived outside the fence of Paulownia House. She stood the clean tools neatly in a row beside a sickle against the earthen wall and then went out of the house with a broom and the dog to sweep the footpath leading from the road to her thatched hut. When the morning chores were done, she stretched her back to take a brief rest and looked along the narrow patch of green onions and all around at the golden patterns of the rice paddies. When her eyes reached the road sloping down to the ferry, Ollye quickly turned back to go into the house and sweep the front yard; she was afraid to look at the town beyond the river.

Presently the sun rose over the rolling skyline of the eastern hills. Here and there scarecrows stood guard, sunk in the yellow expanse of rice up to their chests. A soft breeze stirred the endless strings of tin "bells" that had been hung on poles in the rice paddy dikes to scare away crop-stealing birds. Made of crooked nails in empty cans, they clattered as the wind turned them. In these few remaining days of summer, the forsythia around the onion patch looked like a species of bleached death. The dancing cosmos and scarlet salvia blossoming in the back yard of the Chestnut House were signs of autumn.

Mansik's house, called the Chestnut House because the tallest chestnut tree in West County stood by its twig-woven gate, was located at the end of the footpath lined with rose moss some fifty yards away from the log bridge. It was right next to the ferry. The stream flowed only a few yards in front of it and at night when the whole village turned quiet after the farmers had gone to bed early to save expensive lamp oil, Mansik's family could hear the gurgling noise of the water. Chestnut House did not have its own well and Mansik's mother washed almost everything—her face, clothes, the rice—at the stream. She used the well in the Hwangs' courtyard only for their drinking water.

The well was not the only thing for which Mansik's family depended on the Hwangs. Three generations of Mansik's family had been provided for by the Hwangs in one way or another. Mansik's grandfather had been a servant to Old Hwang's father until slavery was abolished by the Japanese colonial rulers in the nineteenth century. Even after the social reformation, Mansik's grandfather lived at the Hwangs' for quite some time, although he was paid by the month instead of receiving an annual sum and everybody was strictly instructed not to call him "the servant" but "the house manager." But Master Hwang did not give him any land

23

to sharecrop. He needed to retain at least one of his four servants, preferably the most obedient and diligent one, because he could not shed his habit of keeping someone at hand to run and bring him a toothbrush or deliver a message to a charcoal-maker.

It was Master Hwang who gave Mansik's father the aristocratic name of Kim Indong instead of a common rustic one like "Pau" (Rocky) or "Tolswe" (Stone and Steel) when Mansik's grandfather finally moved out of the Paulownia House, got married and had a son. However, Mansik's father rarely had a chance to use that dignified name (written in Chinese letters) because he also was a servant to the Hwangs most of his latter life and nobody needed or bothered to express any great respect for him; they simply called him "Mansik's Father" or just "Kim." Yet when Indong, in turn, became the father of a son, he, too, consulted Old Hwang as to the naming of the boy. The old man told Kim to call the child Mansik, meaning, in Chinese, "Maturity and Solidity."

At the time of Mansik's birth, Indong lived in a riverside mud hut at Kamwa village, fishing and sharecropping a bit of land provided by Old Hwang. Then, one summer, most of his corn patch was washed away during a torrential rain. Indong also lost his fishing boat. And the roof of the mud hut collapsed. He searched downstream for several days after the swollen muddy river had ebbed only to find the broken half of his shattered boat washed ashore on the shingle at Paegyang village. Having lost land and boat at the same time, Indong had no way to support his family. He had no choice but to move back to Kumsan, build a kitchen and two rooms onto the community hearse shed next to Paulownia House, and settle down there for good.

Since then the Kims had worked virtually as house servants for the Hwangs. They had worked hard enough to be able to buy a little piece of land on which to plant sesame or cayenne pepper. They might have bought even more land and cherished some hopes for the future if Indong had not spotted a cow floating in the flood one fateful summer day. He could not resist this unexpected opportunity. The animal could buy them quite a few handsome rice paddies right away, if he could rescue it. The villagers on the riverbank tried to stop him because the swollen current was very rapid, but Indong would not listen. He swam out into the river in the pouring rain, somehow put his rope around the cow's neck, and struggled with the animal in the water for about half an hour, until he was completely exhausted and went under.

After her husband's death, Ollye took over his domestic chores at the Hwangs'. Now Mansik was nine years old and big enough to help her with some work, but she could not find enough to do in the village to feed and clothe her son and daughter properly. Last fall Ollye had been forced to sell her sesame patch back to the Hwangs for three bags of rice because she had nothing to feed her two children during the slack winter season. If Old Hwang had not sent her some free barley or potatoes occasionally, she could never have managed. It had become a habit for her to glance over at Paulownia House first thing in the morning in the vague hope that Old Hwang would call her over and give her some work. This morning she glanced over at the house expectantly because she knew the Hwangs would need some hands to dig potatoes on their large patch near General's Hill.

Paulownia House, about thirty steps away from Chestnut House, was also called "the Rich House" or "the Scholars' House." The name Paulownia came from the huge shade tree that the old man had planted by the northern fence next to the well in the year of Sokku's birth to celebrate the arrival of a precious son in a family which had had few sons for several generations. This big house with its tiled roof and brass-decorated gate was the only place in the county where farmers could find books, ink slabs, writing brushes and other rare scholarly objects handed down by the Confucian students of earlier generations. Whenever she looked up at the majestic tiled roof of the Paulownia House, Ollye felt hopelessly small. The appearance of the house intimidated her so much that she always winced when she entered it or went to draw drinking water at the well.

When they moved to Kumsan from Kamwa, Indong did not dig a well for his own family because he thought it was not necessary; Lady Hwang told them it was perfectly all right for the Kims to use the Hwangs' well because they were like her own family. Indeed Indong and Ollye were a part of the Hwangs then; they went over to the Paulownia House almost every day to work and the two houses were located so near each other that Old Hwang would only have to open the door of his room and call to summon anybody at the Chestnut House.

But the situation changed with Indong's death. Ollye felt it was not proper for a widow from another house to draw the first bucket of water for the day when nobody in the Hwang family had used the well yet. She tried to go to the well as late as possible in the mornings, but she could never be sure that someone in the family had preceded her even if she went almost at noon. Her trips to the Paulownia House were even more uncomfortable after the death of Old Hwang's wife. Old Hwang offered the main room in the house to his son and daughter-in-law because the biggest room should be occupied by a couple, and moved his quarters to the guest room by the gate. Ollye was afraid that the old man might hear her approaching and open the outside door to see the young widow enter his house early in the morning, perhaps leading a train of evil spirits. She tried to draw water in the afternoons, but sometimes she worked from sunset to dusk. She could not go in the evening either, because a woman was not supposed to visit after dark.

She also felt guilty visiting the Hwangs for free drinking water now that the Paulownia House had practically stopped giving her any domestic chores. Ollye and Indong used to take care of most of the housework for the Hwangs because the old lady had suffered from a chronic lung disease. She would gasp, wheezing painfully, if she did so much as mop a room or move the mortar a yard, so she had needed Ollye for many hours a day. Ollye had pickled their cabbages and turnips every kimchi-making season, boiled beans to make soy sauce or hot pepper paste, peeled the skin off the persimmons to dry for winter snacks, and washed and mended clothes, while Indong had removed the thorny burrs and packed chestnuts in straw bags, collected twigs and leaves in the woods with a rake to store for use as tinder during wet weather, twined straw ropes until his palms were cracked and done hard labor in the fields as well. Sometimes even Mansik had been summoned by the old man to be given such minor tasks as keeping the chickens out of the vegetable patch.

When the lady of the house passed away about six weeks before Indong's drowning, Old Hwang had wanted his son to get married quickly, for there should be at least one woman in a family to bring warmth to the house. A county matchmaker soon found a very healthy young girl from Toktuwon village for Young Hwang's bride; both Old Hwang and his son deeply appreciated the virtue of good health in a woman, for they had gone through enough unhappiness and inconvenience on account of Lady Hwang's weakness and constant illness. The Toktuwon Woman was certainly healthy. In fact, she was so healthy and strong as to distress Ollye. This young woman worked so hard and fast that Mansik's mother lost almost all employment from the Paulownia House. The Toktuwon Woman single-handedly took care of the domestic chores as well as a large part of the field work, and rarely, only when she was too busy to do all the work by herself, did she ask Ollye to come over to help her for an hour or two. That was why Ollye was so worried about the coming winter.

As Ollye was going back to the kitchen after disposing of Fluffy's droppings in the onion patch, Mansik emerged from his room, rubbing his eyes. With a loud yawn the boy entered the kitchen, sucked his index finger to wet it with spit, pressed the finger on the small pile of salt in a cracked little saucer at one corner of the cooking board, and brushed his teeth with the salted finger.

"Do you have any work to do for the Rich House today?" Ollye asked routinely, opening the lid of the cauldron to check the boiled rice.

"Today, I have," said Mansik cheerfully, taking the towel hanging on the kitchen wall to go down to the stream to wash. "Old Hwang told me to go to Charcoal village, take his ox to carry the load of charcoal and graze the animal on the way back home."

"It may take the whole day if you have to make the trip with the ox."

"Not more than a half day, Mother. I am leaving after noon."

Fluffy hopped back and forth playfully circling around Mansik as the boy walked out to the footpath. "I see Chandol's mother coming," he called to Ollye in the kitchen as he went down to the stream.

Old Hwang sent his son for Kangho's father and told the miller to go to Chunchon and find out what he could about the progress of the war. These days the old man sent Han to town for information more and more often; Kim Indong had run such errands when he was alive, but the miller did them now. Han spent all morning in the town and came back late in the afternoon to report what he had observed to Old Hwang.

When he returned home, the miller told the same story to his wife, who showed no interest at all in the gory tale of dead bodies and gutted buildings along the downtown streets, until he mentioned in passing the destruction of the National Grange storehouse located next to Chunchon Railroad Station, where the incoming grain from the nearby counties was kept until it was shipped to the big cities.

"You mean the granary was bombed, too?" Kangho's mother asked, suddenly alert.

"I already told you about it, didn't I? I saw the building on my way down to the town ferry."

"Was it on fire?"

"No, it wasn't burning, but half of the roof and the walls had collapsed."

"How about the rice?"

"Rice?"

"When I went to Castle village the other day, I heard some farmers talking about the truckfuls and truckfuls of rice that the People's Army had confiscated. They took rice from every village in South County and piled it up in the Grange storehouse. If the granary was destroyed by bombing, what happened to that rice?"

"Oh, that," the miller said. Bags of rice and barley had rolled down and burst open on the ground, the grain spilling out all over the place, he explained. Some townspeople had gathered with baskets and sacks to take away the abandoned rice, but did not dare to go near the collapsed walls because Communist soldiers armed with submachine guns were standing guard around the ruin to protect their military provisions.

"The Red soldiers?" she said doubtfully. "But you said they had started to run away to the north early yesterday evening, didn't you?"

"Some of them did, but there are still quite a lot of them left in the town," the miller said. "I saw a dozen soldiers guarding the storehouse until their trucks come to take away the rice. But the townspeople are waiting, hoping that the People's Army may leave at least some of the spilled rice behind."

"If the World Army is really arriving in a day or two, the Reds will have to leave tonight," said Kangho's mother, as if to herself, calculating. "Or tomorrow morning at the latest."

Realizing what his wife was scheming, the miller warned, "Don't even dream of going to town to get that free rice, woman. The Reds are now as mad as rabid dogs because they are losing the war, and at this very moment, they say, they're killing everybody in sight in many towns, out of sheer anger. If you hang around the storehouse, they might just start shooting and. . . ."

She had experienced too much poverty in her childhood, surviving on nothing but potatoes and corn for months, to give any heed to his warning. Now the Hans were quite well off, running the only rice mill in West County, and some villagers suspected that the miller had secretly bought rice paddies and vegetable patches here and there, and the Hans were even richer than the Rich House these days, but she would never be rich enough to overlook any morsel she could get for free. At least she had to see the granary with her own eyes.

Without telling her husband, Kangho's mother sneaked out of the mill about an hour later, went over to the widow who lived with her six children next door, and briefly explained about the free rice piling up in the street. The two women headed for the town. They came back so late that although they shouted and screamed for more than half an hour the boatman, sound asleep on the opposite shore, did not hear them. They might have spent the whole night on Cucumber Island if the worried miller, suspecting his wife had gone for the rice after all, had not come to the ferry around eleven o'clock to check with Yom.

Both women, of course, wanted to go back to town for more rice but Kangho's mother had to stay home; the miller beat her with a broken piece of old conveyor belting until she foamed at the mouth for ignoring his warning and swore that he would kill her if she left the mill by so much as one single step. The neighbor woman went back to the ferry at midnight and woke the boatman up to take her across the river again, but Yom refused. A woman without a husband was a half person, and few people respected a widow's wish. The widow had to wait until daybreak.

Chandol's mother found out about this when she went to the ferry very early to take a dozen bamboo baskets she had made to her sister-in-law, who ran a general store at the Central Market, so that she could return home before the day's work began at the rice paddies. She met the widow at the bench before the boatman's cabin and they waited together for a male passenger to arrive. Yom, like any other boatman, never took a woman as the morning's first passenger because it would bring him bad luck; shops, inns, bathhouses, and all other public places never served a woman as their first customer for the same reason. While they waited for the boatman, the widow told her what had happened the previous night, and Chandol's mother hurried back to the village to deliver this good news to some of her friends.

"The widow said rice is abandoned in heaps and piles on the street for anyone to take, but it won't last too long if everybody swarms there," Chandol's mother said. "Don't you think we should hurry and take our share before it's too late?"

Ollye glanced over at the rice jar buried in a dark corner of the kitchen. The rice remaining in the jar was only one knuckle deep. What would she feed Mansik and her three-year-old daughter Nanhi during the long cold season?

"Mansik," she called. "You go into the room and tie Nanhi to the door handle. I'll put away the cooked rice so that we can have breakfast when we come back."

"Come back?" Mansik said.

"We are going to town. Hurry."

"I guess I'll take my boy along with me, too," said Chandol's mother.

The word that the miller's wife and her widowed neighbor had brought rice from the granary got around among the Kumsan villagers. By the time Ollye, Chandol's mother and the two boys went to the ferry, a small throng of villagers was waiting for the boat to come back from the island. The crowd increased as time passed and the boatman had to skip his breakfast because of the women constantly howling at him to hurry. More than twenty Kumsan women had brought rice home from town before breakfast, and by this time the news had reached Hyonam and Castle, too. The boatman was furious because nobody listened to him when he shouted that it was dangerous for them to rush into the boat all at the same time, that the boat would capsize and sink if anybody else came aboard, that he had to stop to take a breath for five minutes, just five minutes.

Except for some young boys, however, very few male villagers joined this column of human ants making trips to the granary. Men were hesitant to go to town for two reasons. First, the farmers feared that they might encounter the Communist soldiers, who, it was rumored, recruited every man in sight under sixty to join the People's Army to fight against the pursuing World Army. The Communists executed anyone resisting the conscription order on the spot. The other reason they were reluctant to go was that a proud man would not do certain things, such as begging or stealing, even if he starved to death. They knew the rice was abandoned on the street, but they did not want anybody to see them taking Communist rice. They stayed home and pretended that they did not notice their wives going to town.

Women did not care about pride or dignity, because only men were supposed to possess these qualities. Women could not afford to starve to death on account of anything as absurd as honor.

When Ollye, Chandol's mother and the two boys reached Chunchon Railroad Station, the townspeople were swarming around the National Grange storehouse like bees collecting around peeled persimmons spread on a mattress to dry. More than half the rice was already gone. Mansik glanced at the column of people streaming back and forth along the road. Most of them were heading back to the town. The whole column looked like one big golden centipede moving away from the granary, only moving legs visible under the straw sacks, hemp bags or large vessels being carried on heads or backs. Some families were loading sacks on the small carts they had brought, and some women, for whom a rice sack was too heavy, charged into the turbulent granary with kitchen knives in their hands, stabbed open the bulging stomach of a straw sack, and let the white rice pour out of the opening into their baskets or bags. Inside the granary it was as noisy as a night pond alive with mating frogs in summer. Young and old women scooped and stuffed the rice into their pails and buckets, bamboo and wicker baskets, their legs sunk in grain up to their shins.

"What are you waiting for? Fill your bag quickly!" shouted Chandol's mother, looking back at the two boys, who stood in a daze amidst the pandemonium. With her open palm she began to scrape the rice into the bag she was holding.

"This is really something," said Chandol, scooping up the rice with his gourd dipper. "Look at these people. Just like maggots thriving in a rotting corpse."

Mansik knelt down on the grains, that slipped under him like sand, clamped the opening of his bag between his teeth and pulled in the rice with both hands.

"Seems they're taking everything in sight," said Mansik, tilting his head to point at a thin woman in her fifties, who had just hurried out of the stationmaster's office, hugging a tall grandfather clock in her arms. The townsfolk were looting not only the granary but the neighboring railroad station building as well. Chandol saw two middle-aged women dragging a plank desk out of a station warehouse, followed by an old man carrying a sawdust stove on his shoulders. The boys even spotted a young woman stealing cabbages from a patch behind the granary.

"The whole town is crazy," Chandol whispered to Mansik, knotting the top of his bag. "I heard some women over there a minute ago say the Reds left a lot of confiscated goods behind. At the buildings they've abandoned there are more valuable things than a lousy sack of rice. And then the women left . . ."

All of a sudden, everybody started to run away, the women clustering on top of the rice pile sliding down backwards in panic, the whole mountain of grain crumbling with them like a sand castle washed away by a big breaking wave. The women fled desperately, screaming, some of them abandoning their bags or baskets. Mansik and Chandol and their mothers, puzzled, stood there, not knowing why everybody else was running away so frantically. Then somebody shouted "Air raid!" and they finally understood. Although the two boys and their mothers had not noticed it, the townspeople had experienced enough bombing to instantly recognize, even amid all the other noise, the faint purr of the bombers coming over the mountains. "Air raid!" women shouted, fleeing breathlessly. Some tripped and tumbled down, their baskets bouncing and rolling and spinning on the sidewalk, and a little lost child wept by a telegraph pole, her nose bleeding. Hemp bags and wooden receptacles were abandoned on the street, spilt grain lay on the pavement like the bleached remains of cow dung. A woman, carrying her baby on her back, threw herself into a roadside turnip patch, several women blindly ran into the open field, and several others rushed back into the granary to hide behind the rubble of the demolished wall. The old man threw the heavy sawdust stove away and ran for his life.

The two boys and their mothers dug into the rice piles because they did not know what else to do. Now Mansik heard the airplanes at last. Snoring slowly and monotonously, a formation of twelve breezed in over Saddle Mountain from the direction of Hongchon. These planes were very big and each had four propellers. A dozen women lying exposed on the road, too frightened to run any more, wept and shrieked louder and louder as the planes came nearer and nearer. Her mother finally found the little lost girl with the nosebleed and both of them, hand in hand, jumped into the cabbage patch to seek shelter. Everybody hiding or fleeing or screaming in the fields or on the road or behind the collapsed granary wall waited for the bombing to begin.

The airplanes reached the sky over the town but did not drop any bombs; they kept on flying and slowly vanished over the northern mountains in the direction of Hwachon.

Mansik craned his neck out of the rice to peek around like a cautious turtle. He was breathing heavily, bathed in sweat. The women who had been hiding behind the demolished wall looked at one another and asked in surprise and disbelief:

"Why didn't they bomb us?"

"What's happening now?"

"They passed the town, I guess, because they know the People's Army is no longer around."

"That must be the reason."

The townsfolk who had scattered quickly gathered again at the granary and continued to fill their bags and sacks much faster than before. The old man returned to claim his sawdust stove.

"These planes looked very strange," Mansik said to Chandol. "They are different from those we saw the other day."

"Haven't you seen those planes before?" asked a town boy who had just started to fill his pail beside them.

"No. I've never seen such big planes before," said Mansik.

"They are called B-29s," the town boy stated, importantly. "A B-29 has four propellers. The plane with one propeller is called Mustang.

And you've seen the strafers that have something like sweet potatoes attached to their wing tips, haven't you? Those are Spanglers."

Their conversation was interrupted by Ollye, who asked Mansik to lift her hemp bag and place it on top of her head. "Let's go home before other planes show up, Mansik. I want to get out of this place as quickly as possible," Ollye insisted. "Whether they bomb us or not, I just hate that piercing sound. You'd better hurry too, Chandol's mother."

The four of them waddled out of the granary, carrying their rice, and hurried along the alley which was littered with debris, burnt shreds of clothes and broken cement slabs from previous bombings. Then they skidded down the steep path to the Soyang River. Ollye kept urging them to hurry, hurry.

When, breathlessly, they crossed the shingle and reached the ferry, three Hyonam women were loading their rice and barley onto the boat. The wall-eyed boatman watched them offhandedly, standing aside and puffing at his long bamboo pipe. When all seven were aboard with their booty the old man pushed off with a long pole. They heard two or three automatic weapons burp intermittently in the direction of Kongji Creek.

"What is that? What is that?" Chandol's mother gasped in a frightened voice. "What was that noise?"

"The main force of the People's Army in Chunchon and on Phoenix Hill has fled to Hwachon, but another unit is retreating from Wonju. Maybe some of them are fighting over there," the boatman explained calmly.

The passengers in the boat kept silent. The boat was loaded so heavily that the water almost reached the place where Mansik was sitting. The seat of his pants was getting wet. When Mansik tried to move forward to the bow, Chandol grabbed him by the elbow and signaled with his eyes for Mansik to come closer so that he could tell him something privately. Mansik leaned toward him.

"When we get back home," Chandol whispered so that their mothers would not hear him, "you go and tell the boys to come to the sand under the bridge right after lunch hour."

"What for?"

"You know what for."

Of course Mansik knew. Chandol was planning to come back to town with the other boys for some sort of adventure. "But I won't have time to find all the boys and pass the word," Mansik said. "Maybe I won't even have time to come to the bridge at all."

"Why not?"

"I have to go to Charcoal village on Old Hwang's errand today."

"It won't take more than two hours for you to make the trip to Charcoal, if you really walk fast," said Chandol. "I will tell Toad to pass the word to other boys."

———— • ————

Bong watched the four boys strip themselves by the sand dune near where the village stream joined the river. They could not use the boat because the boatman would tell their parents. Squatting on the white clean sand, he looked at the river and the boys in turn, and then down at the clothes strewn before him, crestfallen. He had been ordered by Chandol to stay behind and watch them. If Bong had been as good a swimmer as the others, Chandol might have allowed him to join the expedition; they did not really need anybody to look after clothes that they could easily hide in a bush or bury in the sand.

Bong threw a pebble into the river. He was sad because he was going to miss the big adventure. To go to watch a real battle fought by grownups was something far greater than going to a hill to pick acorns and chestnuts or to a waterfall to swim. It was an adventure even greater than the expedition to search for the General's Cave, or the Autumn War the Kumsan boys fought every year against the Castle village boys. Bong wanted to watch the grownups' war.

Peeling his pants from his fat legs with a grunt, Kijun glanced over at the unhappy little boy. "Keep a good watch over the clothes," he said. "You know we'll punish you if you lose any of them."

Bong nodded dejectedly. The boys would not only watch the war and the real soldiers, but they would steal clocks and shoes and toys and marbles and everything from the empty houses and shops in town, too. Chandol said the whole town was open for anybody to loot. And Bong was the only boy at Kumsan who would miss all that fun.

"Let's go," Chandol said to the naked boys and started to wade into the river.

Bong watched them splash into the water, chattering and giggling. Chandol was in the lead, as always. Bong liked Chandol very much. Sometimes Chandol gave him a punch or two, but Bong did not mind that very much. Chandol's punches were punishment for some wrong Bong had done, while Toad would punch him when nobody was around for no reason at all. And Chandol knew more about the town and grown-ups and animals than anybody else did. Even if they were lost in the woods and Toad and the other boys were frightened to tears, Bong was never afraid as long as Chandol was with them, because he was sure that his captain would somehow find the way to the village before dark.

Chandol swam out, kicking like a frog. Mansik followed next, his head bobbing up and down. Kangho and Kijun swam side by side behind them.

With a quiet sigh Bong lay down on the sand and looked up at the mild sky.

The four boys, stark naked, trudged across the sandy shore, somewhat tired after the swim. Then they followed a desolate path through the tall reeds along the riverbank. Two parallel ruts made by cartwheels stretched out along both sides of the dirt road crossing the islet; this trail was frequented by cows and by carts carrying West County vegetables and grain to the Central Market in town. Yellow dust puffed up at their feet as the boys plodded on along the track littered with dry cow dung. Rustling softly, the reeds waved as the hot breeze hit them.

"Do you think it'll really be all right for us to go to town naked like this?" Kijun asked Chandol again.

"I told you not to worry about it, didn't I!" Chandol snapped impatiently. "Nobody will see us because all the people are hiding in their homes. There's nobody on the streets but the fighting soldiers. We will find a safe place near the market to hide and watch the war."

They trudged on toward the Soyang ferry. The sun blazed in the silent sky.

"Mansik," said Kangho, walking with his toes curled inward because the scorched dust was too hot for his bare soles, "I've got a sort of queer feeling."

"About what?"

"That we may not see any fighting in town. It's so quiet. I don't hear any shooting."

"Maybe they are using guns that don't make much noise."

"And we haven't seen any airplanes this afternoon," Kangho persisted.

"Hush!" said Mansik, suddenly halting.

Kangho also stopped. "What is it?" he asked. "You look scared."

Chandol looked back at the two boys and asked, "What's the matter with you two?"

"I don't know what it is," Kangho said, "but something is wrong with Mansik."

"Hush, boys, and listen," Mansik said in a choking voice, waving his hand.

"Listen to what?" Chandol asked, frowning.

"Just listen. Can't you hear that sound?"

"What sound?" said Kijun, flustered.

"That sound."

The boys listened attentively, standing in the hot sun on the deserted trail, transfixed. Their tanned shoulders reflected the sunshine. It was dead silent except for the distant peaceful murmur of the flowing water.

"I can't hear anything but the river," said Kijun.

"I can hear it!" said Kangho, shock and fear in his voice. "I can hear it. It's a very peculiar sound. Like a great big monster growling somewhere."

"What do you think it is?" Mansik asked Kangho.

"Now I can hear it too!" said Chandol. "I think something is rolling around. Or it's dry thunder rumbling underground." Or the silver stallion galloping through the cavern, he thought.

"I'm afraid," said Kijun, recoiling from the other boys as though the mysterious sound came from them. He was more afraid because he could not hear what everybody else did.

"To me it sounds like a big grindstone rotating at a rice mill," Mansik said.

"I know what it is," Kangho said, his expression still tense but more confident. "It's a tank."

"What's a tank?" asked Mansik.

"A steel wagon with lots of wheels and a cannon," said Chandol. He always knew something about everything.

"What should we do, Chandol?" asked Kangho.

"It's coming closer!" Kijun said.

"Let's hide," Mansik suggested.

"Hide!" Chandol said. "Quick!"

The naked boys dashed into the reeds. They did not dare to come out for several minutes even when they could not hear the crunching sound any longer.

Their shins were scratched by the grass as they plodded on toward the Soyang River. The boys could hear the occasional crack of rifle shots amid the rustling sound of the weeds. The sounds of rifles and machine guns and tanks grew more and more frequent and louder by the time the boys reached an abandoned dugout on the thistle-covered wasteland where a Hyonam farmer used to grow strawberries. They turned left around the dugout and headed for the ferry upstream.

Finally they saw the tanks. Majestically decorated with twigs and broad leaves, six steel giants and countless trucks rolled along the road between the railway station and the river toward the Soyang Bridge. It was obvious that no tanks had yet crossed the river to Cucumber Island, but the sound was so loud now that the boys felt they were only a few yards away.

"So, there they are," said Chandol, pausing among the sticky thistles. "Tanks and soldiers and everything."

"But we can't see much from here," said Mansik, shadowing his eyes with his hand. "It's too far."

The boys hurried through the weeds, concealing themselves behind clumps and sand dunes from the soldiers on the trucks. As the sounds of war grew louder, they grew more excited. Then they heard people shout at one another nearby.

"Did you hear that, Chandol?" said Kangho, halting again. "Don't you think we'd better hide again?"

At Chandol's signal, they threw themselves into the reeds. They listened cautiously for a while. Chandol motioned them to follow him. They crawled through the reeds closer to the ferry. They stopped again. Holding their breath, the boys silently pushed aside the reeds and peeked out.

A hundred soldiers in green uniforms and green helmets carrying knapsacks on their backs swarmed down the sloping path from the bank to the ferry.

"These are not Red soldiers," Kijun whispered. "Their clothes are not yellow."

"They're either the National Army or the World Army then," said Kangho.

The soldiers gathered around a very tall man, who stepped out to the water's edge and pointed at Cucumber Island, giving an order to his men. As they sat or lay down to rest, the tall man climbed back up the path and disappeared into an alley near the National Grange storehouse. Several minutes later, twenty more soldiers appeared in the alley, carrying three round rubber boats on their shoulders.

"Look at that, Mansik," Kangho said. "They brought *boats* with them."

"What should we do, Chandol?" Kangho said. "I mean, if they come over here."

"We've come here to watch the soldiers, and that's what we are going to do. Stay where you are and watch what the soldiers do."

The soldiers fell into lines and started to cross the river in the green rubber boats.

"They must be the World Army," Chandol murmured.

"How can you tell?" Kangho said.

"They don't look like Koreans. Too tall and too big. And some of them have a strange dark color on their faces."

"You mean they are the foreign soldiers who came to liberate us from the People's Army?" Mansik said.

"Yes."

"Are we liberated?" Kijun said.

"That's right."

Kijun said, "While we've been sitting here, naked? That's funny."

Chandol explained, "We just watch the war. It's grownups who decide whether we are liberated or not."

"That's confusing," Kijun said. "It's so different from our Autumn War."

"It's really a very simple matter, Toad," said Chandol. "Whether we're liberated or not is decided by which side wins the war. If the World Army wins, we're liberated from the People's Army. If the People's Army wins, we are liberated from the World Army."

As soon as they landed on the islet, the soldiers fanned out and took their positions. While this first batch of soldiers was guarding the ferry, one of them roped the three boats together and went back to fetch more soldiers.

Kangho whispered, "They're too close. We have to be very careful."

"Quiet," Chandol said. "They may hear your voice."

"We can't stay here," Kijun said. "They have guns. They may shoot us, if they catch us hiding here."

"But they're our liberators."

"Then how come the Reds did so many terrible things to the Southerners?" Kangho asked. "They were liberators too, weren't they?"

"That's what war is all about—killing a lot of people," Chandol said wisely. "The team that does more killing than the other wins the war and takes the country, you see."

"Does that mean the World Army will become our masters if they win this war?" Mansik asked.

"They say General Megado is a very good person. I'm sure he'll return our country to the National Army," said Chandol, somewhat dubiously.

Kijun said, "The general may be a very good person, but these foreign soldiers look too weird to be nice."

Indeed, the World Army soldiers were grotesque.

"They sure look like monsters," Mansik chimed in, resting his chin on the dirt. "I never expected the liberators to be giants with such long ugly faces."

"They are as tall as telegraph poles," Kangho said. "It must be quite uncomfortable in bed if you're so tall."

"And some of them have black skins. What do you think has happened to them?"

"Too much sun, maybe," Mansik said.

"Hush!" Chandol said. "The last batch of them has finished crossing. Looks like they'll move again."

The *bengko* soldiers stood up, slinging their rifles and knapsacks over their shoulders, and assembled around their commander. The captain discussed something with his second-in-command and pointed towards West County. They shouted some terse orders and the soldiers lined up and began to move towards the cart trail.

"They're coming this way," said Kijun, frightened all over again. "What should we do?"

"Why don't we go out and give three cheers to welcome the liberators?" Kangho suggested.

"But we're naked," Chandol objected.

As the soldiers came closer, the boys could see them better. Their faces were dirty with dust and sweat. Mud crusts were peeling from their boots and helmets. They had almost no eyelids and their green or blue catlike eyes glinted dangerously in hollow eye sockets under the heavy mushroom helmets.

"Why are their eyes so blue?" Kangho asked, surprised. "Did blue paint get in their eyes?"

"Maybe they ate too many vegetables and the green color got to their eyes," Chandol guessed.

"Look at their noses," Mansik exclaimed quietly. "They're real *bengkos*, aren't they? Such huge noses. Must be pretty heavy to carry around."

Kangho felt his own flat nose tentatively, chuckling softly. "Don't the high bridges bother them when they wash their faces?"

The liberators turned into the trail stretching westward through the reeds. The boys were now about one hundred yards away from the marching World Army and Mansik heard a soldier with hooked nose in the leading group say something to his friend in a queer language. The soldier trudging beside him answered in the same peculiar language and both of them laughed a subdued, tired laugh.

"Did you hear what they said, Chandol?" Mansik asked in a whisper. "They speak very odd words."

"What kind of a language is that?"

"I don't know. How can they talk to each other with those funny words?" Mansik worried.

"They're coming too close!" Kijun panicked once more. "They'll find us for sure. Let's run away before it's too late."

Mansik and Kangho also looked apprehensive this time. Chandol squinted at the other boys to read their expressions before making a decision. Mansik looked away evasively. Kangho kept quiet, unsure of himself. Chandol licked one corner of his lips and then the other, reflecting, grinned uncertainly, stopped grinning, and licked the corners of his lips again.

"Well?" Kijun urged. "What are we going to do?"

Chandol stared at Kijun for a moment. "You just stay put," he said at last. "It will be more dangerous for us to run than to stay still. They'll spot us more easily if we move."

"Looks like they're heading for our village," Mansik said after a short silence. "I wonder why."

"There're no Reds in West County," Kangho said. "Everybody knows that."

"Maybe the liberators want to make war against our village," Mansik said.

"I don't believe they will do anything like that," Chandol said.

The naked boys hiding in the reeds watched the foreign soldiers march on toward their village.

THREE

"The U.N. soldiers are coming! The U.N. soldiers are coming!" The stocky boatman ran to the village, shouting and waving his long arms, "The U.N. soldiers are coming! The U.N. soldiers are coming!"

"Where?" the miller shouted back at the boatman across the log bridge. "Where are the *bengkos?*"

Yom told him the foreign soldiers, about five hundred of them, were assembling on the shore of Cucumber Island to cross the river by rubber boats. The boatman ran on to the Paulownia House to report this news to Rich Hwang.

The old man was not sure how he should behave toward these visitors, the foreign soldiers. Old Hwang knew he should not be too rash and openly express delight at the coming of the foreign troops; the Communists might somehow defeat the World Army and come back to punish and execute everybody who cooperated with their enemy. Besides, the old man did not have the vaguest idea what kind of people *bengkos* were. He was totally unprepared to encounter them.

"So, five hundred of them are coming," the old man murmured, still brooding.

"Yes, Father," Young Hwang said, stealing an inquisitive glance at his father.

"How are the villagers?"

"They seem to be worried because some Communists are still in the area and a big battle might break out. Besides, they're suspicious of the liberators."

"Why?"

"Because the *bengkos* are total strangers and you never know what to expect from total strangers."

A short pause ensued.

"Will they come across the river soon, Father?" asked Sokku, hoping his father would give him some definite instructions. "I think they're preparing for some sort of an attack."

"Do you think the liberators might mistake some of the villagers for Communists and kill them?"

"We can go out with national flags and welcome them so that they will know we are not their enemy."

"That is a reasonable idea," Old Hwang said. "We may need banners, and streamers, too. Come."

When they entered his room, Old Hwang took out the stationery and a roll of rice paper. He spread a sheet of paper on the floor and told Sokku to grind the ink block on the watered slate to make black brush ink. He held the paper flat with jade weights and opened his brush casing.

"Sokku, do you think they can read Chinese letters?" asked the old man.

"I don't think they can, Father," said Young Hwang. "Occidentals have different languages from ours."

"What languages do they speak?"

"They must speak many languages. The World Army is made up of soldiers from sixteen different nations."

"If they can communicate with one another in so many languages, they may understand Chinese, too," the old man said, dipping his brush in the fresh ink. "Do you know what Chinese ideographs represent the foreign words 'U' and 'N'?"

Young Hwang explained that "U.N." was an abbreviation for "the United Nations." When the old man finished writing "Welcome United Nations Forces" in Chinese calligraphy on the paper, Sokku cut out a rib from a bamboo rake and glued the top side of the paper to the bamboo rib, which he fixed with a hemp string to a long pole. The father and the son came out of the Paulownia House, carrying the streamerlike paper banner.

"You must go to the rice mill and tell Kangho's father to organize a welcoming delegation," Old Hwang told his son. "They must join me at the ferry to meet the U.N. soldiers. I'm going to the river now to wait for the liberators to arrive."

The delegation assembled by the boatman's cabin at the ferry. However, nobody approached the *bengko* soldiers or spontaneously cheered them when they arrived. The villagers were too appalled and embarrassed by the grotesque appearance of the foreigners. The delegates stood by the boatman's cabin, silently watching the soldiers, who, on their part, showed no interest in the Korean spectators. The tall *bengkos* in loose green uniforms had strange bright colors in their hair and eyes and some of them, especially those with charcoal-black skin, looked horrible, like beasts, when they grinned. The soldiers waited, scattered around the ferry and along the dikes of the riverside rice paddies, filling the water jugs they carried on their hips, scraping mud crusts from their enormous boots, smoking the cigarettes contained in packs with a big red circle or the picture of a quaint humped animal on them.

"Should we go down there and offer some welcoming remarks, Father?" asked Sokku, awkwardly holding the paper banner.

Old Hwang frowned. He was offended because none of the young soldiers had come up to the cabin to give formal greetings to the aged village chief, who had troubled himself to come out this far to welcome them. It was an obligation on the part of the visitor to seek his host upon arrival and ask for his forbearance for the trouble the guest might cause during his stay. The host was then obliged to express his warm welcome and offer hospitality. The old man, however, understood that the soldiers might have some reason for ignoring protocol. He was not annoyed enough by their bad manners to abandon his own manners.

Old Hwang decided to go down to the *bengko* soldiers to say something, but he was not sure what he was supposed to say, and to whom.

Followed by his son, Kangho's father and the boatman, Old Hwang started to go down the bank, but halted halfway down the sandy shore, for he realized that there was no way for him to identify the commander of the soldiers. Sokku gazed at his father, equally lost. The miller and the boatman were helpless.

The frustrated old man looked around the soldiers, not knowing what to do, until he found a *bengko* with incredibly long legs, who was smoking his cigarette, sitting alone on his combat gear and leaning against an aspen tree. He chose to speak to this man because he thought it would be easier to get the attention of a man who was alone. The old man and his party approached the *bengko*, who indifferently glanced up at the four Koreans. Old Hwang stopped and frowned again, for this was the first time that he had ever come across a younger man who was rude enough not to stand up in an elder's presence.

In order to show the good intentions of his party, Old Hwang pointed at the paper banner his son was carrying behind him. Puzzled, the soldier stared at the banner and then at the four villagers, one by one. The old man tried to smile but could not, for he suddenly found himself not liking these soldiers very much. The soldier waited, curiously gazing at the old man. Hwang remained standing stiffly, making no further attempt to express himself. The young soldier fumbled in his pockets, and fished out a flat rectangular slab wrapped in shiny brown and silver paper from his breast pocket and gave it to Old Hwang.

The bewildered old man took the slab, bowing, because he did not know what else to do. He studied it this way and that curiously, for he had never seen anything like it before. The soldier noticed his perplexity and gestured for the old man to unwrap it.

"Why don't you open it, Father?" Young Hwang said. "It looks like something important. The envelope is beautifully decorated."

The old man unwrapped the packet, but he had absolutely no idea what he was supposed to do with the brown slab inside. The soldier gestured for him to put it in his mouth. Finally Old Hwang understood that the soldier had given him something to eat.

The old man's face flushed in shame and anger. He threw the chocolate to the sand and turned back. The soldier gazed blankly at the infuriated old man.

"Come, Sokku," said the old man. "Such impudence."

The Western soldiers streamed along the road, their uniforms white with sand and dust, their armpits dark with sweat. They marched on straight to General's Hill without bothering to check the houses at Kumsan or other neighboring villages. There was no one outside the silent huts and hovels to welcome the liberators, for the villagers had been strictly instructed by Old Hwang to stay in their homes until the *bengkos* left the county. Old Hwang felt relieved when the soldiers who had treated him like a beggar at the ferry passed through the village without any mishap.

At dusk the sound of flying bullets came from beyond General's Hill. The combat raged violently, cannon shells fell. The battle noise sounded so near to the villagers hiding in their shelters that it seemed the fighting was going on right outside their houses. Near midnight it dwindled and stopped at about two o'clock. The villagers heard no more gunshots the rest of the night, but they could not fall asleep until dawn.

Early next morning, refugees from Castle village began to arrive to seek shelter in the homes of their relatives or acquaintances in Kumsan and Hyonam. The farmers were extremely worried about the harvest because their rice paddies and vegetable patches had been destroyed, trampled by tanks and trucks and countless boots.

Rifles and cannons resounded louder the second night, and on the third morning, the Kumsan villagers could see the foreign soldiers digging into new positions far down the northern ridge of General's Hill. Worrying that the U.N. troops might retreat to the village, Old Hwang sent his son to observe.

Both on the slopes and at the base of the hills, hundreds of Yankee soldiers were working, carrying things, unloading ammunition cases from the trucks and piling them among the tents, everybody working everywhere. But contrary to Sokku's anticipation of a major battle, uneasy quiet returned to West County. The villagers squatting in their shelters heard only occasional rifle shots. By daybreak total silence fell. In the morning, the glad news traveled fast among the county villages that all the Communists had fled to Hwachon in the dark of night. In the afternoon, the Castle villagers started to return home.

Not a single rifle shot came from the hills on the fourth day. But the foreign soldiers did not show any sign of leaving the county. At dusk threads of smoke curled up from the ridge. The soldiers were building cooking fires.

Peace was returning.

———•———

"Mansik. Wake up, Mansik," Ollye said in a choked whisper, fretfully shaking her son. "Wake up. Wake up."

She gasped in a raspy voice, frightened by something, but Mansik was still too sleepy to notice; he had fallen into a deep, exhausted sleep after swimming all afternoon with his friends at the river. He had been swimming in the sun again, laughing with the naked boys, and collecting rainbow-colored pebbles on a sandy shore, when she interrupted his dream, and he resented it.

"What is it, Mother?" Mansik muttered, sitting up reluctantly.

"Hush," she said in a quivering voice. "Listen."

He rubbed his eyes. "Listen to what?" he said, befuddled.

"That. Fluffy."

Mansik listened. The paper of the door looked pale blue in the moonlight. It must be far past midnight, he thought, and he heard the dog whimper. The dog did not bark, perhaps because someone was trying to choke it. Mansik suddenly became alert. Fluffy kept whining outside in the yard.

"What's wrong with the dog, Mother?" he whispered.

"It's been whining for some time like that."

"Why?"

"Somebody is outside. A visitor."

"At this hour?"

"Maybe a prowler."

"A thief?"

That could not be, Mansik thought. For generations there had been no thieves in West County. Ollye and Mansik cautiously crept to the door and listened, not moving, not even breathing. The dog kept whining, sidling from one corner to another and then back, as if it was being chased by a malicious, slow-moving beast.

"Fluffy is terrified, Mother. Has he seen a ghost?"

"I woke up a minute ago, heard a nervous bark, and then footsteps. Fluffy barked a few times at first and then began to whine like that."

Suddenly the dog's noise was cut short.

"Fluffy is quiet. Do you want me to go out and take a look?"

"No. Stay in the room. If there's somebody outside. . . ."

"I think Fluffy is dead."

Mansik felt his mother's grip tighten on his arm. She was trembling. It was difficult for her to breath.

"We'd better shout for help," she said.

"Shout what, Mother?"

"Scream. Scream for help."

Mansik tried, but no sound came out of his throat. He swallowed. "I can't, Mother."

"Scream."

"I can't. You try it, Mother."

She could not scream either. They heard someone approach the room on tiptoe. The man outside paused for a moment, as if trying to decide what he should do next. He started to move again. His shadow fell on the paper of the door. It was a tall soldier with a helmet on. The shadow grew bigger as the man came nearer.

"It's a *bengko*, Mother. I can tell by the sound of his boots."

Another helmeted shadow appeared on the paper door and the first shadow stopped. They discussed something. The second shadow went away.

"They're *bengko* soldiers, Mother, and they brought guns with them. Why are they here?"

"Scream, Mansik. Please."

"Maybe they'll kill us," the boy said, terrified.

Ollye moved closer to the door and finally called out in a quavering voice, that was barely audible outside, "Who is it?"

The soldier stopped again. He did not answer.

"Who is it?"

Still no answer. The soldier waited.

"What do you want from our house?" she said, a little louder this time.

The door burst open. A flood of light blinded them and a flashlight beam searched the room for its prey. The giant soldier jumped into the room, his arms wide open. No sooner had Mansik risen to his feet, instinctively, in defense, than the soldier grabbed him by the neck and hurled him out of the room. Mansik lost consciousness even before he landed on the ground. Then the man pushed Ollye down. She tried to scream and run, but he gripped her shoulders, uttering strange words that she could not understand at all, and mounted her like a wild animal.

Trying to fight off the rapist, Ollye kicked the basket by the door. The rice she had taken from the town granary spilled on the floor. As she struggled desperately, trying to scream, the soldier tore off her underpants, and stuffed them into her mouth. Pinning down the gagged woman with his knees, the soldier stripped her and opened her legs by force. Ollye fainted when a long, slimy tongue licked her face and a wet rubbery thing slid up her naked thigh.

Outside under the chestnut tree, a black Yankee was standing guard, waiting for his turn.

When he came to, Mansik tried to turn himself over. He could not. His left shoulder ached. Lying listless and motionless, he looked up at the stars and the yellow moon. It was long past the Eighth Full Moon but the dim moon was still bright enough to etch the contour of the chestnut tree against the graying sky. A chilly breeze rustled the leaves in the early dawn silence.

Mansik drove his hand across his nose, and felt something sticky on his palm. His nose was stuffed with lumps of blood; he could not get enough air through his nostrils. His jawbones gritted as he tried to breathe through his mouth.

Nanhi whimpered inside the house. His head ached, and he felt pain in every joint as he tried to push himself up again. Nanhi whimpered again.

He called softly, "Mother."

There was no answer.

"Mother?"

Something moved in the dark room and then his mother sighed, a deep long sigh. But Mansik soon realized that it was not his mother who had just sighed. It sounded like the sigh of a man after heavy labor. Mansik turned his stiff neck. Through the open door he saw someone, a tall dark figure, buttoning his clothes. Nanhi whimpered in snatches. The dark figure glanced down at the sniveling child, fished something out of his pocket, unwrapped a candy bar and gave it to her. The soldier, who had kept his boots on, picked up his helmet and rifle which were lying by the door and clumped over to the gate. He paused to glance at the dead dog and stooped down to check the squirming boy. The soldier smelled of burnt fur and damp. Kneeling on the ground, the boy blankly looked up at the black soldier, who smirked, his teeth and eyes flashing white in the moonlight. Although he had on the same green uniform as other liberators, this black *bengko* had a flat nose with cavernous nostrils. Mansik had never seen such porky thick lips. The black man strode to the chestnut tree and joined the other Yankee waiting there. The two men whispered something to each other and walked away along the road stretching to Castle village.

When the soldiers were gone, Mansik raised himself with a painful grunt and staggered into the house. He heard Nanhi sucking the candy bar in the dark. Otherwise it was deadly silent.

"Mother," he called.

Ollye did not answer.

He saw the faint shape of his mother, half naked, lying on the floor.

"Mother, are you all right?"

She still did not answer.

Mansik fumbled about the lamp stand to find the match box. He struck a match and lit the kerosene lamp. He saw his mother. She was lying there, limp like a corpse, her mouth agape and her eyes dazed in disbelief. Her hair was disheveled like a woman who has just had a violent fight with a neighbor. She did not even attempt to hide the dark bushy hair exposed between her open thighs.

"Mother, what happened?"

She gazed up, dumbfounded, her breasts showing under her torn shirt. Nanhi was lying beside the spilled pile of rice, sucking at her candy bar.

"Put out the light, Mansik," Ollye said weakly.

FOUR

"**J**un! Jun! Wake up!"

It was long past midnight and Kijun, only half awake, wondered why his uncle had come to see him at this late hour. Kijun did not answer because he was too sleepy to say anything and because he would have had to wake up if he answered.

"Brother! Brother!" Uncle called Kijun's father, his voice still a muffled whisper but a little louder.

Annoyed by the untimely visitor, Father coughed twice to express his intention to rise and go out to see his brother. Kijun decided to go back to sleep.

Kijun heard his father say, "What on earth is up? Don't you know what time it is?"

"Don't talk so loud and come on out here. I've got something to tell you."

Grumbling, he stepped down to the yard. The door slammed shut, and the two men went into the shadow under the eaves outside the children's room. Kijun was suddenly alert.

"Is your wife all right?" Uncle said.

"Of course she is. What kind of a question is that?" Father said, irritated.

"So she is safe. Your wife, I mean."

"Sure. What's the matter with you, anyway?"

"Maybe the *bengkos* didn't notice your house back here. They must have passed by along the road."

"What are you talking about? What *bengkos?*"

"Two Yankees came to the village tonight, and I have a suspicion about their intentions."

As his uncle went on buzzing just outside the room, Kijun became absorbed in the story. He quietly crawled toward the door to overhear the whispered conversation better. He had to trample on his four younger siblings to reach the door, for the room was crowded not only with the five children but with the sacks of potatoes that were kept indoors at night lest wild animals should come down from the mountains and steal them.

"Two *bengkos* came to my house earlier tonight," Uncle said. "I woke up because Brownie barked so I looked out the window to see what was wrong with the dog. I saw a white *bengko* standing by the twig gate, searching for something with a flashing stick lamp, and another *bengko*, a black one, trying to drive away the dog with his rifle. They wanted to come into my house, and I thought I knew what they were after. So I woke up the whole family and we crashed through the bush-clover fence behind the house to escape to the woods. But we didn't have to run too far. The dog kept barking so furiously that the *bengkos* soon gave up. They left and came down along this road. Probably they did not try to break into this house because they didn't see it. Your house is well concealed by trees and bushes."

"Why do you think the *bengkos* came to this village?" Father asked.

"I am not sure but I have a fairly clear idea what they are after."

"Oh."

They paused for a while. Kijun wondered why they kept silent.

Uncle went on, "At any rate, I think they headed for the ferry, because I didn't see them cross the stream to go to Inner Kumsan."

"Old Click Beetle lives over there and the *bengkos* must have passed by his house," Father said. "I wonder if anything happened to him."

"But there're no women in his house."

"I know. Maybe the *bengkos* are after something else."

"Shall we go to see him now?"

Kijun, engrossed in their conversation, was already fumbling in the dark for his clothes.

"Click Beetle" was the nickname of a cranky old widower in his late sixties, who used to sharecrop vegetables for a living until he made an enemy of almost everybody at Charcoal village and moved to Kumsan. In his first year in Kumsan, he tried to raise barley but all his plants died, presumably because click beetles had gnawed the roots. The old man interpreted this disaster in the first year at his new village as Heaven's punishment for his temper which made everybody around him into his enemy.

When Kijun's father and uncle went over to his house, the old man apparently had been awake for some time. Even before they called out to him, Click Beetle lit the kerosene lamp in his room, opened the door, and looked out to see who was coming, holding the lamp high over his head.

"Oh, sure, they were here," the old man said, stroking his gray beard with knobby fingers.

Hiding behind a pile of logs, Kijun listened to their conversation, trying to memorize every word they said so that he could tell the village boys in the morning.

Click Beetle said he had been awakened by the "sound" of the light flashing on the paper door, for he was a very old person and slept lightly.

"I called out, 'Who is out there?' but nobody answered," the old man explained. "I opened the door to see who had flashed the light and I saw a man who was as black as charcoal standing there, and another man, a white one, standing behind him. The black man stared at me for a while and then asked me, 'Sexy *isso?*' At first I didn't understand what he said, and then he repeated the question. He was asking me if there was any woman in the house. Those *bengkos* didn't know how to say *seksi* properly. Now I knew what they wanted and I said '*Opso.*' They didn't believe that there was no woman, and no other man besides me either for that matter, and searched for a while. I think they came to this village to find some women to rape."

Kijun wondered what "rape" was.

"That's what I told you, didn't I?" Uncle said to Father. "That's the reason they came."

"But I can't believe it," said Father. "They have come such a long way across the ocean to fight for us, and many have even lost their lives for us. How can our worthy liberators do such a thing to our women?"

"Well, those things happen in wartime," Click Beetle said. "Always. That's what the Japanese did to our women when they invaded this country, and that's what the Mongols and the Chinese did when they were here. They raped every woman in sight—virgins, widows, housewives—every living thing with a skirt on. I don't think the Occidentals are any different as far as raping women is concerned."

Father was not fully convinced yet and said, "But they're in the middle of a big war. . . ."

"They're doing it because they're in the middle of the war," Click Beetle retorted promptly. "You never know when you'll die in a war, and you do a lot of unpredictable things when you know you may die today or tomorrow."

"Where did they go then?" Father asked.

"That way. To the ferry."

"They must have gone to the Paulownia House next," Father said in a worried voice. "I hope the Toktuwon Woman is all right."

"Should we go to the Hwangs' now?" Uncle asked. "If anything happened. . . ."

"No. You must not pay a visit to your elders or seniors late at night. And in case something terrible did happen there, the Hwangs would be embarrassed to see anybody or to discuss it."

"But we have to report to Rich Hwang that a suspicious incident happened tonight in this village."

"We can do that after daybreak. Bad news can wait for daylight."

When Kijun's father, accompanied by his brother, hurried to the Paulownia House at daybreak, Chandol's parents were already there, discussing something seriously with Old Hwang and Sokku. So, instead of reporting what they had gone through during the night themselves, the brothers listened to what the couple had to report to the Hwangs.

Yesterday, Chandol's mother had loose bowels because she had drunk sour rice wine; the farmer apparently did not know the wine had spoiled, for he had offered it with good intentions to express his gratitude to Chandol's mother and two other neighbors who had helped him repair his tobacco-drying shed. Late at night, on her way back to her room from the outhouse, she happened to see two *bengkos*, helmeted and armed with rifles, come out of Click Beetle's house and head for the Paulownia House.

"The *bengkos* came here to this tree," she said, "and paused here for a moment to discuss something. Then they went over to the Chestnut House." The soldiers decided not to enter the Hwangs' home, Chandol's father guessed, because they had been overawed by the house with a tiled roof. With her own two eyes Chandol's mother saw the soldiers go over to the Chestnut House and snoop around for a while. Then one of them jumped inside, brandishing his flashlight. She was not sure what the *bengkos* had done to Fluffy, or to Mansik and Ollye, but she heard no barking, no screaming, no extraordinary sound at all. She went over to the log bridge for a closer look, but did not dare to cross the stream, for a *bengko* was on guard by the twig gate of the Chestnut House. Although she was at some distance, Chandol's mother had a fairly clear idea what was happening to Mansik's mother.

"And suddenly I was so scared that I ran home and hid in the bomb shelter until morning. I've come with my husband, Master Hwang, to report to you what I saw last night."

When Chandol's parents and Kijun's father and uncle finished their reports and returned home, Old Hwang stood by the gate, blankly gazing at General's Hill, his hands on his hips, confused and perplexed.

"What are you going to do, Father?" said Sokku, standing, at a loss, a step behind his father.

"About what?"

"The Chestnut House. Shouldn't we go over there and find out what happened to Ollye last night?"

Old Hwang did not respond, for he was too distracted by the turmoil of thoughts swimming in his head. Then he blurted, "Unclean."

"What?"

"Nothing. Forget it," the old man said. "You go over and see if Ollye is all right."

The old man strode back to his room, frowning as if he was trying to repress something squalid nagging at him. Sokku stood under the paulownia tree for a while, confused, before he hesitantly went over to the Chestnut House.

"Mansik's mother!" Sokku called out over the twig-woven gate.

Ollye did not answer. The door of her room remained closed firmly.

Sokku called out again, "Mansik. Come on out here if you're home. I want to talk to you or your mother."

There was still no answer. Young Hwang waited. While he was trying to decide whether he should go on calling to them until one of them came out of the closed room or just go away and leave them alone, Young Hwang heard someone inside, moving slowly. The door opened and Mansik, listless and pale, stepped into the yard. Avoiding Sokku's eyes, the boy plodded out to the gate. He stopped and gazed over Sokku's shoulder at the rice paddies around the mill.

"Did something happen at your home last night, Mansik?" Young Hwang asked.

The boy did not answer.

"What happened?"

The boy did not answer.

"Is your mother all right?"

The boy still did not answer.

Sokku realized that he would not be able to find out anything from this boy. After a pause, he said, "Go tell your mother to come here. I want to talk to her."

Mansik plodded back to the room, opened the door, thrust his head inside and murmured something. Mansik remained motionless, leaning forward, waiting for his mother's response, and then returned to Young Hwang at the gate.

"I told Mother to come out but she wouldn't say anything."

Silence followed.

"I see," Young Hwang said with a sigh. "You may go back to your room."

Mansik slowly trudged back, entered the room and quietly closed the door. A heavy silence hanging over the Chestnut House was broken only by the soft gnawing sound of the rabbits in their cage in the yard.

Chandol's father, scrubbing the mud off his black rubber shoes at the dew-wet roadside grass, called to Choe, a farmer who was coming down the rice paddy dike with a shovel and a pickaxe slung over his shoulder on his way home for breakfast. He told him what had happened last night, his voice filled with shock and pity. "Oh, I really can't believe it," he said. "Such a terrible thing happened to Mansik's mother . . ."

He went on to relate what his wife, hiding in the brush by the stream, had witnessed, and what he had heard from Kijun's uncle.

When Choe went home, he told this amazing news to his wife over the breakfast rice, his voice hushed lest his children in the other room should overhear the scandalous story. "Chandol's mother actually saw it all happening," he said emphatically. "Although she was too scared to cross the stream, she could watch everything the *bengkos* did to Mansik's mother."

Choe's wife could not keep this stunning account to herself. As soon as she had finished washing the breakfast dishes she hurried to the rice mill to have her red peppers ground.

"I just can't believe it," Choe's wife told Kangho's mother dramatically. "How on earth could such a horrible thing take place in our own village?"

"So you've heard about it, too," said the miller's wife.

"You mean you already know about the incident at the Chestnut House?"

The two women exchanged various details about the incident, throwing in the phrase "that poor woman" and sighing regularly in their conversation which fed on boundless curiosity and sentimental sympathy in equal proportion. Soon they realized that certain minor details or interpretations differed a little, for the stories had started to change as they traveled from one mouth to another. Kangho's mother insisted that Chandol's mother had crossed the stream at a dark spot some distance up from the log bridge, wading in cold water mounting to her waist and pushing through the billowing branches of willows. According to the miller's wife, Chandol's mother had soundlessly stolen to the fence behind the Chestnut House, sneaked into the back yard, and saw as well as heard everything happening in Ollye's room. Kangho's mother was especially well informed about some important facts such as how the *bengko* who was black as a crow strangled Fluffy to death in two breaths or how desperately Mansik's mother, kicking like a mare, struggled, naked, against the giant soldier mounting her.

Later when Choe's wife, on her way back home with the hot pepper powder, came upon the widow from Inner Kumsan on the road to the ferry, she told the wobbling old woman not the account she had heard from her husband, but the more vivid and entertaining version as embellished by the miller's wife. New imaginary episodes developed bit by bit until they became a part of the narrative. The story passed from the hawk-nosed rice bag weaver to an old farmer from Outer Kumsan who spit a gob of yellow phlegm every ten steps, from a sharecropper who kept raking down his long ashen beard with his gnarled fingers to a chunky middle-aged man with narrow inquisitive eyes, from a young farmer with a torn straw hat sitting on an upturned pail to an emaciated tobacco-smoker, from a gossipy woman to her imaginative nineteen-year-old daughter who was picking mushrooms, from a grinning farmer to a sly charcoal-maker, and from the farmer with six fingers on his left hand to the county sorceress. And when Chandol's mother went to the ferry and the boatman asked, "You mean you saw all those things?" with great admiration, she was so amused that she did not try too hard to correct his wild misinformation.

By noon many farmers at other villages in West County had learned of the Chestnut House incident, and almost everybody at Kumsan had heard it at least twice. The same two farmers who had gossiped about Ollye crossing the log bridge, repeated the story when they met again on a dike with several other farmers to have the lunch that their wives had brought out to the field. They relished it anew, from the very beginning to the last word, as enthusiastically as the first time, and nobody minded that some of the details had changed.

When Yun, a farmer of Castle village, appeared at the ferry to go to Central Market to sell his sesame, Yom the boatman, wiping his perspiring chin with the grimy towel hanging from his neck, asked the innocent farmer, "Have the Castle villagers heard about what happened here last night? I mean, what the *bengkos* did with the Chestnut House woman."

There was an obvious lewd insinuation in the boatman's squinting glance when he said this, and his tale no longer reflected any sympathy or compassion for the victim of this incident. When the Castle villager went to town and met his friends at the tavern, he claimed confidently that "a woman at Kumsan village actually watched the whole thing through the back window of the room and she saw this black soldier violating the Chestnut House woman, you know, and this woman saw the *bengko*'s cock, too. She told me that the cock looked like a black rubber stick."

In the late afternoon, the stories evolved faster and faster, and some said that Ollye had bitten the black rubber stick off the Negro *bengko* when she could no longer resist the rapist, and some said that Mansik had been stabbed by a bayonet while trying to rescue his mother from the soldiers, and some said that the *bengkos* had such huge tools that the Chestnut House woman had bled a whole chamber pot of blood "down there." The village women washing clothes at the stream giggled and exchanged delicately bawdy anecdotes and some farmers insisted that Mansik's mother actually enjoyed it a lot, for she had had no man at all for two full years.

All this went on but nobody came out of the Chestnut House to explain to them what really had happened.

FIVE

Sitting listlessly on the walnut stump by the gate, Mansik looked over at the room where his mother had been lying dumb and motionless all night. Nanhi was asleep beside her mother on the littered floor. Mansik had come out of the house at sunrise and did not want to return. The morning fog was thick; it would be very hot this afternoon. The sun loomed whitish yellow like a disc floating in the milky density. On General's Hill, golden and red tints of autumn leaves and violet splotches of wild camomile had already encroached upon a large part of the dark green ridges.

Mansik got up to go down to the stream to wash his face. He stopped by the chestnut tree. He dared not venture out to the footpath. He felt the world beyond had been suddenly forbidden him by some unknown force and he was confined to his house by invisible walls. He was afraid to be outside, to meet anybody.

The morning dragged on and on, interminably. The fog was gone now and white cotton patches of cloud sailed across the blue sky. The acacias by the stream and the tall ginkgo tree at the entrance of Hyonam village were a dazzling yellow. The rice plants in the paddies basked in the sunshine. Dragonflies flitted around the brilliantly colored cosmos blossoms and sparrows swarmed over the field.

Mansik paced on and on around his yard. He fed the rabbits with clover. He glanced at the small mound of dirt by the chimney where he had buried Fluffy. He did not want to go out and meet someone who might ask him embarrassing questions about last night, as Young Hwang had done.

Nanhi whimpered. She was hungry; it was long past breakfast time. Mansik quickly hid himself behind the twig fence when he spotted three women coming down the road from Castle village. The three women, hastening to the ferry carrying reed baskets on their heads, cast curious glances at the Chestnut House. They looked away promptly when they found Mansik peeking out through the twigs in the fence.

Nanhi whimpered again. The boy wondered for a moment if he should cook some rice for his little sister and mother. But he did not want to cook. He did not want to do anything. He did not want to exist.

He went over to the chestnut tree and lay down on the straw mattress spread in its shade. He looked up at the distant top branches of the tree. A hot breeze gently stirred the leaves. Even the leaves seemed to have changed overnight. The boy felt the world was missing something very important to him. Everything was different now. So different. In a single moment his world had been lost.

There was only silence and emptiness around him. And in his heart.

Listening to the monotonous *clang—clang—* of a sledge hammer beating an anvil at the distant Hyonam smithy, Old Hwang had been sitting for over an hour on the plank bench under the paulownia tree, thinking.

He could not make any decision because his thoughts kept repeating themselves, circling in the same rut. He shook his head to clear it.

The old man gazed at the four village boys hunting grasshoppers on the rice paddy dike across the stream, their heads and shoulders floating on the golden sea of ripening crops. Five Kumsan boys used to go around together all the time. There were only four of them today. The old man looked over his shoulder at the Chestnut House. Mansik was still there, squatting on the straw mattress under the chestnut tree, watching the four boys on their grasshopper hunt. Old Hwang sighed.

The old man was not sure what he was supposed to do now. This was a situation that his community had never faced before. He did not know what was proper. If somebody had died or fallen sick, the villagers in this community, who had lived for generations like one single huge family, would have rushed to the house of grief to offer solace and consolation. But they were totally at a loss as to what they should do about the woman of the Chestnut House.

No woman had ever been raped in this county. If Ollye had committed adultery like the flirtatious daughter of Widow Yu and the trinket packman who had been caught naked by two young male villagers one night on the sandy shore of Cucumber Island in the year of the national liberation, Old Hwang and the villagers would have had definite ideas as to what punishment she should be given. Strictly speaking, however, Ollye had done nothing wrong, did not deserve any kind of punishment. She was a victim. Besides, they were in no position to bring justice to the *bengkos* who had intruded on the village to commit the sinful crime. They did not even know from which country the rapists had come, and Old Hwang doubted very much that their decision to punish the soldiers would be respected by the World Army if they somehow caught the perpetrators.

Nor could the old man visit Ollye and offer her words of consolation. He could not free himself from the thought that, victim or not, she was a dirty woman. Loss of feminine virtue, under any circumstance, was the most profound shame for a woman—so profound a shame, in fact, that in the old days, a disgraced woman did not hesitate to drink a bowl of lye to terminate her life. The act of taking her own life symbolically restored the chastity of the defiled woman.

On the other hand, Old Hwang could not help pitying Ollye. The old man knew none of the neighbors went to the Chestnut House to express his or her compassion and sympathy for Ollye's predicament because Old Hwang himself had stayed away from her. Nobody wanted to be known as the first person to contact the unclean woman against Rich Hwang's will. The old man knew all this, and he also knew it was too late now for him to visit Ollye with some neighbors for a belated display of sympathy.

The old man gazed at the four boys hopping along the dike in the peaceful brilliance of sunshine pouring over the golden field.

With nightfall came anxiety that gradually turned to fear, and then to terror. In late afternoon the sky became overcast with dark, heavy clouds and it began to drizzle after supper. Kijun's father, worried, returned home early from the field. They had been safe last night because the *bengkos* had not noticed his house, but he did not believe they would be as lucky tonight if the soldiers came to the village again. Kijun's mother was even more worried, and she had good reason. "If they rape anybody in the family," she said, "I am the one they'd be after. Not you. I heard Mansik's mother enjoyed it with the *bengkos* so much that she yowled like a crazy bitch, but I am different. I don't want to be raped." This woman, whose eyes bulged forward like a goldfish's as far as her nose, shook her head emphatically. "If that ever happens to me, I'll bite my tongue off and drop dead right there even before they put their dirty thing in me." Seized by fear, Kijun's parents did not go to bed until late, restlessly peeking out at the dark ominous road from Castle village again and again. Kijun was finally sent as a lookout to the foot of the hillock. The boy concealed himself behind an oak and watched for *bengko* intruders.

Although it was drizzling, Kijun was rather proud to be the lookout. He was not a bit afraid. What had happened in the village since the strange accident at Mansik's house made him more and more excited. Lookout duty was far more interesting to him than the stupid, exhausting expeditions to General's Hill, the bombing of the town, or even the adventure in the reeds of Cucumber Island watching the arrival of the liberators. Only a few days ago Mansik and Chandol had bragged about their adventure at the town granary, but Kijun realized that afternoon when they were out in the field on a grasshopper hunt that no other boy knew what had happened in their own village as well as he did. Even Chandol, the captain, was so anxious to hear more stories from him that he tried very hard not to call him "Toad". And tomorrow Kijun would impress them again by telling them proudly that he had been on lookout all alone, all night.

He shivered, his drenched clothes sticking to his skin, but he did not mind the chill. He brushed back his wet hair with a wet hand and stared into the dismal darkness.

It was late, around nine o'clock, when *bengko* soldiers appeared at last on the northern road, the beam of a flashlight swishing this way and that in the drizzle. Though they were four or five hundred yards away, Kijun could see by the flashing light that there were two of them. The boy thought that, maybe, they always traveled by two when they came to rape at night. As soon as he recognized them by their rifles, helmets and height, the boy dashed out of the oak grove and, stooping low, hastened back home along the drainage ditch beside an eggplant patch. "They're coming, Mom," he breathlessly reported to his parents, "the *bengkos* are coming, Pop."

With a muffled scream, Mother urged her husband to lead her to safety, quickly, and putting a straw mattress over her head for a shield against the rain, she scuttled off to the pine grove behind the house.

Father hurried out after her, telling Kijun to go to Uncle and warn him that the *bengkos* were coming.

"Oh, oh, they're coming again," Aunt blubbered when Kijun told her. "They're going to hurt me. I know they'll hurt me this time."

"They *will* come after you if you keep making so much noise," Uncle hissed at her and ordered her to go hide in the bomb shelter behind the barn.

Click Beetle showed no fear when the boy told him about the *bengkos*, because he had no reason to worry. "They won't do anything to an old man like me, but run to the Hwangs and be sure to warn them," the old man said, and closed the door to his room to go back to sleep.

Old Hwang, a big man indeed, did not seem to be shaken by the boy's report. He calmly instructed his son Sokku to take the Toktuwon Woman and the child to the safely concealed shelter. "But, Father, the bomb shelter must be all puddles by now," the son said. "We have a big empty jar for soy sauce in the back yard. Maybe she can hide in it with the child." The old man shook his head at his son's suggestion. "No. You have to take them to the bomb shelter," he said. "It's much more dangerous to stay near the house. The *bengkos* will go away soon, and you can certainly stand the wet for an hour." As Young Hwang was taking his wife and child to the bomb shelter on the hillock behind the house, Kijun dashed out and went on to the Chestnut House.

Kijun faltered at the entrance to the footpath to Mansik's house. He was not sure if it was all right for him to talk to Mansik or his mother. He knew that somehow the Chestnut House had been completely cut off from the village. He felt Mansik had turned into someone more remote than the Castle village gang with whom the Kumsan boys had had so many stone fights. The other boys in the village apparently felt the same way. This morning they had been so curious as to how Mansik was doing that they had gone to take a look at him from a distance, pretending they were hunting grasshoppers. But nobody wanted to go over and talk to him. When he saw Mansik, squatting miserably under the chestnut tree, enviously watching the four boys playing in the sun, Kijun had been secretly glad. Unlike Kangho, who never talked much, Mansik tried to act like the vice-captain of the band, and Kijun hated him for that. Yet, he felt a little—just a tiny little bit—sorry to lose a friend so suddenly and completely.

Kijun wondered what Mansik was doing now. Maybe he was peeking out at him through a chink in the door. It was time for everybody to be in bed, but Kijun doubted anybody in Kumsan village was peacefully asleep tonight. He had to tell Mansik and his mother that the *bengkos* were coming, for they might be returning to the Chestnut House. But Kijun felt awkward calling on Mansik at this hour after he had pretended all day long that the Chestnut House did not exist.

Kijun stole to the twig gate on tiptoe and hollered suddenly at the top of his voice, "*Bengkos* are coming! *Bengkos* are coming!"

There was no response from the Chestnut House, not a sound. Jun was sure that Mansik and his mother were awake. They probably kept silent because they were too abashed to reply or look out the door. Or perhaps . . . they might have mistakenly thought that Kijun was mocking them. Sneaking up to their gate in the middle of the night and shouting like this about the *bengkos!* Kijun wanted to convince them that this was no joke.

"*Bengkos* are coming! *Bengkos* are coming!" the boy shouted again and scurried down the footpath.

He stopped by the log bridge and looked back, but he still could not see any movement at Mansik's house. He waited for a while trying to figure out what he should do next. He glanced over at the northern road to see how near the *bengkos* had come. The yellow gleam of the flashlight, bobbing like a glowworm in the misty drizzle, climbed down to the rice paddies from the road near Click Beetle's hut and headed for Inner Kumsan. The soldiers had decided to try a different place tonight. Kijun realized that he had to tell Kangho and Chandol and Bong that the *bengkos* were going toward their houses. He started to run to the rice mill, thinking everybody would call him a hero before this night was over.

By the time Kijun pounded on the plank door of the mill with his wet fists, Kangho's family was already bustling in a flurry, for they had been alerted by the boy's shout at the Chestnut House.

"What should I do? What should I do if the *bengkos* come here?" Kangho's grandmother whined, fretfully entering the room, stumbling out to the mill, and then rushing into the room again.

"You don't have to worry, Mother. They won't bother old women," Father said impatiently.

"Who says those savages care anything about age? I have to run and hide somewhere, too. How can they tell a woman's age in the dark, anyway?"

"Do you know where I left my skirt?" Mother said, tearfully.

"Didn't I tell you many times to keep all your clothes on?"

"Mother, do you happen to know where I left my skirt? Oh, never mind. I found it."

"Hurry. Get out of the mill quickly."

"I have to take an umbrella with me."

"Why do you need an umbrella when you're going to hide in the barn?"

"I don't think the barn is a safe place to hide. I'll find shelter somewhere out in the open field."

"Take me with you," Grandmother said.

"Umbrella. Get me the umbrella."

"Get out. I'll bring the umbrella out to the field for you later. No, no, not that way! Use the back door!"

During this commotion, Kijun beckoned Kangho out to the road and asked him to come with him to tell everybody to run away. The two boys went over to Bong's house and showed his parents the soldiers' flashlight, now crossing the rice paddies.

Fleeing to a willow grove with her two daughters, Bong's mother took out a worn-out tobacco pouch containing charcoal powder she had been carrying in her bosom, and handed it over to her older daughter. "Here. Put this on your face."

"What is that, Mother?"

"Charcoal powder."

"Why do I have to put it on my face?"

"To make your face look black and ugly in case you're caught by the *bengkos*. Many women avoided ill fortune with charcoal powder when the Chinese and the Japanese invaded this country and the barbarian soldiers raped every Korean woman in sight."

"But some *bengkos* have black skins. They might like us better when we paint ourselves dark."

"Look, Mother! They're over there. Can you see the moving light?" Huddling together in the dark under the willows, the mother and her two daughters watched the *bengko* soldiers approach Inner Kumsan.

Kijun and Kangho and Bong hurried to Chandol's house to tell his parents that the *bengkos* were already in the village. Chandol's parents told it to their neighbors over the fence, and soon all the village women, hastily but silently, vanished into the dark outside. After Chandol's mother had fled to safety, the four boys concealed themselves in the manure hut by the tall ginkgo tree to watch.

The *bengkos*, in raincoats, barged into several houses to find *seksi*, but soon realized that the village was virtually empty except for some old men. They paused before the tobacco shop and discussed something, pointing at Hyonam village a couple of times with their stick lantern before trudging away toward Charcoal village.

Kangho's father reported to Old Hwang in the morning that no woman had been assaulted the previous night in Kumsan and Hyonam. But the miller did not like what he had to report about Charcoal village.

"I visited Charcoal this morning to see if anything wrong had happened there."

"And what did you find out?"

"Two girls were raped, sisters. The soldiers found them hiding in a cow shed. The *bengkos* tied the girls' father to the manger when the old man tried to stop them. The neighbors were too scared to go to rescue the girls because the soldiers were armed with guns. The *bengkos* had to knock the old man unconscious with the gunstock because he was howling and fighting them like a madman. One soldier raped one sister while the other stood guard outside to scare away the villagers if they tried to rescue them. And then they took turns. The other sister had to watch the rape going on right in front of her. One girl was seventeen and the other fourteen."

Old Hwang resented his own stupidity in having gone down to the ferry the other day with the rice paper banner to welcome the arrival of the liberators. And he recalled how a *bengko* soldier had treated him like a beggar, giving him a chocolate bar. "Brutes," he said.

The farmers were busy all morning and afternoon because the harvest season was imminent and so much work had been delayed during the uneasy days of the battle on General's Hill. At sunset, however, they hastened home to have their suppers early and prepare themselves for another visit by the soldiers. Quite a few women had caught cold in the rain the previous night, but they refused to stay home in the warmth although their husbands promised to watch for intruders and help them escape in time if the soldiers did come. About thirty women hid, by fours and fives, in secret hideouts that the young villagers had dug along the banks of the stream that afternoon. Although the hideouts had been cushioned with sheaves of straw and old clothes, the women shivered all night in the cold. They wept and trembled so long that most of them felt sick to their stomachs by midnight. There was fear in the air; even the familiar chorus of frogs croaking in the dark frightened them. It began to rain again a little past midnight.

No *bengkos* came that night.

The day broke and the women returned home, sniffling and crying. They shivered even after returning to their dry, heated rooms.

It stopped raining in early morning. Rice plants and ginkgo leaves glistened with fresh moisture in the warm sun. In the evening, flickering glowworms flew through the undergrowth. Though many of them were sick after spending two nights in the open, the women went out to hide again. Stars and the moon slowly traversed the sky. After what seemed to be an eternity, day began to dawn in the eastern sky. Their eyes puffy after the sleepless night, their hair disheveled and their clothes soaked with dew, the women returned home at daybreak.

The day was sunny and bright, but nobody cared about the weather any more.

Squatting on the walnut stump by the twig gate, Mansik looked around the open field of rice ears rippling in the cool breeze. Not even a tiny speck of cloud disturbed the tranquil sky. The silent afternoon hypnotized him into drowsiness. The yellow sun laid a film of yellow over the earth and the yellow landscape of the remote sunny world blurred his sight. Hot peppers, spread on the thatched roof of a hut to dry, glimmered red in the sun. Kangho's parents, alternately raising their bamboo flails high in the air and then beating down, threshed dried legumes on a wide round rush mattress in the yard of their rice mill. Scarlet leaves of wild ivy engraved bleeding patterns on a rocky cliff on General's Hill. The lilac bushes beside the tobacco shop were withering to a dirty color. In the rice paddies, farmers were busy harvesting. The straw hats of two villagers moved slowly as they cut down the beanstalks they had planted on the bank of the stream. A young girl with braided hair, carrying a reed basket loaded with steamed potatoes on her head, hurried along the winding riverside path to Kamwa village. But these familiar fields and mountains and rice paddies and sky and everything else looked distant, unreal and intangible, to Mansik. Outside his house, it was a world of strangers.

Ever since the *bengkos* had made his mother dirty, he had not gone anywhere beyond the stream where he washed himself and drew water. He did all the washing at home now and he had to draw the water for drinking and cooking at the stream because he feared to go to use the well at the Paulownia House. Eventually he lost the courage to find out whether the autumn field still belonged to him. He could not venture any further than the stream. And whenever he had to make the short trip to the stream, he checked up and down the road to make sure there was nobody in sight. He did not want someone to stop him and ask anything about his mother. He was ashamed of her.

His mother rarely came out of her room. She brooded. Sometimes she wept quietly.

Mansik watched several hens clucking and pecking in the dirt by the bush-clover fence around the Hwangs' cabbage patch. The tall red-painted gate of the Paulownia House was latched because the whole family had gone out to the field to work. Now and then Mansik glanced over at the four boys in the distance discussing something under the ancient ginkgo tree beyond the stream. Those boys, who used to be his friends, might be arguing about where they would go to play this afternoon. They could go to the stream to catch rainbow fish with a bamboo basket, or knock down walnuts with stones, or steal chestnuts and dates from the trees in a neighbor's back yard. The boys had many games to play in autumn.

Mansik raised himself from the walnut stump when the four boys finally left for General's Hill. He went to the rabbits' cage to thrust clover and leftover cabbage leaves through the wire netting. After feeding the rabbits, the boy sat down. He remained on the stoop for some time. He had nothing to do. Nothing at all.

Gazing at the closed door of the other room, he called in a languid voice, "Mother."

Ollye was silent. A rustling sound came from the room a full minute later, and she replied, belatedly, in a weak voice, "Yes?"

Mansik bit the knuckle of his forefinger, thinking. He opened his mouth to say something, but changed his mind. Finally, he said, "I've been wondering about something, Mother. I can't make out why they are doing this."

"Doing what?" Ollye said softly through the door.

"Why doesn't anybody come to see us any more?"

She did not answer.

He rose, plodded to the room, cautiously opened the door and peeked in.

"Why doesn't anybody come to see us?" the boy asked again.

"Why do you think anybody should come to see us?"

"Well, you know, they used to come to see us for a chat or something. Everybody started to behave strangely after that night. They must be angry about what happened to you, I guess."

Without any reply, she rolled herself toward the wall.

"Did my words hurt your feelings, Mother?"

Still facing the wall, she said weakly, "No, my son."

"Isn't it strange that people can change so completely in such a short time?"

"That's how people are. You will come to understand the reason why they are like this. Some day."

"I don't think I can ever understand them. I've been thinking about it for a whole week but I still understand nothing," the boy said. "Do you think the villagers hate us? Is that why?"

She gave brief thought to this. "I don't think they hate us," she said.

"Then why?"

She did not answer.

Mansik sadly watched her back slowly heave. A dead fly, pressed flat by her weight, was stuck on her shoulder. She had grown sickly pale and gaunt in the past few days. She looked like a skull with lustreless eyes sunk deep in hollow eye sockets and cheeks pinched to the bone. Mansik was sad whenever he saw her haggard face.

Mansik stood up and quietly closed the door.

Kangho came to Chandol's house about two hours after breakfast and told him that the *bengkos* were going away.

Chandol ordered Kangho to go fetch Bong quickly and then the three boys picked up Kijun on their way to the hillock facing the ridge where the World Army had built its tent headquarters. The four boys perched, like a bevy of quail, watching the soldiers in the woods about five hundred yards away. There were at least a thousand of them. The green grass on the sloping terrain had been ruthlessly marred by the brown pockmarks of fresh dirt piled around countless foxholes.

The boys had never seen so many people assembled at one place before. Soldiers with dangling canteens and cartridge belts, soldiers carrying weapons over their shoulders or in their hands, soldiers with talking machines squealing on their backs, soldiers boiling black water in their mess tins and sipping it, soldiers folding and packing their socks and underwear, soldiers deflating and rolling tents—there were soldiers everywhere, moving around constantly.

"It must be great fun to travel around like that, camping day after day in the woods and by the river and any place you want to spend the night," said Kijun, sitting cross-legged on the rock.

"You can say that again," said Chandol, observing the soldiers closely to memorize every possible detail about real soldier business.

"I guess all the women in our village can sleep in their rooms from now on," said Kangho, squatting at the edge of the rock.

"I wonder why the *bengkos* did their raping only at Kumsan and Charcoal," Chandol said. "Castle village is much closer to their camp."

Kijun thought it over and said, "Maybe the *bengkos* preferred to do evil things at a distant place because they didn't want to be caught and punished by their captains."

"Looks like they're really leaving," Bong exclaimed, pointing at the opposite ridge. "*Bengkos* are climbing into trucks over there."

"Let's get a closer look at them," Chandol said, scrambling to his feet.

By the time the boys climbed down the hillock and reached the northern road to Castle village, the advance party of the U.N. troops was moving around the foot of General's Hill, heading for the North Han River. Trucks with dark canvas covers backed out one by one to carry the soldiers away.

"The *bengkos* must have had a lot of free chestnuts while they were camping in the grove of chestnut trees," Chandol said, halting on the road about two hundred yards away from a large group of soldiers sprawling in and around a bean patch, waiting for their turn to leave, their knapsacks and rifles placed in an orderly row along the ditch.

"Do you think they eat chestnuts?" Bong asked uncertainly. "I heard the World Army soldiers eat only food contained in cans or wrapped in papers."

"They must eat fruits and vegetables and stuff," Chandol said. "They're people like us, after all."

"The owner of that bean patch will get mad as hell," Kijun said, chuckling. "It's been all trampled to mush by trucks and soldiers."

"The U.N. Army has a lot of cars," Chandol said, looking around at the trucks in admiration.

"Look," Kijun said, giggling. "That *bengko* is smiling at us."

"He's beckoning," Bong said in a terrified voice.

"Shall we go over to him?" Chandol asked with a brave grin.

"It's dangerous," Bong said, more terrified. "I think we should run and hide."

"They do bad things at night but it's daytime now," Chandol said. "They do the war—fighting and even dying for us—in daytime. You don't have to be afraid of them as long as there is the sun."

Kijun said, "Look. He's holding out a can."

"Okay. Let's go," Chandol said.

The boys approached a swarthy *bengko* leaning against a broken tree with his helmet cupped on his upright knee. When Chandol halted a few steps away from him, the soldier offered a pack of Chuckles jelly candy to the boy. The children warily watched the colorful pieces of candy wrapped in mysteriously transparent glass paper as if they were dangerous explosives. Then Chandol snatched it from the soldier's big hairy paw and quickly stepped back. While the *bengko* was watching the boys with an amused expression, Chandol removed the glass paper and put one of the candy pieces in his mouth. It tasted good, sweet and gelatinous. Chandol gave each boy one piece and he had the extra one himself because he was the captain.

"I know what this is," Kangho said, chewing. "This is jelly. My father told me about this jelly thing."

"That's right," said Kijun. "My uncle told me about it, too."

"I like jelly." Bong stated his opinion in very simple terms.

"Shall we ask for some more candies?" Kijun said.

Chandol asked, "Do you know how to speak *bengko?*"

"Sure. I learned a lot of English words when I went to town with my uncle. The town boys speak English really well."

"English? What's English?"

"That's the *bengko* language."

"How do you say we want more jelly in English?"

"I just know how to say it," Jun replied.

"Say it then."

Kijun pranced over to the soldier with stubbly chin and said in a flat monotone as if reciting a Chinese poem, *"Hey, bengko, give me chop chop. Jelly give me chop chop."*

The *bengko* said something briefly in English, shrugging his shoulders. Chandol was disappointed when the soldier showed no sign of giving anything more to the boys. But another *bengko* who had been scraping the crusted mud from his boots with a broken twig went over to his knapsack by the ditch, fished out a dark green can and came back to give it to Kijun.

"See?" the fat boy said triumphantly.

The can had a small white metal device attached to its side and Kangho showed the boys how to turn it round and round to open the can. Inside there were salty crackers instead of sweet jelly candies.

"This tastes horrible," Chandol said.

Suddenly there was a ripple of noise among the soldiers by the bean patch. They slowly lined up along both sides of the road. These soldiers started to march, and the last of the liberators on the eastern ridge moved out, leaving behind a devastated slope that looked like bombed ruins. More soldiers were still coming down another ridge of General's Hill further north. The grove of chestnut trees was deserted, littered with empty cans with jagged open tops, ammunition casings and crumpled corrugated cardboard, squashy leftover food and other dumped or abandoned things. As if out on a treasure hunt during a school picnic, the four boys searched for useful or valuable things in the ruins, running among the trees and delving into piles of battle trash. Each of them found a couple of unopened C-ration cans, and Bong and Kijun respectively a dented canteen and a shiny can opener. Kangho came across a long loaf of bread that looked like a pillow.

"That's a pillow bread," Kijun explained to Kangho. "My uncle said some soldiers use it as pillow at night and cut out a piece of it for a meal when they're hungry. The *bengkos* always eat bread. They never eat rice."

"That's a lie as red as a monkey's behind," Chandol retorted, collecting spent cartridge cases under a burnt tree. "Nobody can live without eating rice."

Kangho, who had been sitting on a clump of grass chewing the gum stick he had found in a pile of empty cans and slimy lumps of boiled food and damp sawdust-like coffee grounds, said, "Look!"

A lone jeep, with its windshield down, was driving slowly behind the soldiers marching in two rows along the northern road. No more soldiers or vehicles were in sight.

"We will never see the foreign liberators any more, right?" Kangho said, somewhat relieved.

"Right," Chandol said, somewhat disappointed.

"We will miss them," Jun said, glancing at the captain and trying to be disappointed, too. "We've had really exciting days on account of them."

"Come on," Chandol said. "Let's go."

"Where are we going?" Kangho asked.

"Let's follow the *bengkos* and watch them some more. We may never have a chance to see them again."

"Do you think it'll be all right?" Bong asked.

"Don't worry. They won't harm us. Come."

The four boys, carrying the dented canteen and the pillow bread and other loot, followed the departing army. The soldiers in the jeep paid no attention to the boys. The Castle village farmers mutely watched the passing troops with indifferent or resentful expressions.

Following the marching soldiers, the four boys walked for more than two hours until their legs were stiff. They finally reached a bridge, over which, Chandol reckoned, the *bengko* trucks had entered West County. The U.N. troops crossed the bridge and marched onto a paved highway where they joined another World Army unit coming up from the south. Soldiers and vehicles were all moving toward Hwachon.

When they had crossed the bridge, the boys were too tired and hungry to march with the soldiers any longer. Chandol decided that they would make their lunch, under a poplar, from the cans and the pillow bread they had brought with them. And then they could watch the passing soldiers as long as they wanted, comfortably resting in the shade.

Growling, massive tanks rolled by, their blunt cannons poking into the air. Their heavy caterpillar treads left deep tooth-prints in the hot asphalt.

"There they are," Chandol exclaimed. "Real tanks."

"Yeah," Kijun said. "Aren't they splendid?"

Heavily loaded trucks crept by, some of them dragging fearful howitzers with long shiny barrels, muzzles capped with canvas covers. Some trucks had tent houses rigged in the back. And foot soldiers wearily trudged along the road on both sides of the truck procession.

"Don't they look impressive!" Chandol said, pointing at the plodding soldiers.

"Soldiers are most magnificent when they march," Kijun said.

"Why don't you say something to the liberators, Toad?" Chandol urged. "You're the only one among us that can speak to the *bengkos* in English, after all."

As if stung by that remark, Kijun sprang up, waving his hand, and shouted enthusiastically, *"Hello, bengko! Give me chop chop! Give me chop chop!"*

A soldier driving a heavy truck with huge wheels threw a chocolate bar to the boys and Kijun ran after it.

"Wait a minute," Chandol said. "You said those same words at the camp this morning, didn't you? You say it when you want a *bengko* to give you something to eat. Why don't you stop begging and say something new, something like 'goodbye', to the departing soldiers? Or perhaps you don't know any other *bengko* words, eh?"

"I know other *bengko* words all right," Kijun said, breaking the chocolate bar into four pieces to share it with the other boys. "How about this? *'Hello, bengko, bengko! Sonnomo betch! Sonnomo betch!'"*

"*Sonnomo betch?*" Chandol said, intrigued. "That sounds like Korean. 'Cabbages over the hill,' right?"

"But it is English," Kijun insisted. "My uncle told me that many town boys say it to passing *bengkos* and then run away. It must be a swearing expression because the soldiers always get mad when you say it to them."

"Maybe *betch* is the bad word. Perhaps they hate cabbages more than anything else in the world, because their eyes have turned green from eating too much cabbage and they hate green eyes. They look like monsters because their eyes are such a strange color."

The World Army soldiers were on an endless march, their heavy boots clomping on the tarmac, helmet straps cinched tight on their chins, their expressions glum or forlorn, their lips locked firmly in fatigue and boredom, their deepset eyes staring into the void ahead of them, so many identical helmets and rifle muzzles and loaded shoulders bobbing and streaming on and on.

"If you know any other *bengko* language expression, why don't you teach it to us? I really like *sonnomo betch*. I must remember it," Chandol said.

"I know *gerrary*. It's got something to do with someone going away.

83

When you go somewhere, people say *gerrary* to you. Or you say *gerrary* and someone leaves. I forget exactly which."

"That sounds perfect," Chandol said, "because the soldiers are going away and we have to bid farewell to them."

So the boys used it. Waving their hands goodbye, they shouted to the soldiers at the top of their voices:

"Gerrary! Gerrary!"

"Gerrary! Gerrary!"

Part II

TEXAS TOWN

ONE

The sky was a vast clear glass ceiling that might be shattered by the least vibration. In the willows by the stream, a bird sang. The pine needles had turned dusty green and the shade in the woods looked darker. Sitting on the stoop, Mansik stared at the field over the twig fence.

"Mother," he called.

There was no reply from the other room. Ollye did not stir. She gazed blankly at the ceiling, lying on the floor as usual. Nanhi was playing alone with jackstones by the walnut stump. It was so silent around him that he thought he could hear the silence itself. The boy lived in such absolute silence these days that he sometimes had delusions of hearing things such as the glass sky quietly cracking at noon or the village women skulking around the Chestnut House, with intermittent muffled giggles in the dark, to spy on the cursed family.

"We have nothing to eat along with the rice, Mother," the boy said.

A short silence ensued before Ollye reluctantly answered in a low, drained voice, "I know."

They had not run out of the rice they had taken from the town granary yet, but Mansik could find nothing in the kitchen to eat with it except salt, soy sauce and pickled garlic. "Maybe I'd better go to the hills and pick some mushrooms," the boy said.

After another short silence, her weak voice replied from the room, "Do you think you can go?"

"What do you mean? Of course I can."

Then it dawned on the boy why she had asked him that question. She was wondering if her son had finally summoned enough courage to venture out into the world which denied their existence. Mansik stared at his sister who was trying to grab all five stones at once with her clumsy fingers.

"I'll go to the hills in the afternoon," he said. "I'll go to the bean patch, too. And maybe I can get some potatoes somewhere."

He took a deep breath to brace himself. I can go anywhere I want to, he thought defiantly. Nobody is going to stop me.

Two strange women came up the riverbank from the ferry. Their clothes looked scandalous. The boy had never seen anything like them in West County. Even during his occasional trips to the town with his mother, Mansik had never seen anybody dressed as outrageously as these two. At first Mansik thought they were twin sisters because both of them were in such odd but identical attire—short blue-black skirts that exposed not only the bare skin of their calves but the whole round shape of their hips, and brightly colored blouses without any sleeves at all that revealed the ugly marks of cowpox shots on their shoulders for every-body to see. Their peculiar hair, in permanent waves, resembled upside-down bells, and both of them wore pointed, glossy leather shoes with high heels as sharp as hoe blades unlike the beautiful and elegant white or turquoise rubber shoes with exquisite flower patterns he was accustomed to seeing.

The women, each about twenty years old, paused by the log bridge to discuss something, looking around Inner and Outer Kumsan alternately, and then over at the Chestnut House. Mansik was embarrassed because he did not want to be caught secretly watching them. Then they reached a decision and crossed the bridge. They headed for Inner Kumsan along the road lined with blooming Chinese asters. Mansik stood and craned his neck to watch the women as they went. They paused again before the rice mill, had another short discussion, and one went over to the wide plank door. The woman seemed to hail someone, and a little while later, the smaller side door opened and Kangho's mother peeked out. They exchanged some words and the two strange women disappeared into the mill. Mansik was curious. He wondered why strangers from the town were visiting Kangho's family.

Mansik watched the closed doors of the silent mill for several minutes, waiting for something to happen. The women came out of the mill and went over to the tobacco shop near the old ginkgo tree. Mansik waited again, growing more and more curious. They took a little more time at the tobacco shop. When they came out of the tobacco shop at last, Mansik felt instinctively that these strangers were plotting something. The boy did not know what their scheme was, but he did not like it.

Now the two women retraced their steps along the road lined with Chinese asters back to the log bridge, crossed the stream, and came directly over to the Chestnut House. They stopped by the chestnut tree and one gestured at Mansik to come over to them.

"Mother," Mansik called, sidling to the gate, his eyes still fixed on the women.

Ollye must have heard the footsteps coming up the footpath too, for she replied without much delay this time, "Yes?"

"We have visitors."

"Who are they?"

"I don't know," the boy said. "They look very strange."

"Find out who they are and what they want from us."

The woman in the purple blouse was tall and slim, her left eye conspicuously narrower than the right, and she had a way of looking at people sideways with her chin pulled in. This woman had painted her eyelashes thickly like caterpillars and her lips as red as blood, like a shaman. She also had shiny glass pieces suspending from her earlobes and a pearly necklace resting on her bulging breasts. And she wore a small, personal watch on her wrist, while only four families in Kumsan village even had their own household clocks. She held a large black velvet purse in her hand.

The other woman clutched an identical large black velvet purse. This woman, in a red blouse, was as heavily made up as the first, and had a mole on her high forehead. She had a baby face with chubby cheeks and a plump chin, and her expression was alert although her eyes were bloodshot from lack of sleep. This young woman's blouse, like her companion's, very clearly showed the shape of her big breasts. Mansik supposed they were not decent women, because all respectable ones did their best to completely conceal the existence of their most feminine parts in loose dresses. Most shocking of all for Mansik was the fact that their sleeveless blouses even revealed the shameful hair under their armpits whenever either one of them lifted her hand.

"You must be Mansik," the woman in purple said, tapping his nosetip. At first glance Mansik had recognized her as the leader of the two.

"Who are you?" said Mansik, recoiling. Now he was sure he did not like this strange women. "My mother wants to know who you are. And what do you want from us?"

Ignoring his questions, the woman in purple peered into the house to catch sight of Ollye. "I've got something to talk about to your mother," she said. "Will you tell her that we came to see her?"

"Mother," he called. "Come on out here. They want to talk to you."

Ollye kept silent for a while. She said at last, "Let them come in."

The rusty hinges of the gate opened with a cautious creak and Mansik stepped aside so that the visitors could enter. As they waited in the yard, Ollye, pallid and emaciated, came out to the stoop, tidying herself. She led the visitors into her room and Mansik sat down on the edge of the stoop to find out what these two women were up to. The woman in purple introduced herself and her friend to Ollye.

"My name is Yonghi and this is Sundok," she said.

The woman in red nodded her head hello. Not prepared for visitors, Ollye squatted defensively near the wall without replying.

Yonghi tried to be sociable. "My name means 'Dragon Girl.' My father gave me that name because my mother had an auspicious dream of a golden dragon soaring to the blue sky while she was pregnant with me. But I've never made anything close to a heavenly dragon." She chuckled and so did her friend. She went on, "My friends call me Serpent, because that's the thing I've made closest to a dragon. Some of my friends call me Loach, because they believe I haven't even made a snake!"

These two women were shameless and insolent enough to joke and laugh about their personal lives—intimate matters—at a stranger's house on their very first meeting, and Ollye tried very hard not to look directly at the bare skin of their exposed arms and chests.

"Tell me why you wanted to see me," she said, watching her young daughter trying to feed jackstones to the rabbits in the yard.

"Well, well, well, you know," said Yonghi, stealing a sidelong glance at Ollye. "We didn't know anything about it when we arrived here but . . ." She paused for another quick squint. "We've been enquiring about getting a room or a house in this village and learned of it at the tobacco shop by sheer chance."

"Learned of what?" Ollye said. She did not understand because she was not listening attentively.

Yonghi restrained herself, not too sure how to approach this naive country woman. She glanced at Sundok, hoping to detect a hint in her friend's expression. Sundok offered no clue. The woman in purple turned back to Ollye. It was this hesitant silence, not Yonghi's actual explanation, that enlightened Ollye as to what the visitor was trying to tell her. Yonghi was relieved when she noticed by the subtle change of her expression that Mansik's mother had finally got the message.

"I am so sorry for you," the stranger said solemnly. That was enough compassion for courtesy, however, and she instantly resumed her aggressive approach, getting down to business. "So I thought I might be able to help you somehow and decided to visit you. I have a proposition to offer you."

"A proposition?" It was Ollye's turn to study the visitor's expression to seek a hint.

"Yes. And a good one too," the visitor said. "Since you've gone through such a terrible ordeal, you might want to leave this village."

"Leave this village?" Ollye said, puzzled.

"That's right. Leave. You know. Leave here and forget everything. You can settle down at a new place and start a whole new life, if you want. You must have thought about it a lot."

So far Ollye had not considered the possibility of leaving West County. If she left she believed she would wither and die, like grass uprooted. She could never leave the County. Never.

"Why are you making this offer to me?" Ollye asked, brushing her hair back with her bony fingers. "Why is it your concern if I leave this village or not?"

The woman in purple once more studied Ollye's eyes to determine if she had given too many hints and cornered herself. She did not think so. "You have to dispose of your house if you leave this village," she said. "And I want to buy your house in that case."

"Why do you want to buy my house?"

"Because I need it."

"Mother," Mansik called, rising slowly from the stoop, looking out at the road with a worried face.

"What is it, Mansik?"

"Look," the boy said. "Out there on the road. Master Hwang is watching us."

Ollye looked over the fence at the road and saw Old Hwang, standing in the road staring at the Chestnut House, his face red with anger. The old man must have come from the rice paddies where he had been working, she supposed, for he had a wet sickle in his hand and his rolled-up sleeves were stained with mud.

Mansik was surprised by his mother's indifference to the old man. This was the first time she had ever ignored the old master.

Ollye turned back to her visitors. "Why do you need this house?" she asked.

The woman in purple seemed to vacillate for a moment as if choosing whether or not to tell her the truth. She decided to be honest but discreet. "You'll have some visitors here soon," she said. She wanted to reserve some information for the time being.

"He's going away," Mansik said, stretching to watch the old man strut away.

Ollye did not even bother to look. "What visitors?" she asked Yonghi.

"Why do you care? You must want to leave here with your son and daughter and forget the whole thing. We need a room or a house to do some business with the visitors who will come here soon. We've been looking around this village for a house to rent or buy, but didn't find anything satisfactory . . . until now." It was obvious that Yonghi was determined to buy the Chestnut House. "Now you know the whole story. And I want to know how much you want for this hut."

"I didn't say anything about selling this house," Ollye said. "Nor anything about leaving this place."

The woman in purple was becoming desperate, thinking Ollye was driving a hard bargain. Maybe the prospect of selling was too sudden and her offer too generous for this woman, Yonghi thought.

The harder the strangers tried to persuade her, the more suspicious Ollye became. The woman in red joined in, but Ollye would not change her mind, because she had absolutely no idea where she would go if she sold the house and left the village.

"Well," the woman in purple finally said, picking up her velvet purse and rising to leave, "I'd better admit that I lost this time. Let's go back to town, Sundok."

Ollye was about to say goodbye to the departing visitors when Sundok, stepping down to the yard, spotted a hovel on the riverbank about five hundred yards downstream.

"Look, Sister Serpent," she said to Yonghi. "That's a very nice location, isn't it?"

Shading her eyes from the sun's glare with her hand, Yonghi took a careful look at the distant thatched hut. "I can't see what shape it's in at this distance, but its location is terrific," she agreed. Squeezing her plump feet into her tight leather shoes, she asked Ollye, "Who lives there?"

"A snake hunter," Ollye explained. "An old man who catches snakes to sell at the snake soup house at Central Market. He used to live at a house near that tall ginkgo tree over there, but the neighbors built a new hut by the river and asked the old man to go and live there. They were afraid that snakes might escape from his house one night and . . ."

Sundok, who was not a bit interested in snakes, interrupted Ollye's explanation and suggested to Yonghi, "Why don't we go take a look at the hut, Sis? Maybe that shack is just what we've been looking for, after all."

"Sure," Yonghi said, already hurrying to the gate. "Sorry we pestered you," she said to Ollye. "I'll come back to say hello to you when we open our shop."

Watching the two strange women hurry along the riverbank to the snake hunter's shack, Ollye thought the purple and red colors of their blouses were like butterflies. Butterflies flying free. She stepped down from the stoop, suddenly reanimated, and hurried to the kitchen saying to Mansik, who was washing Nanhi's dusty hands with a wet towel, "I'll go out and find something to cook for side dishes, Mansik. You look after Nanhi while I'm gone."

She took the smudged bamboo basket from the kitchen and a hoe from the back yard. And for the first time in a month, she left the Chestnut House. She looked up and down to see if anybody was watching her. Nobody was in sight. Hugging the basket and the hoe in her arms, she dashed down to the road. Out on the road, she thought it was ridiculous for her to run. Nobody was chasing after her to drag her back to the house.

She tried to compose herself and walk confidently but she could not shed her uneasy feeling. Her knees were shaky. She felt uncomfortable outside the house. Her heart was palpitating when she reached the log bridge. What would she do if she encountered anyone?

She heard a splashing sound under the bridge. She stopped. The splashing sound stopped, too. She looked around once more, and then down under the bridge. Bong, who had been bathing naked, alone, looked up at her, startled, frozen there under the bridge, holding his crotch with his little hands. She was also embarrassed, seeing that the boy was on the verge of bursting into tears. It was obvious that this young friend of Mansik's dreaded her.

For a moment, she thought of going back home. Now she had no doubt that other villagers would react more or less the same way to seeing her. But she was determined not to turn back. She had to go on. Anywhere away from her house. She decided to get as far off the road as possible to avoid chance encounters.

She went down to the rice paddies, made a long detour along the web of dikes around Hyonam village, and hurried to the nearest slope. She went up to the lookout shed by a watermelon patch. The patch owner slept at the open shed on summer nights to keep the watermelon-thieves away, but it was usually abandoned during the daytime. This slope was one of Ollye's favorite spots for collecting herbs like shepherd's purse, fernbrake, and wild lettuce for dinner. She searched among the grass stalks for sowthistle, sagebrush, bellflower and other edible plants. When she had collected enough herbs, Ollye went into a nearby grove of alder trees to conceal herself and rest. She sat on a soft bed of clover and watched the open field and the open river beyond. Withered leaves whirled down in droves from the aspens by the turnip patch at the foot of the slope. She inhaled the cool breeze. A silent, peaceful feeling, bliss, slowly overwhelmed her.

Sitting all alone among the trees, Ollye looked down at the village. The lonely poplars on the riverbank were being stripped of their leaves by the passing wind, and nothing moved on the sandy shore of Cucumber Island. Mudfish Pool looked like a stain of spilt mercury in the middle of rice paddies that were divided into many large or small rectangles by the dikes. She saw Bong hurriedly pass by and head for the ginkgo tree, but could not find the purple and red blouses anywhere. They must be in the snake hunter's shack, she thought.

The soothing sense of freedom she had briefly felt was gradually overshadowed by a consciousness of isolation as she sat there, watching the village and brooding. Why, why on earth had she been chosen as the victim that fateful night? She wondered if she had conceived the *bengkos*' child. What would happen to her, to Mansik and Nanhi, if she gave birth to a child of yellow hair, blue eyes and black skin? She might be carrying the bud of that monstrous creature in her womb. Even now, her skin crawled with shame and pain to think of that horrible night.

Ollye looked over at the Hwangs' rice paddies in the southern gorge of General's Hill, where Old Hwang and his son were shearing the rice with four hired hands. Standing in a file, the six men chewed into the dense rice plants like a silkworm eating away a mulberry leaf. Some distance down the stream two women were hurrying on their way along the road from Outer Kumsan, carrying large wooden pails on their heads. One of them was the Tuktuwon Woman and Ollye guessed that they were taking lunch rice to the Hwangs' paddies. Carrying lunch out to the fields during the busy harvest season used to be Ollye's work, but things had changed. Now everything was different from what it used to be a month ago. One long month ago.

She might have been spared this ordeal if her husband had been alive, Ollye thought. Somehow he would have protected her from the *bengkos.* Living all alone, ostracized, she missed him more and more, often wondering how her life might be different now if he was alive . . . if he was alive. . . .

On summer evenings, she used to shiver in ecstatic excitement as the whole house burst with the intense smell of his sweat when he burned wet grass in the yard to smoke away the bothersome mosquitoes, or when he hungrily swallowed potatoes and rice, or when he smoked rolled tobacco sitting cross-legged on the stoop, or when he cleaned the dirt from under his fingernails with a broken twig, or whenever he was just there near her. She missed his masculine odor, his blunt thumbnails, his front tooth, broken in the middle when he had fallen upon the stepping-stone while moving a big soy sauce jar to the kitchen, and his huge rough hand that fondled her breasts and crotch every night in the dark.

She shook her head to drive away her memories and looked down at the peaceful river. The two women, Yonghi and Sundok, came out of the snake hunter's shack and headed for the ferry. They did not seem to be in a hurry at all. Perhaps they had managed to buy the hut from the old man. Ollye wondered why these two women wanted to buy a house here so badly. And who were the "visitors" they had mentioned?

Ollye had been tempted, momentarily, by the unexpected opportunity to escape when Yonghi had asked her to sell the Chestnut House that morning. But her life had taken root here too deeply for her to break away. Ollye's parents had been sharecroppers for the Buddhist temple on the slope of the Three Peaks Mountain for years until her father started a love affair with a woman worshipper who frequented the temple to seek transcendental peace of mind but never neglected her worldly desires. Their affair lasted too long and she came to the mountain too often, and the suspicious husband finally hired a woodcutter to shadow his wife. This insatiable woman and Ollye's father were caught while engaging in their illicit pleasure in the woods at night. The husband, infuriated by the woodcutter's report, ran up all the way to the temple from the town, barged into the worshippers' quarters in the middle of the night, flogged his wife half to death with an oak stick, and dragged her away like a hog to the butcher. Two days later, Ollye's father, who had hidden in the forest, sneaked back into his room at night, packed his things and vanished, never to return. They heard the rumor months later that the two adulterers had secretly rendezvoused at Kangchon and eloped to Wonju.

Abandoned by her husband and too ashamed to stay at the temple any longer, Ollye's mother came down to Kamwa village and built a shack at the foot of the mountain. But she had no means of support for herself and her young daughter. Then one day, about a month after she had built the hut, a young man came to see her from Kumsan village and told her to remove the shack and go away because that land belonged to the Hwangs. She would not comply with the Hwangs' order, for she had no place to go and she had expended much effort in building that shabby little hut. The argument dragged on for months. In the meantime the Hwangs came to sympathize with her and eventually allowed her to sharecrop a piece of their land near Hyonam village. This was how Ollye first met Old Hwang when she was only ten years old.

It was also Old Hwang who later arranged her marriage with Kim Indong when she grew up. The marriage, at sixteen, brought her glimpses of hope and happiness never known to her before; most of her young years had been spent toiling all day in the scorching sun or shivering all night in winter's cold. Building a new life with a husband of her own filled her heart so she was not as sad as she was supposed to be when her mother died. Although the little river-side hut they lived in was always dark and filled with smoke, she felt her whole body brim over with mysterious strength when her husband was at home with her. She could persevere against all hardship as long as he was there.

She shook her head again to drive away the futile longing for her husband. She was alone now, and she had to learn to live alone. She missed him more at the moments when life was hard, but she would have to be tougher. The more she missed him, the harder she had to try to forget him, for there was nobody in the world who could save her now, except herself.

Ollye watched the four boys climbing the opposite slope toward the Hwangs' graves beneath the Eagle Rock. She could not recognize their faces because of the distance, but she knew they were the four village boys who used to play with her son every day. They did not play with Mansik any longer. She was sorry for her son, the innocent prisoner. She was sorry that he had to suffer along with her.

She looked over at the river. The two women were getting off the boat on the shore of Cucumber Island. Ollye picked up her basket and stood, ready to go home. She was going to cook a nice meal this evening for her children. Engrossed in her own distress, she had neglected them. She wanted to make up for it. Even if she could not free herself from this curse, she had to help Mansik overcome it. She was a mother.

Ollye passed the lookout shed and hastened down the slope. She wanted to be back with her children as quickly as possible. There must be a change, a new start to her life, she thought. And her children's.

When she reached the road, Ollye saw the Toktuwon Woman and the miller's wife coming down the other road from the rice paddies, carrying empty lunch pails on their heads. Ollye was at a loss. She was going to meet these two women at the spot where the roads converged near the log bridge. The two women saw her and faltered, too. The miller's wife said something to the Toktuwon Woman, and then they started to walk slowly again. Even if she could avoid the embarrassment of encountering them face to face at the fork in the road, Ollye dreaded the idea of walking all the way home with the two women staring at her from behind. She slowed down. The two women slowed down too. It was clear that the two women were controlling their pace to meet her at the intersection. Ollye could not run any more. She had to face what was to come.

When they met at the fork in the road, the three women stopped at the same time as if on cue. Ollye hesitated, wondering whether she should greet the woman of the Hwangs at least, if not the miller's wife. But she could not say anything. She did not know the proper words to say at a moment like this. She did not even have the courage to look them in the face. She turned her eyes to her house across the bridge, hoping either of the two women would say something, anything, to her. But they kept quiet, observing her from head to toe curiously. Then they started to run toward the bridge, laughing.

Ollye watched them scamper away, giggling. Perhaps I should have sold the house this morning, she thought.

TWO

Sitting cross-legged in the meditating posture squarely before the door of his room, Old Hwang gazed at the Three Peaks Mountain looming in the morning fog, thinking. Even the trees on the riverbank, having shed most of their leaves, looked chilly, for this was the Day of Cold Dew.

Old Hwang was upset because of the two strange women who had visited his county yesterday. The glaring colors of their outlandish attire had gotten on his nerves from the moment he first saw them from a distance. He was merely curious at first, but he gradually became suspicious as they visited the rice mill and then the tobacco shop as if they were looking for something definite. By the time they went to the Chestnut House, he wanted to find out what kind of women they were and what they were after. But he could not just walk into Ollye's house and ask questions of the strange women. They should have come to see him first if they had any business to transact. He could not tolerate such impertinent persons. When Ollye glanced at him over the fence but ignored him, he was infuriated, for he had never before been insulted by her like that. He had to return to the rice paddies, fuming, "Insolent women! Insolent women!" He could no longer stand there in the road like a fool watching them.

Before returning to the rice paddies, Old Hwang dropped in at the Paulownia House to wash his muddy hands and found the miller's wife at the well with the Toktuwon Woman cleaning the rice for the workers' lunch. He asked why those shameless women had visited the miller earlier. She said the two women had wanted a house.

"Why did they want a house here?" the old man said.

"I don't know, Master Hwang. They didn't tell us why."

On his way back to the rice paddies, the old man saw the two women hurry along the riverbank to the snake hunter's hut. He concluded that these outsiders were very serious about their business, and decided to send his son for the snake hunter to ask him why they wanted a house.

When Old Hwang asked him if the women had wanted to buy his hut, the snake hunter, averting his eyes guiltily, said that he had sold it.

"Sold it!" the old man said, his fury already mounting. "Did you by any chance ask them the reason why they want to buy your hut?"

"I did, Master Hwang."

"Well?"

"They wouldn't tell me, Master Hwang."

"So you don't have any idea why they want to have a house in this village."

"No, sir."

Old Hwang exploded. "You, you—gutless idiot!" he roared. "Why didn't you come to consult me before selling the hut to them? If you had any sense at all in that head of yours, you could see at one glance that they are women of dubious nature—women who travel without husbands or chaperones and make business deals by themselves!"

Old Hwang told him to go find the women at once and cancel the deal if he could not prove that they were decent respectable persons, which they certainly were not. That evening, while playing flower cards with the villagers at the tobacco shop, the snake hunter complained about the old man interfering with his right to sell his own house. The women must have paid him quite a chunk of money, or the snake hunter, one of the lowest men in the community, would not have complained so openly about Rich Hwang, risking a severe rebuke for challenging the old man's authority. Nobody had sold or leased a house in the county for generations and they had no idea what a house was worth these days, but the villagers were sure that the women had offered the snake hunter a staggering sum, one so large that he would piss in Old Hwang's face if he had to. The women had paid the whole sum in cash and asked the snake hunter to vacate the hut as soon as possible. These strange women seemed to work very fast.

Old Hwang was about to leave his house the next morning after a light breakfast of sesame soup to go to ask the miller if the snake hunter had canceled the deal yet when he spotted three strange women coming to the village from the ferry. "Sokku," the old man called his son, who was feeding the ox. "Fetch those women here. I want to talk to them."

These new visitors were dressed, and even walked, the same way as the two women who had been there yesterday. Hurrying to the log bridge to intercept the three women before they could cross the stream and head for Inner Kumsan, Sokku had a gloomy premonition that some evil spirit was hovering in the air over the village. Two women yesterday and three more today — women with painted faces in gay blouses and leather shoes were invading, crossing the river to steal something away from the farmers. But he could not guess what they were after.

"Wait, women," Sokku said, hastening to the bridge, waving his hand.

The women in bold clothing stopped on the road, staring at the young farmer, who was now, gingerly, approaching them.

"Will you three come with me?" he said. "My father wants to talk to you."

The three women looked at one another, affronted and amused at the same time. Then a woman with a hooked nose whose huge breasts drooped like a cow's in her persimmon-colored blouse, the one who looked the most aggressive of the three, stepped forward.

"Who on earth is your father that he wants to see us?" she asked.

After a momentary hesitation, Sokku simply pointed at his father who was standing before the Paulownia House, for he was not sure how to introduce his father to these women. The visitors seemed to show more interest in the imposing house with its tiled roof than the old man with grey hair and whiskers standing before it. The three women exchanged glances; the hooked nose one nodded her head. They obediently followed him.

The tall woman walking next to Young Hwang asked him in a sweet voice, "Is your house the biggest one around here? Have you lived here long?"

"Yes," Sokku said uncertainly. He could not understand why she was trying to be friendly with him.

"You must know this village very well," she said. "I wonder if you can do us a favor."

Sokku did not reply because he was not sure what favor she was talking about.

The tall woman did not give up. "We heard that Sister Serpent had bought a house in this village," she said. "Do you happen to know if there are any other houses for sale around here?"

Sokku was so amazed by her brash inquiry that he did not say anything more to them until they arrived at the Paulownia House. These women looked as tough as any man and Sokku wondered where and how they had earned so much money that they were able to walk into a village and buy houses on the spot. Old Hwang did not waste any time when his son brought them to him.

"I want to know who you are, and for what purpose you are visiting this village," the old man said point-blank.

The women were dumbfounded for a brief moment. Then the third woman, who looked not a day older than eighteen, retorted, "We're looking for a house we can stay in for some time. Anything wrong about that?"

"What do you want a house for?" Old Hwang demanded.

The women remained silent.

"Two other women like you came here yesterday to buy a house, and I want to know the reason why so many women are suddenly interested in buying houses here," the old man went on. "Tell me. Why do you need a house in this village all of a sudden?"

The woman with a hooked nose spoke for her companions, "We need a house because we have to live here. We don't know how long for, but we will have to stay here at least three or four months. Maybe longer."

The old man kept silent, waiting for a further explanation.

She continued, "You'll have real prosperity for several months at least. We plan to settle down here for some time and enjoy business. Are you satisfied now, old man?"

Old Hwang frowned at the young woman's insolent tone.

Glancing at his father, Young Hwang decided to intervene. "What business is there for women like you to do at a country village like ours?" Sokku asked. "What do you do for living, anyway? You don't look like farmers to me."

The three women stared at Sokku, wondering if this young man was making fun of them. They soon realized he was not. Then the hooked nose one blurted, "We're whores."

At first the old man and his son did not believe what the woman had told them. "What did you say?" asked the old man.

"Whores," the hooked nose woman repeated. "You know. Prostitutes. Anything else you want to know about us?"

The old man, breathless from astonishment, said in a choked voice,

"You mean you're going to open pleasure houses here and do that business with the villagers?"

The three women burst into laughter.

"What is so funny?"

"Sorry we laughed, old man, but we couldn't help it. You see, we don't do our business with farmers. There's not much money in it. Maybe you two really don't know anything about us. People call us 'U.N. ladies' or 'Yankee wives.' We work only with the Yankees."

"Yankees? But we don't have Yankees around here."

"You will have them all right. A lot of them. And soon."

"What do you mean by that?" Sokku said.

"An American unit will arrive soon, and when they move their base here . . ."

"Wait a minute," the old man said. "You mean the foreign soldiers are coming here again?"

"Sure. That's the reason we're in a hurry to find a place to open our shop."

"So you're planning to make money by being prostitutes for the foreign soldiers in this village," the old man mumbled as if to himself.

"Yes, sir. This godforsaken village will prosper and become a boom town. Every miserable farmer in this area will get rich if he makes the right moves quickly enough. In wartime, you have to work for soldiers in every business. And *you* should be grateful to God in Heaven that a whole unit of them is going to be stationed here."

Old Hwang was stupefied by this unexpected news. Why should he, or anybody in the county, be grateful to God for the coming of foreign soldiers? That a whole bunch of the *bengkos* was coming to stay for months was bad news enough, but this time wicked women would swarm to his village, too. They would invade this community and infest it like dung flies with houses of shame right under his nose.

"What a disgrace," the old man muttered. He resumed his usual stern manner and ordered his son, "Sokku, take these women to the ferry and send them back to wherever they've come from."

The old man spat angrily and strutted into his house.

The three women did not leave the village without putting up verbal and even physical resistance. Sokku had to drag them to the ferry by force. The shameless women kept kicking and scratching and screaming and swearing all the way to the river.

"What the hell do you think you are? Do you own this village or something? No son of a bitch ever drove us out of any town. You bastards won't be able to keep us out of this damned place for long either."

Even while they were being carried away to Cucumber Island by the boat, they kept shrieking and cursing at the top of their voices. "Fuck you, old man! You will pay for this. We'll come back and fuck everybody in front of your gate! I'll fuck your son and piss in your face!"

When they were gone, the old man ordered the snake hunter never to let the women set their feet in his hut because they were immoral, sinful creatures who were determined to corrupt and destroy the community. The snake hunter said, with a displeased grunt, that he understood what he was supposed to do quite well. Then the old man instructed Pae, the official village chief, to pass the word to every farmer of Kumsan, and to all the other villages in West County, not to sell any house to the undesirable outsiders. He also dispatched the miller to the town to confirm the rumor that the Americans were coming.

What the Yankee wives had said proved to be true. The Yankee wives were on the move constantly, traveling up and down the country with the *bengkos;* whenever the soldiers moved to a new place, they would pack up and migrate with their "steady customers" or "temporary husbands." They were scouting for their new business sites near the base the Americans were about to build on Cucumber Island.

That afternoon and the next morning, more "U.N. ladies" came across the river looking for a house to let, but not a single farmer would discuss the matter with them. The villagers respected Old Hwang's instructions. Besides, nobody wanted the indecent women, who associated with the rapist soldiers, to live next door. In the meantime the villagers, especially the women, discussed the imminent arrival of the

Yankees and their prostitutes with apprehension and fear. The adults were embarrassed by their children's question, "What's a whore, dad?"

When they realized that West County was completely closed, the new Yankee wives had to find places elsewhere. But Old Hwang, as well as the other villagers, had the snake hunter's shack to worry about.

The boys enjoyed the war more and more as the days passed. Before the war, they were happy enough to play all day with a water beetle or a mole cricket. When war broke out they realized that the world was full of wonders they had not even dreamed of. They looked forward to the arrival of the Yankees. When they actually appeared, the boys were so delighted that they went across the river every day to watch the *bengkos* build their camp.

Prior to the arrival of the soldiers themselves, huge trucks brought steel beams and plates and a lot of soldier-workers began to construct a bridge between the town and Cucumber Island. When the bridge was completed, trucks rolled onto the islet early in the morning and unloaded hundreds of *bengkos*, both black and white, who pitched their A-tents and started to dig ditches and erect frame structures. Bulky plywood crates piled up on the sand and among the thriving weeds. The soldiers also installed a fence of barbed wire around the highest area of the islet. Weird, heavy machinery with caterpillar wheels and huge plough-like blades came next to remove the dense grass and level the ground outside the fence. Then they started making roads and building Quonset structures at the southern end of the camp.

On the first day of the *bengkos'* arrival, the village women hid again in their shelters at night, but no Yankees came across the river. The next night and the third night passed. When the new Yankees had done no harm to the county for a week, some farmers came to Old Hwang to seek advice as to whether the women should continue to hide all night so long as the foreign soldiers were stationed in the islet. The old man told the village chiefs of the county to let their wives and daughters sleep at home, for it was getting very cold after dark these days. Hwang also instructed them to organize lookout patrols of the young men of the county, who would guard the river every night in shifts, spot any *bengko* coming across the river and alert the farmers.

The *bengko* soldiers camping on the islet behaved very differently from the savage army that had gone north. None of the newcomers ever showed up at Kumsan, not even in the daytime. They were busy constructing a small town within the barbed-wire fence.

One day the four Kumsan boys went to Cucumber Island as usual to yell "hey, *bengko*, give me chop chop, give me chop chop," to the soldiers guarding the fence and get some C-ration cans or chocolate bars. It was a bad day for the boys, because they met no *bengkos* at all until they reached the main gate near the Soyang ferry. The two guards at the gate had nothing to give them either.

Then Chandol saw a plank sign nailed atop a long pole by the guardhouse. The sign carried the *bengko* letters "OMAHA," and underneath it, the equivalent Korean letters in clumsy handwriting.

"O Ma Ha?" Chandol said. "What is O Ma Ha? Sounds like somebody's name. Anybody know who O Maha is?"

Nobody did.

"Hey, Toad, how about you? Do you know who O Maha is?"

Kijun said he had no idea.

"Hasn't your uncle told you about it?" Chandol asked.

Kijun managed to save his face later because it was his uncle, after all, who found out that Omaha was the name of a town in America.

"Omaha" was not the only sign that was put up in the islet. Somebody erected a sign in the shape of a milepost that, like the Omaha sign, carried both in English and Korean the words "Texas Town," at the entrance to another village a few hundred yards distant from Camp Omaha's main gate. This second village was not constructed by the *bengko* soldiers, but by dozens of Korean carpenters and workers brought in from the town. With broken planks from ammunition boxes, tin plates from beer cans and sturdy cardboard from C-ration cartons, a team of two or three carpenters worked a miracle, creating one shanty a day. Built wall-to-wall, the board shacks on the barren slope looked like one big beehive.

As the shanties were completed one after another the Yankee wives, carrying big bulging suitcases, came to Texas Town. Soon the shanty town was fully occupied by the prostitutes.

Sister Serpent and Sundok returned to Kumsan around the time when the soldiers and the Yankee wives started building Camp Omaha and Texas Town.

Old Hwang summoned the snake hunter once more. "Let me have the money you received from those women," the old man said. "I'll return the money and tell them myself to stay away from this county." The snake hunter went back to fetch the money, grumbling, and did not come out of his den again all afternoon. The boatman came to the Paulownia House late that night to report that the snake hunter had left the village in secret.

"He said he was going to town for the night, but I doubt he will ever return, Master Hwang," the boatman said. "He was carrying two bundles, and one bundle rattled with bowls and kitchen stuff when he put it down on the boat, and the other bundle contained clothes and bedding. He sure looked like he was leaving here for good. He even carried a bag with wriggling snakes in it."

The old man told Sokku to go and check the riverside shack. The boatman was right. The snake hunter had packed everything worth taking with him and cleared out.

When Yonghi and Sundok showed up at the village again, Old Hwang had to go to see the two women himself, accompanied by his son, to tell them his wishes. The women were sorting and hanging their colorful clothes on the wall of the musty room, while an ancient carpenter, who was as emaciated and wizened as a dried fish, surveyed the shack to decide what repairs were needed.

When Old and Young Hwang were both present for a discussion or negotiation with another party, it usually was the son who did most of the initial talking so that his father need not waste his breath on trivial details before making his major statements. Naturally, Sokku tried first to politely persuade the women to show some consideration for the community, to find another place to open their business. Yonghi ridiculed his request that they leave. Then Old Hwang offered to reimburse them for whatever money they had paid the snake hunter, but the women did not seem to understand that they should be ashamed of themselves.

"What the hell does this old cock think he is anyway?" said Sister Serpent, not a bit intimidated. "An MP or something? What right do you have to tell us to stay away from this place? I bought this house with my own money, and nobody is going to drive me out of my own house. You think you can treat me like dirt because I'm a whore, but, you fucking bastard, you'll see that you have it all wrong."

Old Hwang, his face flushed with shame and rage, strode back home, for he realized logic would not work with these degenerate animals. Half an hour later, the boatman was summoned to the Paulownia House.

"If those two women who bought the snake hunter's hut or any other women at Texas Town ever ask you to row the boat for them to cross the river, you may not do it. You must never let yourself be tempted by any offer they might make. If the filthy women or the foreign soldiers reach this side of the river on your boat, that will be the last day you'll see this village. Do you understand that?"

"Yes, Master Hwang."

Yom, the boatman, knew well enough serious consequences might arise if the *bengkos* came to Kumsan again, but there was another reason—possibly the most important reason imaginable for him—that he had to follow the old man's instructions. This was harvest season, and the villagers would soon collect and give him his yearly payment in crops. He could not afford to offend Rich Hwang or the villagers at this time of year.

When the two women showed up at the ferry the next morning to go to Texas Town to fetch a carpenter to fix up their shack, the boatman flatly refused to serve them.

"If I let you set as much as one of your toes on my boat, Rich Hwang will throw me out of the county," Yom said.

Sister Serpent tried to coax him into rowing the boat for them, but no smiles, no offers of money, nothing worked. Yom kept repeating "no way, no way," without even looking at the women. While the two women were arguing with the boatman, Pae, the village chief, came down to the ferry to go and look at Cucumber Island on Old Hwang's instructions, to see if it was safe for the village women to pass through on their way to town. As Pae scrambled onto the boat and Yom raised the pole to push the boat off, Sister Serpent grabbed the mooring rope.

"Look here, boatman," she said. "You have to cross the river anyway because you have a passenger. Why don't you just let us go along?"

The village chief decided to intervene. "Listen, women," he said. "This boat is a public property of the West County inhabitants, and *we* decide who can use this boat and who cannot. It has been decided that nobody from Texas Town will be allowed to use this boat. So, if you can't swim, you can fly across the river."

"Did you hear that?" Yonghi said in anger. "Did you hear what that son of a bitch said?" An outburst of colorful oaths followed.

Appalled by the foul language gushing out of the painted lips of the young women, Pae told the boatman to get going. "Yes, chief," said the boatman, snatching the rope from Yonghi's hand.

"Chief?" Sundok said. "How about that, Sister Serpent? That cripple must be the village chief around here. No wonder these people behave so strangely. Let me ask you something, chief. What's wrong with you folks here? I don't see anything but asses around here. Does your tribe eat hay? And who the hell is old man Hwang? Why does that old cock put his nose in everybody's business? Tell me, chief, how many times a day do you have to lick his shoes?"

But all the ranting in the world did not help them. Left alone at the ferry, tired from screaming and not knowing what to do next, the two women agreed that they were hungry. And then they recalled that there was a woman in the village who might be able to help them out of their ridiculous plight. They hurried to the Chestnut House.

Yonghi barged into the house, hailing Mansik's mother noisily, faking delight and surprise as if she had come across one of her best friends in a strange town. "How have you been, Mansik's mother?" She climbed up to the stoop without waiting for Ollye's invitation. "I told you I'd come to see you soon, didn't I? Friends in need are . . ." Then she breathlessly swore at Old Hwang and the cripple of a village chief and the boatman. "How on earth could they do this to us?" she asked in a conspiratorial tone, suggesting that they were sharing persecution by a common enemy. "This village could make a lot of money if you had a few bars for the American soldiers, you know, but these hicks are simply too stupid to see this God-given opportunity to get out of their miserable life of digging the dirt like worms until their last day. We're bringing luck and business to this place, but these ungrateful bastards treat us like filthy rags."

Then Yonghi told Ollye what had happened at the ferry. She wanted to know if there was some other way they could get across the river. Ollye said there was a bridge far upstream, but it might take one full day to get to the islet by that route.

Yonghi said, "By the way, what is your name?"

"Ollye."

"Ollye? Sounds too rustic. Anyway, you must get a lot of grief from these characters all around you. Oh, I almost forgot to ask you. I wonder if you have some rice to sell us. We ran out of the bread and ham we brought with us yesterday, and we have nothing to eat until we get back to Texas Town. I doubt if anybody else in this village will sell us anything because they're afraid of being punished by old man Hwang. You are not afraid of that old man, are you?"

Ollye was not afraid of Old Hwang, not any more. For Ollye, Old

Hwang was no longer a person to fear or avoid. Like everybody else in the village, the old man had ceased to exist for her. But she really had little rice to share with them.

Ollye gave the Yankee wives one gourd dipper of rice as well as a handful of sesame leaves, dried mushrooms and some hot pepper paste.

Yonghi paced before the shack, glancing now and then at the boat crossing the river, back and forth, with only one or two passengers aboard. Sundok was taking a nap in the dark humid room that still seemed to smell of snakes.

Yonghi was aware that the old man's tactic was working. She wondered what Old Hwang had in store for her next, and whether she should fight back or give up and go over to the islet to build her own shanty in Texas Town. Fighting would consume her time and energy, and she was not sure if this seedy shack was worth that trouble. But she would not give up the shack unless she was sure to get all her money back. She cursed her own stupidity. Why had she not thought first of building a tent house or a shanty on the islet, like everybody else? She could have started there, small, and then expanded her business later on. She used to think she was one of the best at her trade, but apparently she still had a lot to learn. These days there were many smart girls who knew how to get ahead. When the war broke out few women had heard of prostitution, not to mention whoring for foreign soldiers, but competition was now getting tougher every day.

Like an incorrigible gambler who keeps promising himself that he will never touch the cards again after one more big win, she had vowed to herself over and over again that she would quit when she made enough money to start a new life. When she made enough money to begin a "new" life, however, she always found a bigger new life to go after. When she'd left Hongchon for Chunchon, she was determined to make enough to be able to go back to Haeundae Beach in the southern port city of Pusan and open a club at which to entertain Yankees. She would be the mistress of the best whorehouse in that town. That was her latest ambition. She had gone through hard times, so she certainly had the right to enjoy a better life, but her dream was being thwarted by that impossible old man.

Sometimes Yonghi herself could not believe all that had happened to her in the past half year. Last spring, her parents and relatives at her hometown of Kumchon, Kyonggi Province, had been busy arranging her marriage with the fourth son of a pear orchard owner at nearby Yongju village. The wedding was scheduled for the lunar tenth month. Yonghi went down to Chochiwon to stay for three weeks with her aunt, who had volunteered to provide the whole trousseau for the bride.

War broke out while she was visiting her aunt. She hurried north to get back to her family, but all the territories north of Seoul had already fallen into the hands of North Koreans by the time she reached Anyang, a township thirty miles south of the capital city. She fled back to Chochiwon only to find that her aunt's family had taken refuge in Pusan. With little hope of finding her aunt, she made the long journey to Pusan, skipping meals more often than she had one, sleeping in abandoned houses or out in the open, sometimes begging on the road for food. Traveling on foot most of the way, she reached Pusan in a month, but she had no means of surviving in that city which was crowded with refugees from all over the country.

Most of the time she could not even find a decent place to sleep. One night she went to sleep among the rocks on Haeundae Beach, a favorite spot for vagrants and homeless refugees. Three men came to the beach and had a drinking party. One of these men noticed her and came over. Her brief life as a refugee had already turned Yonghi into a shameless woman; she no longer believed in the virtue of chastity in the face of the need to survive. For food and transportation, she had slept, on separate occasions, with two strange men whom she had met on her way down to Pusan. If she had not offered herself to them she might have never made it to the city. She did not mind lying with a third man, if he could provide her with a room and warm meal.

Yun Piljung was the name of this beach bum. He turned out to be a professional thief. That night, and every night after that, he took her to a cheap, bedbug infested back-alley inn. They lived together at this cheap inn near the railroad. Now and then he pilfered from the American military base and Yonghi was responsible for selling the stolen goods on the black market. They barely managed to pay for the room and food by selling C-rations and Hershey chocolates and Chuckles and Lifesavers and instant coffee and chewing gum. Yonghi thought they needed one big break. To steal one big container stuffed with radios and electric machines from an American cargo ship—that was their biggest dream. It did not take long for Yonghi to realize that this man had taken her in hoping she would support him later on. When he found her a job at Bichuku on Haeundae Beach, he stopped working. At this club for American soldiers she worked as a maid, cooking and washing and cleaning, and made barely enough money to pay for their room.

It was only after she began to learn English that she found out "Bichuku" was in fact "Beach Club" garbled by the beach area inhabitants. This club opened a whole new world of wonders to her. She used to think all adult women wore the loose *chogori* coat and long *chima* skirt or baggy *monpe* pants, but the girls working at Bichuku pranced around the beach in tiny pieces of cloth called "bikini" that barely covered their nipples and the hair of their groins. She was fascinated by these half naked girls, with their permanented hairdos and colorful clothes.

Every night the club held a strange show called "strip tease" in which the girls undressed on the stage before the audience of foreign soldiers. The locals, including the children, swarmed to the barbed-wire fence around the club at night to watch the stark-naked girls making strange suggestive motions. Sometimes a drunk or two would try to climb over the fence to have a better view of the show, and American MPs were called in to drag them away. Some day, Yonghi dreamed, she would dance like that, applauded by many foreigners.

Yonghi admired and envied Hwaja, the most popular U.N. lady on the beach, who was always surrounded by several Yankees whenever she showed up at the club. Better known by her American name of Helen, she slept with a different man every night. And she was paid for all that fun, too! Yonghi compared the luxurious, happy life of Helen with her own miserable existence.

One day Yonghi asked Big Sister, the club owner, who also ran a brothel at Sombat, to let her work there as a U.N. lady. She was soon allowed to move into a shack at Sombat "U.N. Town." This shack in the Red Light alley, like many other shacks owned by Big Sister, was called a "box house" because it looked like a box topped with a slate roof. Within the four walls, the box house had two rooms and a latrine. It had nothing more — no kitchen, no hall, nothing at all. Every door opened directly into the alley. They could hear what was going on in the next room and even in the next shack, through the thin walls. Sundok occupied the other room of Yonghi's box house. They had stayed together ever since.

Yonghi was soon busy collecting steady customers among the Yankees who strolled into the alley so that she could quickly make enough money to buy the box house for which she now had to pay weekly rent to Big Sister. She served every customer as best she could to keep him coming back to her, for she wanted to be an independent U.N. lady.

When the logistical unit moved to Wegwan up north, she had to move along with the Yankee soldiers because all her steady customers belonged to that unit. By this time, she had made enough money to buy a house and run her own small business. Sundok came to Wegwan with Yonghi but they were no longer colleagues. For some time, even before they left Haeundae Beach, Yonghi had been working as a madam for Sundok; Sundok was in debt to Yonghi because she always spent too much money, while Yonghi had so many customers that sometimes she had to send some of them into Sundok's room.

They moved again to Hongchon following the soldiers. At Hongchon Texas Town, Yonghi was known by the English name of Dragon Lady, and she was as famous and popular among the GIs as Helen had been at Bichuku. The nickname "Dragon Lady" had been given to her by a master sergeant called Jimmy, but she did not know it had been the nickname of a horrible empress in Ching China until she was told by a Major Kim Hijun, a Korean information officer, who used to entertain *bengko* friends at Yonghi's house. Major Kim told her that Jimmy must have given her that nickname as a joke, but Yonghi decided to keep it.

Now Yonghi envied nobody. She believed she would get everything she had ever wanted. When she made her first trip to Chunchon, her business sense had been sharpened by experience so she saw the potential of this riverside village. Most *bengkos* did not mind filthy rooms as long as they had women underneath them, but there was no doubt that the customers would prefer a decent house by the river to a sweltering pigsty. She could charge a few dollars more if she opened a really high-class sex house at Kumsan village.

The snake hunter's hut had only one room. They had to convert the snake pen to a room for Sundok. Then they would expand the kitchen, install a plywood partition, place two tables in the new hall, and Dragon Lady Club would be ready to begin its business. Yonghi planned to build at least three more rooms with plank boards and sand bricks in the back yard to house more Yankee wives later on. She might even build a small stage in the front yard for the strip show. By the time this Yankee unit moved away, she would have made enough money to go back to Pusan. She had planned it all out and the future looked promising, as far as she could see. But she had not foreseen this idiotic blockade by Old Hwang. At the least expected spot, the enemy had been lying in wait for her.

"It's all gone wrong because of that old cock," she muttered, gazing across the river at the two trucks driving into Camp Omaha, raising a cloud of dust behind them. She stood up with a sigh and went to wake Sundok. "I think it won't work," she said. "Maybe we should clear out of here and move to Cucumber Island, after all."

They cooked the rice, quickly finished lunch, packed their things up, and went to the Paulownia House to see the old man.

"All right, old man, you win," Yonghi said to Old Hwang, putting her trunk down under the massive tree. "We've decided to leave this village. Just pay me back my money, and we will be gone forever."

Old Hwang, carrying a roll of new wire screening under his arm, went over to the chicken coop to mend the rusted door. Ignoring the presence of the two women, he took his time slowly removing the crooked rusted nails one by one from the door frame and then straightening them one by one and then scraping the rust from the straightened nails by rubbing them one by one in the dirt. He knew he was winning the fight now and he did not need to hurry.

"I can't pay you back the money right now because the snake hunter ran away with that money," the old man said. "I don't keep that much money at home. But you don't have to worry. I'll pay it to you when the harvest is over."

For over half an hour Yonghi screamed and swore at Old Hwang, but he did not mind her foul language much, for he was enjoying his revenge. Yonghi and Sundok returned to their shack, swearing that they would not leave until they got the money back and that they would bring in all the whores from Texas Town to this village to turn the whole county into the biggest brothel in the world. But both the old man and Yonghi knew she would have to leave soon.

That evening, the old man instructed the boatman to let the women use the boat if they wanted to go to the islet.

THREE

Ollye, who had been brooding in the dark, crouching motionless on the stoop outside her room with her chin resting on her raised knees, finally stirred. But she did not return to the silence of her room. She could not sleep. Slowly she stepped down from the stoop and squeezed her feet into her black rubber shoes. She quietly crossed the yard and cautiously pushed open the twig gate. Although she moved noiselessly so as not to disturb her children, she was nonetheless resentful that she had to sneak out of her own house like a thief.

She quickly passed the chestnut tree and hastened down to the stream, gasping in fear and anxiety lest anybody should spot her.

She passed the log bridge under which the little boy Bong had looked up at her with a frightened expression several days ago; she reached the willow bush by the brook where she could hide herself safely in the dark shadow; she breathed slowly to calm herself.

Like a bad farmer prowling in the dark, trying to steal some sheaves from the stacks of harvested rice in a neighbor's paddy, she scurried from one dike to the next along the stream, concealing herself among the willows and bushes. There was no definite reason for her to go to the river but she headed for it anyway, driven by a vague instinct which told her that she would find shelter — or a way out — somewhere by the river, if anywhere.

She stopped now and then to take a look around. She had seen this landscape hundreds of times both at night and in the daytime, but tonight it looked so strange that she felt as if she had just returned home from a long journey. The full moon was yellow in black space and the overlapping contours of the peaks and ridges loomed frosty grey at both sides of the river to the south. The wild chrysanthemums glinted in clumps of lilac-violet and silken-silver on moonlit West Hill. The brook chattered noisily but the rest of the village was silent. This silence and the moonlight over the rectangles of harvested rice paddies reminded her of an abandoned cemetery.

This deserted nocturnal landscape, this world of darkness, now belonged to her for nobody was there to accuse her of intruding. Ollye was free for she was alone.

Ollye stopped under the aspen where the brook joined the river and glanced over at the snake hunter's shack. The shack was deserted; Yonghi and Sundok had left Kumsan that morning to go to Cucumber Island. The two prostitutes had decided to rent a room at the shanty town for the time being rather than waste any more time waiting for the old man to pay them back for the hut.

She had been invited to the snake hunter's shack for supper the previous night by the two women who insisted on expressing their gratitude for the rice Ollye had shared with them. She told Mansik to look after Nanhi and went to the hut after dark, for she did not want any villager to see her visiting the whores. It did not take long for Ollye to learn that the two women had another purpose for inviting her besides expressing their gratitude; they asked her to find someone who was interested in buying the shack. They did not mind taking a small loss, for they had no other choice but to move to Texas Town, and they were not sure Old Hwang would ever pay them for the hut. At supper they served their guest with *bengko* cans containing boiled sweet beans, juicy mashed meat, and potatoes dipped in gravy soup. Ollye had never tasted anything so delicious in her whole life. They also offered her a cup of brown water called coffee, but she did not like it as much as cool fresh water. They urged her to take some cookies and candies and a can of honey-tasting jam to her children at home. Ollye was surprised to find that there were so many novel and palatable things to eat in the world.

While Ollye was indulging in those delicacies, Yonghi cursed the hostile Kumsan villagers. "I've never seen people like them, really," she said. "Bad neighbors are worse than wasps."

"She's telling the God's honest ruth," Sundok affirmed. "You should know who your real enemies are. And who your true friends are."

Ollye was easy prey for Sister Serpent's words. But she was so shocked by Yonghi's next suggestion that she could not even swallow the potato in her mouth. Sister Serpent wanted to know if she would be interested in working with them. Ollye coughed several times in quick succession and wondered if she had understood the question. Yonghi asked Ollye to come to see her at Texas Town some afternoon if she wanted to become a U.N. lady and entertain *bengkos*.

"People say lots of foul things about us, but whoring isn't as bad a business as you think," Yonghi explained. In wartime, the best way to survive was to stick around with soldiers and there were certain benefits if you did business with foreign soldiers. "I can tell you many easy ways to make a lot of money, if you're interested." She declared that she was doing much better than anybody she had ever known in her hometown. "You never know what will befall you tomorrow at a time like this, and you have to consider yourself blessed if you know where your next meal is coming from while other people do not even know if they will still be around tomorrow. Think smart," she said. "Smart people enjoy the war while other people get killed in it."

"Hear, hear," Sundok chimed in. "You've got a lot to learn, Ollye."

Yonghi said the business would not last forever and they had to work a lot while they could, because nobody knew when the war would end and the *bengkos* would go home.

"Think hard, Mansik's mother, and don't waste this opportunity," Sister Serpent advised, squinting at Ollye to see how well her words were working. "Even grasshoppers don't miss their own mating season, and you'd better not let this precious chance slip through your fingers. Of course I know you have Mansik and . . . what did you say your daughter's name is? Nanhi. That's right. I know you have Mansik and Nanhi to think about, but you can't just sit here and starve to death. At Bichuku I knew a woman who was older than thirty and had a child. And she knew how to conduct her business! Age and children don't matter a bit if you know tricks to drive the *bengkos* nuts in bed. And to please a man is the easiest thing in the world, believe me."

It was much easier for Ollye to imagine herself starving to death than becoming a Yankee wife. She doubted if she was capable of becoming a proper whore even if she wanted to be one. To offer her naked body to every man . . . that was simply unthinkable to her. Moreover, Sister Serpent was talking about whoring with *bengko* soldiers. She could never do that, never.

"What's wrong with the *bengkos?*" Yonghi retorted. "All men are the same. Especially in this business. Nobody, not even the vilest-looking soldier, has more than one cock. I understand perfectly well how you feel about the *bengkos* that assaulted you. But soldiers are the same everywhere whether they're Yankees or Mongols. Combat soldiers fuck and rape any women they find on their way to their deaths. What's the big deal if a girl or two gets raped, they say, when soldiers get killed every day? But not all of them are rapists and murderers. There're some nice guys too. If you find a really nice guy, your whole life changes overnight to an eternal feast. I hear they used to forbid Yankees to marry Orientals, but that law does not exist any longer. If you're lucky, you can marry a Yankee and go to America. You don't have any idea what a paradise America is. Lots of canned food. Nice warm blankets. And they say almost every family has its own car in that big country, *Migook*. They say *Migook* folks even shit better crap than us *Hangooks*. Think about the opportunity of going to Yankee country! I personally know several girls from Pusan Texas Town who married GIs and made their way to America. Play it smart and you will come to thank heaven for this war for bringing the *bengkos* to this country."

Then Yonghi went on to explain black-market operations. Ollye found herself puzzled and lost in a fantastic world that she had never imagined. She felt a sense of expectation, and even a faint hint of hope, as she listened to Yonghi, who seemed to know the secret formulas to tide one over the worst in life. Yonghi seemed to know more about Ollye's life and future than Ollye herself. This uncanny faculty inspired both fear and curiosity. Perhaps Sister Serpent was the only person who really knew what was in store for the future.

"You just wait and see," Yonghi promised. "I'll show you soon what it is like to have a real great time. If you come to see me at Texas Town in a few weeks, you'll find a very prosperous bar with a big shiny sign 'Dragon Lady Club.' That's me—Dragon Lady. I'll become the biggest madam in Texas Town in no time and you will see with your own eyes what a glorious life a good U.N. lady can enjoy."

Crouching under the aspen on the riverbank and gazing over at the ferry, Ollye vividly remembered the expression on her face when Yonghi said that.

She stared at Cucumber Island, where Yonghi and Sundok might be entertaining their *bengko* friends at this very moment. The bright electric lights from the camp, the new concrete bridge, and Texas Town's shanties were reflected in the rippling water creating yellow wriggling patterns.

Ollye shuddered from the chill. She was conscious of time passing her by. She had the frightening thought that she might be dead even now, sitting there under the tree in the dark, watching the bright artificial lights of another world across the river. Breathing, but dead with her eyes wide open. She had been confined in her home, dead, while the world, ignoring her existence was busy living.

She slowly inhaled the cold wet night air, and she thought about the past month. During that month, a frightful animal had seemed to be lurking around her, invisible, waiting for a chance to pounce, but now she realized there had never been such a beast threatening her, after all. What a waste, she thought, what a waste.

With disbelief she wondered why she had cared so much about the villagers anyway. She had feared that the villagers would sneer at her if she met them by chance. But why had she cared so much about their attitude? She and the villagers lived in different worlds.

She decided she would not mind from now on if the farmers treated her like a disgraced sinner. But Mansik's sickly pale face haunted her. Why did she have the feeling that her own son was also turning into an enemy? Was she imagining things out of guilt?

And Nanhi. A three-year-old girl was too young to understand what was happening to her mother. Yet the little girl's innocence further burdened Ollye, for she felt as if she was cheating her daughter.

Ollye had an urge to run away, abandoning Mansik and Nanhi, to run far far away to some place where nobody would recognize her. She knew she could not do that, but she still wanted to.

When she rose to her feet, staring at Cucumber Island, there was anger in her face. She did not know the exact reason she had to be angry, yet her anger gradually turned to sizzling hate. And she knew that the will to fight and survive thrived on hate.

At the repeated suggestion of the village chief, Old Hwang finally went over the islet one late afternoon to inspect Texas Town. The chief was convinced that the whoretown would bring some harm to West County sooner or later.

When Yom pushed his boat ashore so that the old man could step

down onto the dry sand without getting his feet wet, hundreds of
swallows were training their chicks for the long journey south for winter,
twittering noisily and crowding the sky over the northern shore. The old
man asked the boatman why they were not using the regular landing
farther south and Yom explained that the villagers, especially the
women, preferred to use the northern detour to risking an accidental
encounter with the *bengkos* or the prostitutes on their way to and from the
town.

"It's only natural for the village women to be afraid of the *bengkos*,"
said Pae, holding the boat steady for the old man. "The soldiers might
mistake a passing village woman for a whore and you never know what
they will do."

"You wait here until we return," Hwang told the boatman, checking
his horsehair hat and long-sleeved robe before advancing. "And you
lead the way, Mr. Pae. I want to take a look at the army camp first."

Following the limping village chief, Hwang trudged up the sandy
slope. The old man paused to glance over the river at West County like a
soldier looking back at his hometown for the last time on his way to war.
Patches of white cloud, that would melt in one's mouth as sweetly as balls
of cotton candy, were suspended in the turquoise sky over hills covered
with the flaming crimson and dazzling yellow of autumn. It was the
season of calabashes fattening on the thatched roofs, soft sponge gourds
dangling heavily on the twig fence, bees collecting the last honey from
the purple chrysanthemums, refreshing cool breezes and pleasantly
sunny afternoons. The branches of the persimmon trees sagged with
scarlet fruits, and the farmers had a lot of work to do to prepare for the
cold season. They worked from morning star to evening star, harvesting
and threshing and winnowing and packing and storing the crops in their
barns and kitchens and jars. They had to repair the cracks in earthen
walls, fill the ratholes in rice barns, clean the ceiling closets in which
fruits and nuts were stored, replace the decomposing thatch on their
roofs with straw from the recent harvest, restore the rice paddy dikes
destroyed by the trucks during the battle at General's Hill, haul in

weeds to make winter fodder for cows or compost to use in spring, twine ropes and weave straw bags, hang corn cobs under the eaves to dry to use as seed next year, and pickle cabbages and radishes for the lean months. The farmers were busy, but this was the happiest season for them. They would have already organized a farmers' band to play music and dance around the villages to celebrate the bumper crop, if there had not been a war going on.

The villagers had almost forgotten the war. They were too busy these days to wonder what was going on outside their county. Yonsil's mother, who grew lotus root at Mudfish Pool, had given birth to her third daughter, but nobody bothered to go to see her because the birth of a girl was never worth a congratulatory visit at a busy time like this. But Old Hwang was never so busy as to forget the existence of the war. He doubted that the *bengko* army would requisition crops from the farmers as the Japanese had done in another war years ago, but he would have to warn the farmers to hide away some of the crop this year, for nobody knew what might happen in wartime.

The villagers did not know what was going on at the Chestnut House either, nor did they care enough to find out. But Old Hwang could not ignore Ollye's existence. Ever since he had heard of her secret visit to the snake hunter's shack, he suspected that Ollye was conspiring with the two whores. Although he was somewhat relieved when the two women left Kumsan, he knew the matter would not be settled for good until he paid them back for the riverside hut. He was not a bit happy, suspecting that Ollye might join forces with the outsiders—perhaps even to fight him. He wanted to summon Ollye and ask her what business she had discussed with the prostitutes, but the whole month which had passed made him hesitate to resume communication with her. And he feared that he might not like what Ollye had to tell him.

Then the boatman reported the shocking news that Ollye had made two secret night trips to Cucumber Island in the past week, and the old man was sure that she had not gone to the islet for any reason he would approve of. He had to know what had impelled her to go among the

Americans, whom she had every reason to fear, when she had not ventured out of her house for more than a month. When outrageous rumors about Ollye and the Yankees started to circulate, the old man found it impossible to regard those tales as baseless slander, although reason suggested that those far-fetched stories had probably been invented by imaginative villagers for idle amusement. Ollye was easy prey, she could be wantonly disparaged, for she had been already victimized and condemned to shame. The old man understood that perfectly well, but . . . he could not help suspecting that there must be a fire if there was so much smoke.

Led by the village chief, Old Hwang strolled along the barbed-wire fence, closely observing Camp Omaha—the large tents with their flaps rolled up, huge wooden crates lining the main road which crossed the camp, Quonset huts painted sand color, the Korean flag and the American flag and the United Nations flag drooping side by side, lifelessly, on the tall pipe poles, scattered bunkers for heavy machine gun emplacements, ugly dark green plank tables and benches in the mess hall, a jeep with a tall radio antenna, and lots of soldiers everywhere.

"I didn't think there were so many *Migook* soldiers at this small camp," Old Hwang muttered, his hands clasped behind him as he watched the *bengkos* moving around inside the fence.

"Hundreds of them live here," Pae explained. "In fact, so many soldiers stay here that they have to dispose of their leftover food and garbage by the truckload every day."

With a frown, the old man looked around at the soldiers setting out chunks of turf atop the sandy soil around the Quonset huts, at the soldiers raising a telegraph pole near the main gate, at the soldiers playing basketball, a cloud of dust rising all around them like an early morning river fog, at the soldier with stubbly chin drawing something in white paint on the wider flap of a tent, at the two helmeted soldiers standing guard by the entry gate, at a barefoot soldier crossing a patch of grass with an armful of folded blankets, and at a soldier scraping his mess kit into a garbage can. The old man was frustrated because there were too many soldiers for him to do anything about, because the army camp was too big for him to do anything about, and because the world had grown suddenly too big and too complicated for him to do anything about.

Many of the soldiers were naked to their waists, shiny dog tags dangling over chests that were as hairy as beasts'. Watching the half-naked *bengkos*, Old Hwang recalled the savage Japanese who used to strut around the town with nothing on but loincloths. Savages, savages, the old man thought with a sigh. A gentleman was never supposed to expose any more than his face and hands in public under any circumstances, but the world was obviously full of savage nations.

Old Hwang hoped the war would be over soon one way or the other, so that Sokku would not have to be dragged away to fight side by side with these naked barbarians. But Sokku would surely be drafted if the war lasted many more months. The townsfolk said even boys of sixteen or seventeen had been conscripted, and a lot of those untrained students had been killed at Pohang in August. The Hwang family would end if Sokku were to die. The family was in decline and the old man had hoped Sokku would be able to rebuild it. The villagers would be shocked speechless if they were to find out his situation. Rich Hwang—why he could not even pay back the prostitutes for their riverside shack, and he had been deeply indebted to the miller for several years. If he lost his only son, what would be left of the Hwangs?

Shaking his head, Hwang said to Pae, "Take me to the place they call Texas Town."

"Oh, it's right down there."

The shanties had been built in haste. The whole town could be moved to a new location in an hour. The place looked as dull as a country market by daylight. At the entrance stood a big plank sign saying "Welcome to Texas Town" both in English and Korean with a gigantic picture of a reclining naked woman displaying her huge breasts, nipples and all, like pink watermelons for sale. Some shanties had similar but smaller signs mounted on their roofs. These signs showed *bengko*-looking women with blue eyes and golden hair, their loins barely covered with slips of cloth the size of handkerchiefs. The roofs and walls of the shacks were mostly built from the wood of used ammunition boxes and still bore black stencilled English letters and numbers. The walls were papered inside with old Korean newspapers and Yankee comic books, creating a motley collage of columns of printed letters, colorful pictures and bubbling word balloons. Thin black electric wires hung like clothesline between one shack and the next, the whole cobweb of lines converging and running back to Camp Omaha. Electric bulbs hanging inside and outside the shacks were painted yellow or red. There were many nails on every interior wall used as hooks for hanging up scanty female clothing in cheap, bright colors. On the washlines behind some shacks, enticing underwear and bras made of transparent or suggestive black material hung like the banners of sin. The latrines, each used by four or five shanties, emitted the stench of gasoline or kerosene, which the U.N. ladies had poured into the pits in order to kill maggots. The zigzag alleys were littered with waste paper, crushed beer cans, and dark patches of sand stained by urine. Around the shanties stood metal ammunition boxes used as substitute safes or miniature ice boxes or even as dressers for storing clean clothing and underwear. Dented helmets were used as washbasins, and cans of all sizes were used as dishes and containers for miscellaneous items.

Venturing into this bizarre landscape, Old Hwang watched the strange Yankee wives, many of whom had their hair either dyed yellow or permanented into small close curls to imitate *bengko* women. Others let their hair cascade loose over their shoulders. Some had on black glasses or heavy bracelets or extremely short pants so as to stand out from the other girls who dressed, behaved and painted themselves like nobody the old man had ever seen before. Idling in the shanties or playing strange card games as they sat out front on benches, the girls glanced indifferently at the two uninvited inspectors from West County and resumed what they had been doing. They knew Old Hwang and his companion were not prospective customers.

"They say there are at least fifty of these women here," Pae explained, alternating a worried glance at the old man with a curious leer at the girls.

They turned a corner and found three Yankee soldiers and two laughing girls around a plywood table drinking beer outside a shanty whose sign pictured a tall cactus.

"It really worries me, sir, to think of the village children who come here and watch these things," the village chief said.

"The children?" the old man said. "Do the children come here?"

"Yes. They come almost every day to snoop around the camp and this place," Pae said. "Some of them come to beg the *bengko* soldiers for C-ration cans and chocolates. Other boys come to watch the whores play with the foreign soldiers."

"We should tell them to stay away," the old man said "This is not a place for children."

"I doubt if the children will listen," Pae said.

"I'll tell the boatman not to let any child use the boat to get here."

"I already tried that, sir, but it didn't work. The boys swam across the river and got here anyway."

Hwang felt disappointed and depressed for he was unable to do anything to fix the deplorable situation. As time passed he had to admit that he was losing more and more of whatever power he had possessed. He could not help noticing that he was gradually being shunted aside.

A woman with round flat face and puffy eyes, who was sitting on a rolled straw bag before her shack and washing peaches in an LMG ammunition can, was apparently amused by two country gentlemen in proper ramie attire snooping around the brothel. With an easy grin she came over to the awkward visitors.

"Want to have a good time?" she asked. Her hips were as fat as a sow's. Then she bit into a juicy peach. "The girls here seldom play with natives, but I don't mind making you happy as long as you pay me enough. Which one of you wants to have me first? I guess I have to serve the older one first because Confucius tells us to respect our elders. Right, old man?"

Two women who had been playing flower cards on a plank bench laughed, glancing at the old man with his prim aristocratic horsehair hat and his single crippled follower.

"Don't tease him too much, Sis," said the one in a thin orange-colored blouse. "Maybe he really wants to have a good time. He must have all the equipment he needs to play with, even if his instrument is a little rusty. Why don't you help him rub the rust off his tool?"

Then, out of nowhere—the old man really could not tell from where it was coming—a scream rang out: "That's him! That's the old cock!"

It was Yonghi.

"That is the old cock that took my house away and wouldn't even pay for it!"

Surprised by the sudden verbal attack, Old Hwang turned to see Sister Serpent wagging her fist at him. Her face and hair were covered with soapsuds—she had been washing her hair—but the old man instantly recognized her.

"I told you girls about this fucking dotard, didn't I?" Yonghi was furious. "I told you about the bastard who wouldn't even let me get on the boat, and look, that old cock is here!"

Sundok, who had been laundering her brassiere, dashed forward to join Yonghi. "What is that son of a bitch here for?" she said, drying her wet hands with her apron. "Does he want a girl, or what?"

Neither Hwang nor the village chief had had a chance to defend themselves as the other prostitutes joined in the barrage of accusations.

"So that's the old guy who stole your house, ha?" a snub-nosed girl scoffed. "Why don't you kick him in the balls, Sister Serpent? He doesn't look like much of a man, anyway."

"A big man indeed—stealing a house from a whore," said a tall slim girl with her dark glasses stuck in the waistband of her skirt. "This is for you," she added, making an obscene gesture with her hand.

"But why is he here, anyway?" said another. "He's got your house already. What does he want next?"

"You want me, old man?" said the tall slim girl. She lifted her skirt to show her red panties to Old Hwang. "Short time or long time?"

Several girls laughed.

Old Hwang, finally recovering from his amazement at the bombardment, cleared his throat several times in succession and then addressed Yonghi. "I have no intention of stealing anything from you. I asked you to wait because I don't have that much money now."

"And I trust your words as much as I do a cat sitting in front of a fish," Yonghi snorted.

There was no point in arguing with these filthy creatures, the old man thought as he turned to leave. But he could not help noticing Pae's disappointed expression. And the old man thought it was all getting to be too much for him to handle.

FOUR

Squatting on the walnut stump before the Chestnut House, watching the village which loomed bluish in the moonlight, Mansik wondered about his mother's recent behavior. He was not sure what exactly was happening to her, but there was no doubt that some change was taking place in her life. Why did she leave home secretly at night, and where did she go?

She had sneaked out of the house again tonight. Pretending to have fallen asleep early, Mansik had been waiting for her to make a move to confirm his suspicion. He became alert a little past nine when he heard his mother quietly rise from her bed in the next room.

She crawled to the children's room and listened through the paper door to the sound of their breathing. When she was sure that Mansik and Nanhi were sound asleep, she stepped down into the yard and noiselessly approached the twig gate. Mansik crawled to the door and watched his mother through a chink. She looked up and down the path before skulking out of the house.

Mansik quickly slipped out of the room; he had gone to bed with all his clothes on. There was a half moon in the sky over the Three Peaks and he heard the faint sound of music wafted by a breeze from the islet. Mansik saw his mother hurry to the ferry. He followed her down to the tobacco-curing shed, but he could not go any farther because the rice paddies provided no concealment. He did not need to shadow her any more, for he had a fairly clear idea where she was heading.

This was the third time that Mansik caught her sneaking out of the house at night. He was awakened the first time at midnight by the dogs barking somewhere in the distance. A while later he heard someone cautiously open and close the twig gate of his house. Suddenly frightened, recalling the night a month earlier when the two *bengkos* had attacked his mother, he crept to the door and peeked out. The boy was so relieved to see it was only his mother that he did not even wonder why she had been out of the house in the middle of the night. He went back to sleep and completely forgot next morning to ask his mother why she had gone out and scared the dogs.

The next time, however, he was stricken with an uncanny premonition when he heard the dogs barking. He was wide awake and very alert by the time his mother came up the footpath to the house. He watched her through the chink of the door as she tiptoed to her room, carrying what looked like a bundle of clothes. He had an urge to open the door and ask her where she had been, but somehow his whole body stiffened in fear and his throat was paralyzed. He feared that she might give him an answer that he was not yet ready to hear.

This morning when he went to his mother's room for breakfast, Mansik noticed a strange smell. He could not tell where the smell was coming from—her clothes or the room itself—but he recognized the sour odor of wine and vomit. But his mother had never touched a single drop of rice wine even when her husband used to drink it at home.

During breakfast, she tried to avoid Mansik's eyes and he recalled that she had been nervous for the past several days.

Mansik also found that the rice jar in the kitchen was half full. Lately their meals had consisted of nothing more than a handful of boiled wild greens with little grain. Suddenly there was plenty of rice to eat. The side dishes were remarkable too; for the first time in years, Mansik enjoyed such delicacies as acorn curd, buckwheat jelly and even cow tripe. His mother would have had to go to Central Market to buy such things and Mansik was not sure when she had managed to find time to go to town and where she got the money to buy them.

After lunch—they never missed the noon rice these days—while Mansik was looking for a coil of hemp string, he accidentally discovered four *bengko* C-ration cans in the straw basket hanging on the kitchen wall. Unlike rice or relishes, the discovery of the *bengko* things in the house prompted Mansik to ask questions.

"Where did you get the rice and the Yankee cans, Mother?"

Ollye was embarrassed. "Well, you know," she mumbled, "I got them—somehow. I can explain everything to you, but not now. Don't ask me anything, because you're not ready to understand me."

Squatting on the walnut stump before the Chestnut House, Mansik tried to guess how his mother had gotten hold of rice and the *bengko* cans. He feared she might have stolen them. If she had earned them doing some proper job in town, his mother would have told him about it. Mansik had a strong suspicion that his mother worked at the *bengko* town on the islet. What did she do there in the middle of the night to be paid with rice and cans? He was glad that they did not have to go hungry any more, but he was not sure if he should be happy.

A chill streaked through his body and gooseflesh bristled up on his arms and shoulders as he felt a foreboding. Something ominous, something like a hovering shadow, was approaching, and he looked up in fear, in apprehension, sensing imminent danger. He saw a boy coming from the direction of the log bridge. The boy stopped short, startled, as Mansik slowly rose to his feet, staring.

Mansik did not recognize the boy at first because the moon was behind him. When the boy started to move again Mansik knew he was Kangho. The lanky boy had sloping shoulders and chopstick legs that were easily recognizable even at a distance. Kangho turned into the footpath and stopped a few paces away from Mansik. They stood facing each other. They said nothing for a moment. The noise of the brook sounded loud in the silent dark. Mansik wanted to say something about this surprise visit by his friend, but he was too startled to decide what reaction he ought to have. The best Mansik came up with was the simple question, "Are you Kangho?"

"Yes, it's me," said Kangho in a flat emotionless voice. He did not seem to have decided what attitude and tone of voice he should assume either.

For want of anything better to say, Mansik asked another stupid question, "What are you doing here?"

Kangho said nothing; perhaps he had not been prepared for that question.

Mansik rephrased his question. "Why did you come to see me?" He did not want to drive his friend away with unnecessary antagonism.

"I've been to the ferry on an errand for my father, to see the boatman," Kangho explained. "My father wanted the boatman to come to the mill first thing in the morning and pick up the rice the villagers contributed for him."

Kangho paused to study his expression. Mansik was puzzled as to what the boatman or the rice had got to do with Kangho's visit.

"As I was about to cross the bridge on my way home," Kangho went on, "I spotted you sitting here and decided to come to see you and say hello."

"We haven't talked to each other for such a long time," said Mansik. He thought his own remark incongruous and wondered if he had intended it to sound like an accusation. He thought he had better say something else, something more friendly. "How are the boys?" he said.

"Well, fine," said Kangho. "They're fine."

Mansik was nervous, afraid that their conversation would peter out and Kangho would leave. Mansik had to keep the conversation alive somehow. "The harvest season is over and I guess you boys have to prepare for the Autumn War with the Castle village boys," he said.

"Sure. The war will be on soon."

"Going on expeditions, too?"

"Oh, yes. We're going to the dumping place tomorrow," Kangho said.

"Dumping place? What dumping place?"

"Lots of Yankee have arrived on Cucumber Island, you know, and they built a whole new village there. There's a great big dumping place at the southern part of the island where the *bengkos* dispose of their garbage. The Yankee trucks come to unload their garbage at this place twice a day and that's where we're going tomorrow."

"Anything special about the dumping place?" asked Mansik, intrigued.

"Yes, but we didn't know it until Jun found out that the Castle boys made secret trips there every day."

"Secret trips?" said Mansik, wondering if his mother had gone there tonight.

"Those boys did not want anybody besides themselves to know about this place, but we found out about it and now everybody in West County knows what nice things you can find in the garbage."

"What kind of nice things can you find in the garbage?"

"Oh, this and that. Sometimes you can find unopened cans containing slices of peaches in sweetened water or candies or powdered milk. You can find chocolates and chewing gum, too."

"Sounds like fun," said Mansik, recalling the unopened *bengko* cans his mother had hidden in the kitchen.

"It is fun. So we keep going there. If you pick through the garbage carefully enough, you can sometimes find some pretty cellophane papers in various colors. And razor blades. And cardboard boxes and envelopes, too. Once or twice a week, the *bengkos* throw away lots of leftover chicken pieces, and on those nights, many families in West County have a feast. Even some grownups come to the dump at night secretly when the *bengkos* dispose of chicken and other meats."

"Don't the *bengkos* stop you if you take those things?" Mansik said.

"Of course not. They don't mind anybody taking them, because they are throwing them away. No Yankees guard the dump."

"Must be great fun to go there."

"It is," Kangho said. "Will you come along with us tomorrow?"

Mansik was tempted by the spontaneous invitation, but on second thought, he knew it was impossible for him to join the boys now in any kind of expedition.

"I don't think I can go," he said.

"Why? Don't you want to play with us?"

"Well, I don't think it's a matter of what I want to do," Mansik said. "You see, nobody'll want me to come along. What would Chandol or Toad say if I just showed up uninvited?"

"Since when have you ever needed an invitation to come to play with us? We're friends and you can come to play with us whenever you want to."

"That's what you think but the other boys would think differently. Things have changed, you know."

"You've become a very strange boy," Kangho said. "What good does it do you if you stay away from everybody? You shouldn't avoid us like this."

"You think *I* am avoiding you?" said Mansik, his voice turning sarcastic.

"Well, I haven't come to see you for quite some time," Kangho admitted. "I don't understand myself how come I have been that way to you, but it just happened, you know. Anyway I came to see you tonight."

"Do you think they really won't mind if I come?"

"Uh? Oh, sure. Of course they will be glad to have you back. So, are you coming tomorrow?"

After a short pause, Mansik said with a sigh, "No. I can't go."

"It's up to you whether you come or not. If you decide to come, you will find us around noon on the southern shore of the island. You can't miss the dump if you just walk down the shore along the reeds. I hope I will see you tomorrow."

Kangho turned to leave.

"Thank you," Mansik said to Kangho's back. He spoke in such a soft voice that Kangho did not hear him.

Seated on the sand at the edge of the reeds, Mansik hurled a pebble into the river. The stone landed on the surface with a *plop* and sank into the water. He sighed and glanced over at the cow browsing through the grass on the opposite riverbank. The brass bells on the cow's collar jangled as the animal waved its head this way and that to drive away the flies. He picked up a withered twig and nervously snapped it into little pieces.

Mansik was waiting for the boys to come across the river but he was not sure what attitude he should assume when they did come. He had had little sleep the night before trying to decide whether or not he should join the boys for the raid on the dump. He finally made up his mind to come, for this was a chance he could not afford to lose, perhaps the last and only chance for him to end this depressing life, confined to the small sunny yard, ambling back and forth, doing nothing, day and night, and day and night again, and then again day and night, with no friends to play with, not even one. If he were to be accepted back by the boys . . . If they would really welcome him back as Kangho had said they would . . . He wanted to be one of the boys again. He knew nobody would expect him unless Kangho had told them about last night, and he was not sure how they would react to his appearance, uninvited. But he had to take the chance.

When Mansik went to the ferry, everything—the shallow rippling water, the blueness of the river and the sky, the boat bobbing at the end of the rope, the dazzling golden sand on the opposite shore—everything looked new and foreign to him, because he had not seen them for so long. The boatman apparently felt the same way about Mansik.

"Haven't seen you for quite a long time," said the boatman with a knowing smile, squinting at the lone passenger on his boat inquisitively. "Going somewhere?"

"Over there," said Mansik. "Across the river."

"Across the river? You mean you're going to Texas, too?"

"Texas?" the boy said. "What's Texas?"

Pushing and pulling the oar slowly with a rhythmic grunt, the boatman stole a glance at the boy once more and grinned. "You should know," he said cryptically. "I thought you were going there on your mother's errand."

"What errand?"

"Never mind," the boatman said. "Maybe you really don't know."

About ten yards away from the dump, the four boys watched a truck unload garbage into a deep oval pit. At the back of the truck a muscular *bengko* soldier, his soft cap tipped back halfway, grunted while turning a big aluminum dustbin upside down as he emptied coffee grounds, that looked like steaming brown sawdust, into the sloping pit. The other soldier, in a sweat-soaked shirt, placed the emptied dustbins on one side and pushed the next one over to the first *bengko*.

Kijun watched closely to see where something he might like to pick up later landed. "I hope we find some meat again today," he said. "Do you boys remember what I found in a can last time? My uncle said it was 'ham.' It really tasted good when my mother made a piggie stew with it."

"What's piggie stew?" Chandol asked.

"You collect everything you can eat from the *bengko* garbage — meat and cheese and chicken bones and everything — and boil them together in a pot. That's piggie stew," Jun explained. "Some people call it U.N. soup. My uncle saw the town folks sell it on the streets the other day. He told my mother the piggie stew recipe."

The Yankee soldiers slammed the tailgate shut after emptying all six garbage cans, climbed back into the truck and drove away, waving to Bong and Kijun, who called "hello, hello", "gerrary" and every *bengko* word they knew. Then the boys swarmed into the pit to dig and stir and scoop off the warm wet coffee grounds with sticks and their bare hands, searching for anything they could salvage. They shook and emptied every open can they found to see if anything to eat was left inside. Chandol and Kijun and Bong enjoyed the treasure hunt, their legs sunk in slimy garbage up to the knees, their faces and hands soon stained with brown slops, but Kangho was not as excited as the rest today. Hoping Mansik would show up any moment, Kangho kept restlessly scanning the ferry and the sandy shore.

They were going through the garbage for the second time, more thoroughly now, because they had found few things to take home on the first go-round.

"Look, Chandol," said Kijun, standing in the middle of the garbage, all movement suspended as he stared at the sandy shore.

"What?" said Chandol without lifting his head to look at anything. He was busy shaking the trash out of a large carton.

But Kangho, who had been turning over wet, dirty papers with a piece of steel pipe, did look up; he knew what Jun's tense voice might mean.

"Over there," Kijun said. "Mansik is coming."

"Who?" Chandol said, finally raising himself to look.

"Mansik is coming," Kijun repeated.

Bong, who had been picking through the garbage with two long broken pine branches, operating them like a pair of chopsticks, looked back over his shoulder, surprised. Chewing a piece of Chuckles jelly candy he had found earlier, Chandol stared at Mansik, who was hesitantly advancing toward the pit.

Kangho had not yet mentioned his invitation to Mansik. Several times he had tried to, but Chandol seemed to be in a foul mood and Kangho did not want to aggravate him for fear he would be ordered to go to the Chestnut House and cancel the invitation. Kangho had decided to let Mansik and Chandol face each other and hope for the best.

Mansik stopped about a hundred feet away from them when he saw Chandol's expression. Then he continued to approach the boys; he knew he could not turn back now.

"Why is that son of a bitch coming here?" said Chandol, his face creasing into a frown.

Now Kangho feared his plan would not work but he had to give it a try anyway. Pretending he did not know anything, he said in a composed and innocent voice, "I think he came to play with us."

"Play with us? Who says we will play with him?"

"Well, he is here, anyway. Why don't we play with him?" Kangho suggested tentatively. "We haven't played with him for a long time."

"Are you crazy?" said Chandol, glaring at Mansik who was still walking towards them. "The villagers make such a big deal out of our coming to this island, as it is. Can you imagine what they'd do to us if they found out that we were chumming around with him? Anyway, how did he find out that we were coming here this afternoon?"

"Yeah, how come that bastard knew we would be here this afternoon?" Kijun reiterated.

"I guess someone must have told him," said Chandol, checking the boys one by one with an interrogating glance. "Who was it?"

"I don't know," Kijun said quickly. "I haven't played with Mansik since the arrival of the *bengkos*."

When Chandol's stare fell on him, Kangho said, "I did." The three boys gaped at him in amazement. Kangho went on, "I went to his house and told him to come here this afternoon if he wanted to play with us."

"Who said you could make such a decision for us?" said Chandol.

"Yeah, who said you could?" Kijun chimed in. "You think you're the captain or something?"

"Mansik used to be such a good friend to us," Kangho said, ignoring Jun. "Why don't you give him a chance and try to understand—"

"We don't have to understand anything about him," Chandol interrupted Kangho. "And you stay out of this business, Kangho. I'll take care of him myself."

Chandol beckoned Mansik over. Mansik hesitated for a moment, sensing something was going wrong, then went over to Chandol.

"Stop there," Chandol said. "That's close enough."

Mansik stopped.

"Why are you here?" Chandol asked.

Mansik said nothing. He knew he should not have come. He had known all along that things would turn out this way. It was too late now.

"I guess you came here to play with us, but we can't play with you," Chandol said. "We all know that your mother fucked a nigger. And you still expect us to play with you?"

"Yeah," Kijun added. "My mother told me your mother will have a black baby because she fucked a black man."

"You shut up, Toad." Chandol silenced Kijun and then went on. "I know that Kangho went to see you last night and told you to come here today, but Kangho's words are cancelled by me. I heard your mother is whoring in Texas. Think, boy, think. How can you expect us to play with a whore's son?"

Later, Mansik could not remember exactly what had happened after that. He was running across the sand. He ran like a whipped dog. He did not cry. He was too confused to cry. He just ran. And someone, perhaps Kijun, chanted at the top of his voice somewhere in the distance behind him:

Mansik mommy U.N. lady,
Mansik mommy Yankee whore,
Mansik mommy U.N. lady . . .

.   .   .

Ollye and Sister Serpent entertained their *bengko* customers in a narrow room illuminated by a red-painted electric bulb. On one wall there was a pinup poster showing a young American girl in short pants doffing a military helmet coquettishly. The bare planks of the opposite wall were decorated with a one-page calendar. Several dresses in bright colors hung from nails on the rear wall.

"You mean beer still tastes bitter to you?" said Yonghi maliciously, maintaining a false snaky smile on her lips so that the Yankee soldiers would not notice that she was berating Ollye in the middle of their drinking party. "You should be quite used to all sorts of strong liquor by now, much less this mild beer. Look, Sis, you shouldn't frown like that in the presence of the customers." She poured another cup of beer for her soldier and went on, "You should give a smiling impression to all your customers all the time and you have to keep drinking a lot. You can charge them for all the beer you drink, remember? Smile, I said. I've told you a hundred times to keep smiling, haven't I?"

Yonghi's room had a regular door with a latch and a handle, but the room she rented to Ollye had no door of any sort. They had not yet been able to get plywood to make one. A single straw mat was draped over the entrance like a curtain to screen the room from the alley. They were sitting on the board floor around the low plank table loaded with beer cans, bottles, dried cuttlefish, salted peanuts and anchovy mixed with roasted kelp.

"*Hey, drink can do?*" said Ollye's customer, whose nose looked like a clenched fist. In Texas Town, the *bengko* soldiers spoke Konglish, Koreanized English.

Ollye understood that the soldier wanted to know if she could drink and she replied with the *bengko* words taught her by Yonghi and Sundok, "*Okay. Can do. Sank you.*"

Sister Serpent displayed a satisfied expression at her answer. Ollye could not see Sundok in the room. Where did she go? Where had she . . . Oh, yes, now Ollye remembered. She had left the room early with Sarging Buffalo, who had preferred to retire to the back room with

Sundok after only one can of beer. That terrible Sarging Buffalo would torture Sundok all night again, and Ollye knew Sundok would be too tired tomorrow to get out of her bed until late afternoon.

Yonghi's tall sarging, who was too tall even for a Yankee, scooped a spoonful of jam from a glass bottle and offered it to her smiling red lips. Yonghi asked her tall sarging, *Where your homutown?* The tall sarging said *Omaha*, and Yonghi asked Fist Nose, *Where your homutown?* Fist Nose also said *Omaha*, and they laughed.

"These sargings are funny guys, Sis," Yonghi said. "I asked them where is their hometown and both of them said they're from Omaha." Ollye could not understand why that was supposed to be funny and Yonghi explained, "They're saying their home is here, Camp Omaha," and Ollye still could not find anything funny about that and Yonghi said, "Why don't you smile, too, once in a while, Sis, when they seem to be enjoying themselves? Just give a cute little smile when they laugh even if you don't understand what they are talking about, will you?"

Ollye simpered belatedly and resolved to try to smile now and then. But she found it extremely difficult to control the timing of her smiles, control herself, or control anything when she had taken a drink. She tried to be a good U.N. lady, although it was difficult. But that was the only way to pay back Sister Serpent for all she had done to help her. Yonghi was, so to speak, her guide and mentor. Yonghi trained and educated her, provided her with a room, brought men and introduced them to her, and even coached her in the tricks and skills which would please the foreign soldiers. In addition to teaching her so many basic things, Yonghi sometimes helped her communicate with the customers, and it was also through Yonghi that she exchanged military payment certificates for real money. Ollye was totally hopeless without Yonghi, and she knew it, so it seemed fair that Sister Serpent took half of her earnings.

Sister Serpent seemed to know everything there was to know about this Yankee wife business. Ollye listened attentively to her lectures every day, but there were always more things for her to learn. "You have to be prepared for the venereal diseases, Sis," she said one day. "You must have heard about 'social diseases' or 'pleasure diseases,' haven't you? The most common ones are clap and pox. *Gonorrhea* and *syphilis* in Yankee words. Be careful not to contract them. If you get one of those horrible diseases, you could give birth to a harelipped baby, and I saw a girl with pox who lost most of her hair. So you have to use this rubber sack all the time." She showed the white transparent balloon to her. "You wrap the male tool with it like this." She showed with her fingers how to fit it and Sundok laughed and laughed during the demonstration. "If your soldier uses this, it will prevent not only diseases but pregnancy, too. Some of them prefer not to put anything on their instruments, so you'd better ask 'Condom okay?' when you have a new customer. If he says okay, you are okay, too."

Ollye noticed they used the word "okay" surprisingly often in the *bengko* language. The *bengko* words Sundok and Yonghi and their soldier friends used most often in their conversations were "*okay, okay,*" "*hubba-hubba,*" "*namba wang,*" "*namba teng,*" "*gerrary,*" "*drink,*" "*kiss kiss,*" "*cock,*" "*cunt*" and "*fuck.*" These were the first American words she learned.

Yonghi taught Ollye the phrases she would need to communicate with and entertain her Yankee customers. "When a *bengko* says '*Slip with me?*' he wants to sleep with you. '*Slip with me*' means the same as '*fuck.*' Then you have to ask '*Long time, short time?*' Long-time customers sleep with you all night but short-time customers have just one fuck and leave."

Ollye had not had a long-time customer yet. At first she had thought it would be too embarrassing for her to hail the boatman from across the river early in the morning to go back home. And she was afraid to stay with a *bengko* all night. Yonghi knew this and assigned only short-time customers to her.

The beer upset her stomach so much that she felt her entrails twirl like eels on a frying pan every time she moved. But she did not feel as nauseated now as she had with her first drink. When Ollye had

had to entertain her first customer, Yonghi gave her a shot of clear apricot-colored liquor, telling her it would drive away fear and anxiety. It did make her feel less nervous, but unbearably queasy too. She dreaded what she was doing during the actual sex, even confusing the customer with the *bengkos* who had attacked her that night, and shuddering in abhorrence and terror. But she could not resist because she felt too weak, her head swimming as if she was stricken with malaria. She passed out in a drunken stupor. When she came to, the *bengko* was already gone, leaving only a pool of slippery fluid in her groin.

Sarging Fist Nose asked Ollye *"How old you?"* and Yonghi interpreted; the soldier was asking her age. Ollye said, as she had been taught, *"Tenti po,"* which meant she was twenty-four years old. The *bengkos* couldn't tell even if she cheated by ten years.

Ollye was too drunk now to hold her slippery glass straight and beer streamed down the back of her hand. Ollye was wearing Yonghi's green satin dress with a large cloth rose on the chest.

"Be careful, Sis," Yonghi said with a fake smile. "Don't spill the beer and spoil my dress."

"I'm sorry," Ollye said. "I'll be careful. I think I'll never learn to drink as well as you do."

"You will learn to drink all right," Yonghi said. "In time you'll get used to everything."

That was true. She was indeed getting used to everything—even to sleeping with the foreign soldiers. But she still could not overcome the shock that had stunned her yesterday afternoon when she had found scribbled on the wall of the tobacco shed near the ferry: *Mansik mommy U.N. lady, Mansik mommy Yankee whore.* What worried her most at that instant was the possibility that Mansik might have seen it. If he had not, she wanted to remove it before he had the chance. She dashed down to a rice paddy, grabbed a handful of mud, dashed back to the tobacco shed and erased the charcoal scribbling by smearing mud over it. Now she blushed again, hot anger surging to her face, as she vividly remembered the scribbling. It was in a child's handwriting. It had been scrawled there by one of Mansik's old friends to humiliate her son.

It seemed the whole village knew what she was doing. Nobody could expect the boatman to keep his mouth shut for long. Ollye had bribed the boatman with American cigarettes to keep him silent about her secret trips to Texas Town but Yom must have decided that her time was up. So what? Though they had branded her a filthy woman, Ollye thought they were all accomplices in her fall. She hated the villagers. She hated the villagers, the *bengkos*, the child who had scrawled the dirty words on the wall of the tobacco shed, and everybody around her. She hated the boatman who must have passed the word around that she had become a Yankee whore.

She considered entertaining long-time customers now that she no longer had anything to keep secret. She could not make much money working with short-timers only. But if she were to entertain long-time soldiers she would have to live at the shanty town. She did not want to bring her children to be raised in such a place. She could not make decisions because everything was so confusing and she was so drunk.

Old Hwang would have heard of her activities, too. He might forbid her use of the boat as he had denied it to Yonghi and Sundok. There was no doubt about it. Sooner or later she would not be allowed to use the boat. What would she do then? They might get a boat of their own, as Yonghi had suggested. It sounded like a perfect plan. When they found a boat, they could leave this shanty and move Dragon Lady Club to the riverside house. They could bring the customers across the river. Old Hwang and the villagers would raise hell. Who cared? Ollye was no longer afraid of anything the villagers could do to her. Maybe she was too drunk to fear anything now, but somehow everything seemed to have become easy and simple.

"I think we will retire to my room, Sis," Yonghi said. "It's not good business to keep them awake when they're not drinking any more. Why don't you give your sarging a good time, too? Looks like he has a great big erection."

The tall soldier and Yonghi scrambled to their feet, the soldier staggering but Yonghi as sober as an icicle, and with giggles and murmurs they disappeared behind the veneer door. As soon as they were left alone, Fist Nose started to take his pants off, saying "*I wanna fuck you. I wanna fuck you.*" Ollye thought it was funny that any man took his trousers off before his jacket; this soldier took his trousers off first, and then his shorts. In a moment the *bengko's* male thing was exposed; it dangled down under the jacket like a greased sausage. Then he took off his socks, his jacket and his shirt. He came over to her and pulled the green dress with its cloth rose over her head. She had nothing under the dress, because Yonghi had told her that was one sure way to win a steady customer fast. Yonghi had also told her to learn to have some fun out of the business.

The *bengko* hastily mounted her, his rubbery thing slipped into her, and the floor seemed to roll and pitch like the deck of a ship in a storm. She recalled what Sister Serpent had told her that afternoon. She did not know why she suddenly remembered her words at this particular moment, but she did. As Fist Nose kept pumping she feared her entrails would squeeze out of her anus under his heavy weight. You should make a careful choice of your customers, Yonghi had advised her. There are two kinds of U.N. ladies, you know—those who entertain the white Yankees and those who entertain the blackies. At some larger Texas Towns, there're even separate sectors for the whites and the blacks. The whites never sleep with any girl who has ever entertained a nigger. The whites treat the niggers like dirt, you know. The girls who entertain whites can switch to blacks any time they want, but the blackie whores can never sleep with a whitey. So, if you ever allow yourself to go with a black soldier, you will be a nigger whore for good. Ollye told her that one of the two *bengkos* that had raped her was black. Yonghi warned her not to tell it ever, ever to anybody, if she wanted to remain a white whore. Fist Nose kept pumping and squeezing her and Ollye could no longer stand the punishment. She started to vomit violently with the *bengko* still on her.

Part III

THE CHILDREN

ONE

The river was silent in the dark behind them, but from the direction of Texas Town the three boys could hear a throbbing female voice on an old squeaky phonograph. At times the sound rose and then faded as it was swept away by the wind. Shivering in their wet nakedness, the boys hurried down a narrow path through the reeds.

"This is an awfully cold night to go to watch anything," said Chandol in a low voice, pressing his navel with his index finger to stop the night air from getting into his insides and loosening his bowels.

"But it's worth the trouble," said Jun with a chuckle, following close behind Chandol. "I've never seen anything like what the U.N. ladies do with the *bengkos*."

Kangho kept apprehensively silent, hiding his crotch self-consciously with his folded hands. He was not too sure about this whole thing. This adventure was unlike anything they had ever done before. Neither the Autumn War with the Castle boys nor the raid on the dump was as dangerous and strange as this new game of theirs. If they were ever caught by the *bengkos*, the soldiers would be so mad that they might shoot and kill them.

The three boys had sneaked out of their homes. They swam across the river to Texas Town when the whole village was asleep, for the boys knew the boatman would tell Rich Hwang of their visit to the islet if he spotted them. Bong had been left behind because he could not swim well enough to reach Cucumber Island and also because Chandol decided that he was too young for this adventure.

They quickened their pace. They wanted to see the whores as soon as possible. The breeze felt as chilly to them as air right before it snows on a winter morning. When they reached a sand dune by the shanty town, they looked at one another, their eyes glinting.

"You boys wait here until I pick the house," Chandol said and crawled up the dune, wriggling his hips sideways like a lizard.

Lying flat on top of the dune, Chandol surveyed the whoretown which was colorfully decorated with signs and painted pictures and electric bulbs, deciding which house they would peep into tonight. There were almost fifty shanties in Texas Town now, and the soldiers, in their garrison caps like *origami* boats, slouched around by twos and threes among the crowded shacks, glancing at the young girls sitting on plank benches in the alleys. The whores, displaying their half-exposed tits and open thighs and whatever they had to offer, invited the *bengkos*, "Hey, Joe, buy me drink, okay? Buy me drink, okay?" A girl laughed shrilly somewhere unseen and a soldier swore "Goddamn!" somewhere else.

Chandol quickly made his choice. He knew there would be a lot to watch with this particular couple. The tall soldier and his whore played with each other in a way conspicuously different from that of other soldiers and U.N. ladies. There was lots of pulling and tugging and pinching and hugging and hand-holding going on among the Yankees and the whores but this lanky soldier and his pancake-faced girl *really* knew how to play with each other. The soldier was so tall that her head barely reached his shoulder and his hand could reach around her neck down to her breasts. He kept squeezing and kneading them through the neck of her loose scarlet blouse all the while he was chatting and laughing and walking with her to her house. The girl, in a Chinese skirt, that was slit on both sides to reveal most of her legs, apparently liked what he was doing to her; she giggled, clinging to his waist tightly with one arm, her free hand playfully rubbing and stroking and jerking the bulge in the soldier's pants between his legs. The couple disappeared through the strings of wooden beads covering the doorway of a frame house which looked like a compost shed.

Chandol quickly slid down the dune backward to the waiting boys. "We're going to have a nice show tonight. Come."

The three boys crawled around the dune and approached the house. Like most shanties in Texas Town, this one had no fence around it. The boys crept to the back of the house and concealed themselves in the dark, pressing their backs against the wall.

"Somebody must be lookout," Chandol whispered.

Kijun cast a furtive sidelong glance at Chandol and promptly looked away, hoping he would not be assigned the first shift of lookout duty tonight.

"I'll be lookout," Kangho volunteered. He had been reluctant to join this game anyway. He wondered why he had come in the first place.

"Good," Chandol said. "You go over there to that outhouse, Kangho, and watch out for anybody coming in this direction. Toad will relieve you in ten minutes."

Kangho hid himself in the shabby outhouse, which was only two canvas walls like a folding screen, and watched the U.N. ladies soliciting and catcalling at the passing soldiers.

Chandol and Kijun positioned themselves among the logs and broken planks and mud bricks at the rear wall of the shack and peeked through a chink in the window frame. The *bengko* and the whore were almost naked now under the bare electric bulb. The girl, clad in flimsy underwear as thin and transparent as a dragonfly's wing, was lying sprawled on the floor like a dead frog; the *bengko* mounted her like a huge white hairless bull. The soldier began to suck the girl's mouth, making a lot of slobbering sounds.

Holding their breath, Chandol and Kijun watched the naked grownups play in the room.

"The girl kept moaning and whimpering all the time that huge soldier was swimming on her stomach to push himself into her." Kijun was telling the boys what he had seen at Texas Town.

The four boys were on their way to the *bengko* dump for another afternoon raid.

"Go on, go on," prompted Chandol who had missed that exciting scene because he had had to go on lookout. "What happened next?"

After a dramatic pause Kijun continued, "When the Yankee was about to force himself into her with his cock like a horse, the girl babbled something, pushing him away. The *bengko* fell down on the floor and lay there on his back, waiting with a grin as he rubbed his balls, and the girl stood up. She was facing the window and, oh, boy, I could see everything. Her breasts were wet, as damp with sweat as if she had just had a bath. And she had such bushy black hair down there. Then she came over to the electric bulb and turned the light off."

"Damn!" said Chandol, disappointed. "I wonder why they always turn the light off when they do it."

"Some *bengkos* keep the light on," said Kangho, drawing an endless line on the sand with his stick. "Like the *bengko* we watched the other night."

"Couldn't you see anything more after they had turned the light off?" Chandol asked.

With a complacent beam, Kijun said, "I could see what they were doing clearly enough because the other girl and her *bengko* drinking in the hall kept the light on outside the paper door."

"Well, tell us what they did, then."

"The girl, giggling, sat astride the *bengko*'s stomach, the way you ride a horse, and picked up a packet of balloons from the sewing basket by the door. She placed the rubber balloons at the tip of the soldier's cock and began to roll it down like this, like this, until the whole thing was covered by the silvery balloon. And then she began to pound him down with her hips, gasping again, and the *bengko* was on top of her next moment, and she began to squeal like a stoned bitch. Watching all that made me have an erection myself. Boy, they really knew how to play."

"It's really exciting to watch them play naked," said Chandol and he began to describe what he had seen. With some inevitable exaggerations, because he was the boss and supposed to have seen more strange and exciting things than any other boy had, he told them about the Yankees and the whores he had watched. There was a lot of repetition, with only slight changes in detail, but nobody minded. "As the Yankee fumbled her tits and cunt, the whore began to pant like a dog in summer. And then they began to suck at each other's mouth."

"What for?" said Bong, puzzled. "Why did they suck each other's mouth?" The little boy had heard so many strange things about the grownups' game, and he was sorry that he had never gotten a chance to watch the whores' rooms at night.

"They just do, all the time," Kijun said. "The Yankees just love to suck and lick the girls mouths, and everywhere else, too."

"Why do they suck the girls so much?" the little boy said, his curiosity still unsatisfied.

"How can anybody know why they do that?" Jun said. "Dogs also suck at each other's muzzles before mating, don't they?"

"Dogs only sniff at each other," Chandol said.

"Imagine sucking out anything from a girl's mouth," Bong said, mystified. "Some girls must smell bad at the mouth. Many people have a foul smell in their mouths, you know."

"Sometimes they do lots of other strange things too," Jun said.

"Indeed there are lots of things to watch at Texas Town if you go there at night. Anyway, Chandol, what did they do when they were through mouth-sucking?"

"The *bengko* stripped down her panties. Her black panties were so beautiful, with lace and frills and everything. Then he took his own pants off and climbed on top of her. In no time he started to thrust his cock into her crotch."

Laughing and chattering, the four boys hurried along the shore and arrived at the dump to find two strange boys picking through the garbage heap of steaming coffee grounds, crushed tin cans, wet papers and soiled chicken bones.

"What the hell is going on?" Chandol said, stopping short and squinting.

"They're stealing our garbage," Kijun said.

"Come," Chandol said. "We have to drive them away."

"Hey, you!" Chandol shouted. "Don't move!"

"Stay there and don't move!" Jun shouted.

As the four Kumsan boys swarmed to the pit, yelling, the two intruders looked up at them. The taller boy holding a "pillow bread" soggy with swill and grease was Sinil, the fifteen-year-old captain of the Castle village boys. Sinil started to climb out of the pit, his feet sinking into the slimy garbage and leftover food and his eyes blazing as he glared back at Chandol. The smaller boy was as young as Bong. Something rattled in the can he carried in his hand as he followed his captain as if he was afraid to be abandoned in the pit.

Chandol blocked Sinil's way at the edge of the pit and, trying to stare him down, said, "Who says you Castle boys can come here and steal our things?"

"We are not stealing anything from anybody," said Sinil. "And nobody can say we can't come here either."

"This dump belongs to Kumsan," Chandol explained. "I cannot let you take anything from this place."

"I think differently," said Sinil, who showed no intention of giving in. "I don't think you should try to stop us from coming here. This is an open place. Anybody can take anything he finds here. And I find lots of things that I want to take home with me."

Chandol quickly examined the situation. He had never had a fist fight, one-to-one, with Sinil yet, but there was no doubt that Kumsan would beat Castle now in a group fight. Kumsan outnumbered them by two to one.

"You'd better watch out," Chandol warned, "unless you're ready for punishment."

"You want to punish *me?*" said Sinil. "All right, Chandol, come on and try."

There was no need to exchange any more words. Sinil had hardly finished his challenge when Chandol kicked him in the groin as hard as he could. As Sinil was about to fall forward, Chandol butted him in the forehead like a charging ram. Sinil collapsed on the bed of garbage, blood streaming from both nostrils. The little Castle village boy trembled in fear, expecting he would be attacked next. Children's fights usually ended when one boy had a nosebleed, the undeniable sign of the loser. But Sinil would not admit that Chandol was the better fighter.

"Don't think this is the end of the fight," said Sinil, wiping the blood off his nose with a handful of sand. "I'm coming back. I'll be back soon, with my boys, and then we will have a real war."

Sinil's announcement meant that this year's Autumn War between Kumsan and Castle would be a contest over the right to the dump. It was going to be a bloody fight, Chandol thought. Up to now, the boys of the two villages had never fought over anything tangible. This time some boys would get hurt for sure . . . But he did not want to give the Castle captain the wrong impression that Kumsan did not want to fight.

"Get going. Quick!" Chandol said. "You'd better not dream of coming back here. If you show up around this place again to steal something, I'll chop your hands off with a straw-cutter."

Staring after Sinil and the small boy walking toward the ferry, Chandol began to worry. He knew Sinil would not forget the shame of his nosebleed in the presence of the other boys. Chandol had won today owing to the success of his surprise attack. Now Sinil would be wary and he had longer arms than Chandol's. Kumsan would need a lot of preparation to win the fight with the Castle boys this year. The annual mock war with stones between the boys of the two villages had been delayed this autumn due to the outbreak of the war among the grownups and the coming of the World Army. Chandol was sure that Sinil would not wait much longer to declare war, because of today's humiliation.

Chandol had good reason to worry. Last year, Kumsan barely managed to win; at one time, Chandol's boys had been driven as far down as the abandoned water mill when the Castle boys attacked them with mud bombs containing bitter peach medicine. If a mud bomb exploded anywhere near you and a puff of the yellow powdered pesticide got into your mouth, you could not eat anything for one whole day. And Chandol had a new handicap this year. The five boys of Kumsan had fought successfully against the seven Castle boys for the past three years, but now, there were only four of them. Mansik was out. They would need a good plan to win this year's war and keep the Castle boys out of the dump. When the Castle village boys were gone, Kijun and Bong and Kangho slid down into the pit and began to rummage through the garbage, but Chandol remained on the sand, looking over at the ferry with an uneasy expression.

———•———

Night after night Ollye entertained customers. She found herself so drunk by the time she was ready to go home that she could not walk. Yonghi had reassured her over and over again that she would soon get used to drinking but she was drunk again tonight although she had only two cups of beer. And when she was sober, she felt restless or depressed most of the time; her skin would crawl all over with self-consciousness when she was at home, sober, with Mansik and Nanhi.

Sarging Mike with his hooked nose grinned at Ollye and said "Korean cunt namba wang" and something else, imitating Korean pronunciation, and Sarging Fist Nose and Sister Serpent laughed. Yonghi kept her left breast hanging out of her white dress because Sarging Mike wanted to suck it after every cup of beer as a "relish." Ollye tried to join in their laughter in time but she missed her cue again. Her belated laugh sounded, even to herself, empty and stupid. Sarging Fist Nose was Ollye's only steady customer. He came to see her every week and Yonghi wondered why he liked Ollye so much since she spoke so little *Migook*. Ollye herself could not understand why he had fallen for her. He kept coming to see her even after she had vomited beer and pieces of ham and *kimchi* pickles and rice on his face and chest at their very first encounter. Sundok believed that the soldier had been utterly fascinated by the totally unprofessional service Ollye offered him.

As she spent more and more time with him in bed Ollye thought of him less and less as one of a kind with the monstrous *bengkos* who had violated her long months ago. She was no longer afraid or suspicious of him. This changing attitude enabled her to follow Yonghi's advice to "enjoy" the work now and then. One night she had totally abandoned herself to him, and was so aroused that she kept clinging to him for almost two hours until both of them were as limp as wet rags, drenched in perspiration. Yonghi, who had been with her own customer in the next room, kept commenting through the wall, "You're driving both of us here nuts. Can't you do it a little more quietly and ladylike?" Sarging Fist Nose had entered her three times but he was not willing to let her go at midnight when she usually went home. The sergeant called Yonghi to Ollye's room and told her that he would not be satisfied with a short-time and wanted to have his woman all night. Yonghi, half naked herself, observed with an amused expression the naked couple under the sheet and the telltale signs of violent passion in the littered room. "Great, Sis, great," Yonghi said. "You're doing really great like a pro tonight." Then she told Ollye what the sergeant wanted and demanded that she give him a long-time. By now Ollye had no strength left to leave. The sheets turned soggy with their sweat that night and smelled musty the next morning.

She had awakened, sober and frightened, at sunrise. The soldier was gone already, leaving only the odor of cigarette smoke and spilled beer in the stuffy room. This was the first time in her life that she had ever spent whole night outside her home. She winced in anticipation of going back to Kumsan in the bright morning sun and facing her children. She vaguely persuaded herself that she had to go to Central Market and buy some vegetables for side dishes at supper. She ambled around town for over two hours after buying some turnips and pickled garlic, because she was afraid to go home. When she finally returned to the Chestnut House around noon, Mansik was sullenly waiting for her by the walnut stump. Nanhi had cried until her eyes had turned red.

"Do we have any more beer left?" Yonghi asked. "I believe there's a case of beer out in the hall, Sis."

Ollye tried to remember but her head kept swimming. "I'm not sure," she said. She tried a little harder to remember and she thought there was still one more case of beer left in the hall. "I think there is," she said. "Yes. We have one more case of beer in the hall."

"Would you bring in five more bottles?"

"I see. I will."

As Ollye staggered up on her wobbly legs, Sarging Fist Nose asked her, "*Odika?* Where are you going?"

"Beer," Ollye said. "Beer. Drink beer."

Fist Nose asked Yonghi, "More beer? You wanna more beer?"

"Yeah," Yonghi said with an apologetic smile. "Ah wanna moa beer. Pibe moa bottle beer. Okay?"

Nodding his head okay, the soldier gestured for Ollye to sit down and wait. "I can do," the Yankee said. "I can do bring more beer." He reeled out of the room.

"He really treats you like a queen, Sis," Yonghi said. "I hope my Sarging Mike will learn how to treat a girl from your sarging."

Mike could not understand what the two women were talking about in Korean but he was obviously pleased that his name had been mentioned. He gulped another cup of beer, pulled Yonghi's exposed breast like an elastic toy toward his pouting mouth and sucked it.

Her mind was turning hazy from the drink, but Ollye still vividly remembered Mansik's hostile expression. She had hurried into the kitchen to cook the late breakfast and feed Nanhi—and to avoid Mansik's accusing glare. She scooped a gourdful of rice out of the buried jar and turned back, and Mansik was there, standing by the door, staring at her, his face frozen as hard as a marble tombstone.

Mansik asked point-blank, "Are you a whore?"

Ollye had been speechless. She could not even move her fingers. In the next room Nanhi was screaming at the top of her lungs.

Ollye had expected that Mansik would find out about her night work sooner or later, but she had not been prepared to face him.

Sarging Fist Nose came in with the beer in his arms and placed the bottles one by one on the table. Grinning broadly he mumbled something and Yonghi and Sarging Mike laughed and Ollye, though a moment late, laughed, too. You get used to anything if you practice often enough, she thought. Anything. Even laughing in time. Now she was quite used to the Yankee names too. The *bengko* names were so strange that she could not even imitate the sounds at first, but now she could say Jimmy, Billy, Duncan and almost all the names of the Yankees she had been in bed with so far. She also learned how to call a passing soldier whom she had never seen before; all she had to do was to just say "Hello, Joe, G.I. Joe, buy me drink," as everybody else at Texas Town did.

One thing that she still did not know how to handle was her relationship with her son Mansik. Sometimes, even while she was in bed with a soldier customer and drunk, the faces of Mansik and Nanhi, always with frigid staring expressions, haunted her.

At Texas Town, there was a twenty-four-year-old girl with the Korean name of Meri as well as the *Migook* name of Mary. She never told anybody much about herself and nobody knew where she was from or

163

what her real name was but she must have had a complicated past, for she had a six-year-old illegitimate daughter. Ollye watched Mary and her daughter, who had the Korean name of Suson, meaning "the Narcissus Girl," as well as the American name of Susan, but Ollye could not find any hints in the mother-daughter relationship that might help in her own relation with Mansik. Susan was so used to the life of the Texas Towns that she played with any *bengko* who came to sleep with her mother. While Mary was working with her customer, Susan would wander around the shanty town, looking for somebody to play with. Everybody, both the U.N. ladies and the Yankees, treated her like a mascot or a human pet.

Ollye could not imagine Nanhi as another Susan, and she certainly did not want her children to grow up in a whoretown. Yet she thought that if she received long-time customers, she could make some real money quickly, leave this place for good, settle down somewhere far away and begin a new life.

"Work like a dog for just one year until you make enough money to open a small shop somewhere," Yonghi would say. "Then you can go and settle down at a remote town in Chungchong or Kangwon Province, open a cotton shop or a noodle house and live as happily ever after as you want with your children. Nobody there will ever find out you were a whore unless you tell them."

So Ollye had asked Yonghi, with pretended casualness, if Sister Serpent would still like to open a club at the snake hunter's hut. Of course Yonghi wanted to, but she knew she could not make the boatman take her across the river. "Suppose you can find another boat . . .," Ollye said. Sister Serpent realized that Mansik's mother had been privately working on a scheme of her own.

Yonghi and Ollye had packed up some American cigarettes, C-ration cans and slabs of chocolates and gone to Kamwa village where Ollye had once lived. At the village, Ollye visited several of her old neighbors to ask if anyone might sell or lease a boat to them. A fisherman suggested that they go down river to Kangchon and find the old man who worked for the Buddhist temple during the winter. He would not need his boat until next spring.

Most villagers of Kamwa and Kangchon shunned the two women because of Yonghi's bold "Western" attire and unwomanly aggressive manners, but the old man agreed to lease his boat to Ollye because he had been a long-time friend of her father. The old man also liked the American cigarettes they had brought for him. Besides, the money they offered him for a lease of two months amounted to the sum the old man would earn by a half year of fishing.

"Why don't you open the window, Sis?" Yonghi said, emptying the full ashtray, a jam jar, onto the earthen floor of the hall outside the door. "The cigarette smoke is suffocating me."

Ollye staggered up, trying to stretch her short skirt with one hand to hide her naked knees. She lifted the window and propped it open with a chopstick. When she sat down again next to Sarging Fist Nose, she felt somewhat cooler but her dizzy head would not clear. She knew she would not last long in this business. She was simply not cut out for this kind of life. And she had to start a new life before Nanhi was old enough to understand what her mother was doing. She did not want her daughter to suffer the way Mansik did now. Mansik was always glum these days and rarely answered her. He even skipped his meals because he was too frustrated and angry to have any appetite. The return of Sister Serpent to Kumsan had certainly been the last straw for Mansik.

The old man had been so pleased with the deal and their gifts that he volunteered to deliver the boat to Cucumber Island. When the boat arrived safely at the islet and the old man had gone to town to return to his home by train, Ollye and Yonghi had loaded their trunks and the sign on the boat and crossed the river. They were surprised to find how exhausting it was to row a boat; it took almost a half hour for them to reach the opposite bank, pushing and pulling the heavy creaking oars as the old man had showed them. They moored the boat by the tree near the snake hunter's shack and went to the Chestnut House where they were going to stay until the riverside hut was ready.

When Yonghi entered the Chestnut House, Mansik had been feeding his rabbits. "Hello, boy, long time no see," she said cheerfully. "But we're going to see each other a lot from now on." Taken aback at the sight of the Yankee whore walking side by side with his mother, the boy looked at Yonghi, at his mother, and then at Yonghi again. "You're not going to say hello to me?" asked Yonghi, reaching out to pat his head. The boy stepped back, dodged, and stopped short when his back touched the wire netting of the rabbit cage. He glared at the woman as if she were a criminal. "What is the meaning of this, Mansik!" Ollye tried to scold her son, but she was not sure if she was entitled to. "She's your mother's friend." Mansik ran out of the house and did not return home until dark.

Yonghi and Ollye went back to Cucumber Island the next day to settle matters such as paying the remaining installments of rent, arranging to purchase drinks and Yankee food, and notifying the steady customers of the new location of the Club. Yonghi instructed Sundok to change the name of the old Dragon Lady Club to Club Goldfish "so that all the customers coming here will drink like fish to make us rich very quickly" and left her in charge. Then the two women went to town and hired a carpenter and two workers to remodel the snake hunter's shack. First of all, Yonghi wanted the kitchen converted to a room with cubicles for entertaining soldiers. They did not need the kitchen because they would have their meals at the Chestnut House and they could cook the snacks which went with drinks with canned solid alcohol fuel. They decided not to entertain any customers at the Chestnut House because Ollye needed a place to keep her children apart from her shame.

The hired hands finished their work in four days, and the two women started working on the house themselves. The rooms where they would sleep with soldiers were papered with comic books and the *Stars and Stripes*. On the rear wall they hung a framed photograph of a *bengko* moving picture actress called Betty Grable. They had failed to locate an inexpensive second-hand wind-up phonograph yet, but they would manage with music from the AFKN Yankee military station on a Zenith radio.

Since they did not have electricity in the county, Sister Serpent lit the main room with two kerosene lamps while paper lanterns with candles inside were placed on tall wooden stands in each of the two "customer" rooms. Yonghi contrived the paper lanterns herself with some pieces of wire and willow branches, and Ollye was impressed by Sister Serpent's extraordinary skill in drawing orchids and bamboo on the wet rice paper with a rat-fur brush.

"Oh, sure, I'm good at many other things besides whoring," Yonghi said when Ollye complimented her on the paintings. "I'm a good cook, too. I would have made a wonderful wife for that son of the pear orchard owner if the war had not broken out." A shadow of resentment passed over her face when she said that. "Well, that's life," she added, cheerfully.

Late one afternoon, Yonghi had rushed into the Chestnut House, excited and happy, laughing and calling, "We don't need to row the boat any longer, Sis! We don't need to worry about drifting away down the river and we don't need to tire ourselves out rowing the boat back and forth."

"What are you talking about?" said Ollye, incredulous but delighted, for she was doing most of the rowing.

"Come on out," Yonghi said. "Look what I've done!"

Ollye went to the new Dragon Lady Club with her and saw a man fixing a thick hemp rope across the river between a steel pole driven into the ground among the reeds on Cucumber Island and the tall plane tree on the river bank near the Club. When the rope was properly fixed and fastened tight, the worker attached big steel rings at both ends of the boat, the rope passing through the rings.

"Look, Sis, you can move the boat this way." Yonghi gave a demonstration. "Instead of rowing, you just sit down here and pull the rope like this. See? The boat glides easily!"

Ollye tried the rope. They could cross the river in five minutes.

"Can you guess where I got this rope and the posts, Sis?" Yonghi said with a playful but proud smile. "I got them from Camp Omaha. Two free fucks."

Yonghi murmured something coquettish and Sarging Fist Nose burst into a loud laughter, the beer glass suspended in the air an inch before his lips, shaking. Sarging Mike also laughed, and Yonghi laughed, and Ollye laughed too with perfect timing. The laughter died down and it turned silent. Nobody said anything. The two soldiers and Sister Serpent stared at Ollye. Ollye wondered what was wrong.

Sarging Mike said something in a low voice and the three stared at her again. Then Yonghi said with a frustrated expression, "He's asking you, Sis."

"Me?" said Ollye, confused. "What did he ask me?"

"Didn't you understand his question?"

"No."

"Why did you laugh, then?"

"You told me I have to laugh when everybody else does. What did he ask me?"

"Never mind," Yonghi said. "Just say you like it."

Ollye did what she was told to do. "Yes," she said. "Namba wang. Okay."

The three laughed again but Ollye, instead of joining their laugh, picked up the glass before her and gulped the beer; she was not sure if she was supposed to laugh now or not. Ollye realized that she did not know what was going on around her and she felt left out. She did not belong here, she thought. Or anywhere.

Sarging Mike chattered on for some time alone. Sarging Fist Nose said something. Yonghi said something. Sarging Mike said something again. They continued chattering for several minutes without laughing. Ollye felt drowsy. She felt her head grow heavy. She would be happy to go to her room with her soldier so she could lie down.

TWO

The more you hate someone the more he haunts you, it is said. It was true for Old Hwang. Day after day first thing in the morning when he opened his gate, he saw the Chestnut House and the snake hunter's shack. He had to start each day provoked by the sight of the two houses he hated most. Exasperated, he would turn back into the Paulownia House, shuddering, before beginning work. When he was doing calligraphy or reading Confucian classics in the guest room, he kept the doors closed not just because the November weather was rather chilly for his aged knees but more because he abhorred the sight of those two hateful houses.

The villagers now called the snake hunter's hut the *Imugi* House. *Imugi* are serpents that have failed to become dragons because of some curse. It was their nickname for the wicked crafty woman who had managed to persuade Ollye to become a Yankee wife.

Old Hwang hated every single thing the Serpent Woman did.

Whenever he watched the two women and the foreign soldiers crossing the river, playfully pulling and tugging the hemp rope suspending over the water, laughing and chanting in unison, "Heave! Heave! Heave!", the old man was so infuriated that he suffered a severe pain in his stomach. The boat that the two women had secured for their own use was an outright challenge to him and his authority. If the drunken soldiers sang a *bengko* song crossing the river on their way back to Camp Omaha, he would be awakened—disturbed not so much by the song itself as by everything it signified—and he could not get back to sleep until daybreak. Whenever the two women and their Yankees sang or played the radio, the raucous sound seemed to hang heavily over the whole village like a dirty cloud of curses. On those occasions he wanted to rush to the Imugi House with the sharpest axe in the house and cut the rope and let the boat drift away, away, far away . . . But the old man was reasonable enough to realize that the Serpent Woman had every right to stay at the shack she had bought with her own money.

Kumsan village used to be so quiet in the long early winter nights that you could almost hear the rustling sound of the moonlight touching the withered trees. But that peace was gone now because of the screeching *bengko* music from the Imugi House. One night when he could no longer stand the noise Old Hwang sent Sokku to the women with an order not to play the music. The noise quieted down a little but even the faintest sound from the riverside house got on the old man's nerves. It was complete silence that the old man wanted back. He felt his skin itch with goose bumps of detestation whenever he heard the women's shrill laughter pierce the nocturnal silence.

One night when Imugi House seemed to have a particularly noisy customer and the old man could not fall asleep, he noticed a very strange sound as if dead leaves were rolling away on ice, or a huge serpent slithering over grass, or a stream flowing through a narrow channel. He did not know what the sound was and woke Sokku up.

"Do you hear that sound too, son?" the old man asked.

Sokku listened and said he could hear it. "Sounds like something rolling, Father," he said.

"No," said the father, turning toward the gate to go out. "I think it's the sound of the river flowing very fast. Can't you feel a sudden chill in the air coming from the direction of the river?"

The father and the son dressed quickly and were about to go to the river and see if anything was wrong when the boatman arrived at their gate, breathless.

"What is happening at the river?" the old man asked.

"I've never seen anything as strange as this, Master Hwang," the boatman said between his gasps. "It has not rained a drop for over a week but the river is now rising as fast as after the most torrential rain."

The news about the mysterious phenomenon circulated rapidly among the villagers; they gathered at the riverside by twos and threes, asking one another in worried whispers what on earth was going on, as they watched the swollen river rush by.

"This must be the doomsday before the new creation of the universe," said an old man. "War is raging in this country and now the river is rising to swallow us all. What more proof do you need?"

"Maybe this is happening because the Imugi Woman has moved into West County," an emaciated farmer said superstitiously. "That evil imugi is gathering the water here from all over the world so that she has enough water to swim around and leap high into the air and turn into a dragon."

"The whole village may be flooded overnight if the river keeps rising this way," said the village chief, frantically limping around among the nervous farmers. "We must stop this. We must stop this somehow."

Nobody knew how to stop it. They could do nothing about the river except watch it rage. The thick, muddy water kept rising throughout the night to the level of the highest summer floods. The water finally started to ebb at sunrise and the villagers returned home, tired and relieved, to make up for lost sleep. The river resumed its normal level late in the morning but the water was still thick with mud. A dirty layer of sediment covered the dead grass and reeds like a slimy skin.

Old Hwang sent Sokku and the miller to town to find out what had caused the mysterious phenomenon. The old man secretly hoped that the *bengko* camp and the whoretown had been wiped out by the river, but Sokku reported on his return that the Yankees were safe and had suffered no damage. The camp was located on the highest spot of the islet. Texas Town had not been flooded either, to the old man's great disappointment. The *bengkos* and the prostitutes had been puzzled and terrified, but that was all, the miller reported. Most of the floating bridge connecting the islet with Chunchon Railroad Station, however, had been swept away and lost.

Some of the Communist elements, whose retreat route to the north had been cut off by General Megado's Inchon landing, were conducting guerrilla activities in the Hwachon area, the townsfolk said. The Communists had launched a coordinated attack on the power plant twenty miles upstream. When they captured the plant, they had opened the floodgates to wash away a National Army unit deployed at the riverside village of Sinpo, downstream.

Old Hwang hoped the *bengkos* had been frightened enough by the unexpected water attack to consider leaving Cucumber Island, but he was disappointed again. In the late afternoon, several helicopters flew in, sputtering noisily, to unload steel beams, and lots of trucks brought hundreds of wooden crates to the town ferry. A swarm of *bengko* soldiers reconstructed the floating bridge in a single day. In the evening, Texas Town was as full of whores and *bengkos* as ever. And Imugi House rang again with shrill laughter.

The old man knew he could do nothing about what was going on on Cucumber Island, but he had to protect Kumsan. He would have to repay the price of the snake hunter's hut in order to drive the Imugi Woman out of his village. If he could expel her, Ollye would not be any trouble. At least that was what the old man thought.

Old Hwang went to town to raise the money to pay the prostitute.

Nobody would lend him such a large sum, so he took a boatload of rice from the harvest and sold it to the grain retailers. Once he had enough money to pay the Imugi Woman, he felt infinitely relieved.

Sitting cross-legged before the red lacquer dressing stand, the first large mirror she had owned in her life, Ollye watched herself combing her hair not with a common bamboo comb but with an expensive yellow horn comb. The house was quiet because her children were not home; the weather was quite chilly but Mansik must have gone out with Nanhi. Dragging Nanhi by the hand, he went down to the stream every afternoon as soon as Ollye began painting her face. It was obvious that Mansik did not want his sister to watch their mother go through her ritual of preparation for a night of sin—the ritual of her transmogrification from an ordinary mother to a woman of shame. But Ollye no longer minded her boy's efforts to keep the innocent little girl away from her; she had become accustomed to other people, including her own son, treating her like filth.

These days Ollye spent many afternoon hours powdering and painting her face. She had never known that "beautifying one's face" could consume this much time, for until her encounter with Sister Serpent she had not experienced this complicated process. Now she trimmed and adorned herself like a flower, using many strange cosmetics and brushes, drawing and rubbing different colors around her eyes and on her cheeks, nourishing her skin every other day by placing cucumber slices and tangerine peels all over her face. Even at her wedding held in the yard of the Paulownia House she had not been painted and decorated as elaborately and extravagantly as this. Dressing and making herself up had become a painstaking routine constituting the most essential part of her life.

When Yonghi bought the first pack of Coty powder for her, Ollye thought it was preposterous to use that heavenly powder to make up her face for a few soldiers, who wanted something other than her face after all. So she used to coat her face first with cheap Korean powder and then dab just one or two puffs of Coty upon it. What impressed her as much as Coty powder was Yankee toothpaste. The toothpaste from the plastic tube tasted so sweet that she could not resist, on several occasions, swallowing it after brushing her teeth; she had cleaned her teeth with salt most of her life.

She shook several drops of oil onto her palm out of the blue glass bottle, replaced the shapely bottle on the nacre dresser, rubbed her hands together and began to feed the oil to her hair, now permanented into numerous small curls the U.N. lady way. She used the fragrant oil contained in a transparent foreign bottle instead of ordinary castor oil. At first she had not believed any woman would use this expensive perfumed oil on something as insignificant as her hair. Now, she was doing it.

She looked at her own profile in the mirror. She always looked younger and healthier after putting on makeup. U.N. ladies had to do everything the Yankee women did at home to attract the soldiers, regardless of the time and money it might cost. She wondered when the Yankee women did work like farming and cooking and collecting firewood if they had to spend so much time every day to look beautiful.

Making up one's face was vulgar, Ollye had been raised to think. But she came to believe that it was something highly elegant and truly feminine. Perhaps prostitution itself was not something as abominable and vile as people said it was. Maybe Yonghi was right in her belief that prostitution was as good for the women themselves as it was for men. Yet nobody but the U.N. ladies seemed to think the way Yonghi did. And whenever Mansik stared at her, she felt as if she had been impaled by the spear of his hatred.

She smeared white cream on her face and wiped it off a while later with thin toilet paper. She painted her lips red with a stick of lip crayon. She drew black distinct crescents upon her eyebrows. Then she vacantly gazed at her reflection in the mirror, her face covered with thick painted lines and stains like an exaggerated portrait. Yonghi had said refined

U.N. ladies were not supposed to paint their faces thickly like Japanese kabuki actors but to accentuate the outlines of the eyes and lips skillfully so that they would look sensually charming. That advice sounded quite simple and easy but Ollye could never master the make-up techniques Yonghi tried to teach her. Whenever she drew another face upon her own and stared at the new one in the mirror, Ollye felt it belonged to somebody else. Every afternoon she changed into a different person before the mirror.

She was gradually familiarizing herself with this new life. She wanted to *lead* her life, and she tried to. She bought a camera and took pictures of Mansik and Nanhi standing before the chestnut tree, standing before the house, standing by the kitchen door, standing on both sides of the rabbit cage, standing side by side on the footpath, standing everywhere. Mansik did not seem to be too excited about the photographs, but the camera was material evidence with which Ollye could prove to herself that she now belonged to a different world from the rustic village that had abandoned her. It was time for her to do her own casting off—of her past life. She tried to become a U.N. lady inside and out. She even wore the nylon stockings that covered her legs to the thighs like large condoms. She came to like the soft touch of the stockings. Her manners toward the soldier customers also underwent a change. Once, when she was very drunk, Ollye attempted a clumsy imitation of the striptease. She even learned to express her displeasure the Yankee way. If somebody tried to tie her down with a rope or tried to force her to do unmentionable things such as sticking a bottle in her crotch and sucking the beer in, she did not hesitate to shriek, "Goddamn fucking sonabech gerrary," and in case her feelings had not been fully communicated by those *Migook* words, she went on screaming and cursing in Korean. If Korean swearing did not work either, she knew how to call the MPs and get the "sonabech" dragged away for punishment. She no longer felt uncomfortable in Western clothes, short skirts and sleeveless blouses, and nobody doubted that she was now a regular U.N. lady.

Ollye also knew how to dispose of the C-rations and other goods that

Sister Serpent smuggled out of Camp Omaha at the town black market. Yonghi, who had many steady customers from Bichuku days, easily got hold of soap, cigarettes, cologne, whiskey and other items popular on the black market. Through black market deals Ollye made as much money for herself and Sister Serpent as by entertaining the soldiers. Ollye seemed to have become a success. But life was not as easy for her as others believed.

What Ollye found very difficult to get used to was walking in high-heeled shoes. She had worn flat rubber shoes all her life. It was impossible for her to balance herself upon precarious pointed heels, especially when she walked along the muddy rice paddy dike or sinking sand of Cucumber Island.

When she finished her make-up, Ollye put away the cosmetic bottles and sat closer to the mirror. She twitched her eyebrows up and down to see if they were drawn in the proper place, and pouted her lips to see if they were neatly painted. The woman in the mirror looked drowsy. Maybe it was because of the false eyelashes. Narrowing her eyes, she gazed into the mirror. She was not sure whose face she saw.

"Mother," Mansik shouted. He was about to bring Nanhi down to the stream to wash her muddy knees. "Master Hwang is here to see you."

Ollye, on her way out to the yard to fetch the firewood, froze by the kitchen door. This is it, she thought. Her feet would not budge. It was as if they had been welded to the threshold. With unseeing eyes she gazed at the old man waiting outside the twig gate; her vision suddenly blurred as her mind groped for something she was trying hard to remember. She had tried to prepare, to rehearse what to say and how to behave in this situation, but her mind was not working now. Although she had foreseen this moment, it was still happening too suddenly.

When he spotted Ollye at the kitchen door, the old man said to Mansik, "You go somewhere with Nanhi and leave us alone for a while. I want to talk to your mother in private."

Nervous and suspicious, Mansik cast a questioning glance at his mother. Ollye nodded her head, saying, "It's all right, Mansik. Do as Master Hwang told you to."

Looking back at the Chestnut House over his shoulder, Mansik plodded down to the stream. Nanhi followed him, noisily sucking a handful of sweet Lifesavers she had stuffed into her mouth.

Shuffling out to the gate, Ollye could make a reasonable guess as to what the old man wanted to tell her, and was relieved by the fact that Yonghi had gone to Cucumber Island early in the morning to get a case of whiskey. She preferred to face the old man alone. She knew Master Hwang would not look away forever from what was going on. It had been merely a matter of time before the old man had to make a stand. This is it, she thought. She had to go through it sooner or later. Now was as good a time as any to make her own stand.

When she stood before Old Hwang, the doubt in her eyes had already been replaced by an air of challenge. "How do you do, Master Hwang," she said, stepping aside from the gate. "Please come in."

Old Hwang averted his eyes; he looked toward General's Hill. "No," he said. "I'd better not set foot in your house. I will stay out here." After a short pause, he went on, "I am not here for a conversation. I came to give this to you." He produced from inside the sagging sleeve of his robe a bundle neatly wrapped in rice paper. "Here."

"What is this?" she asked.

"Money. Give this to—to that woman you're associating with. This is the exact amount I believe she paid the snake hunter for that shack. Deliver this to her with my words. I want her to vacate the hut immediately."

For a moment Ollye looked down at the money. "I think you'd better give it to her yourself, Master Hwang," she said. "And you have to tell her about vacating the house yourself, too."

"I brought this to you because I don't like talking to her," he said. It was obvious that he had observed from the Paulownia House that Yonghi was not home. "I want you to do it for me."

"No," she said tersely. "I can't."

"You can't?" he said, offended. "You mean you won't do what I *tell* you to?"

"I won't."

"You have become not only shameless but impudent as well."

Kijun's mother, carrying sweet potatoes in a large wicker basket on her head, and a woman from Castle village with two puppies to sell at Central Market, were on their way to the ferry when they saw Rich Hwang and Mansik's mother discussing something at the gate of the Chestnut House. Out of curiosity they stopped on the road to watch. Mansik was also watching from the stream.

Giving in to the old man's gaze Ollye finally lowered her eyes but she was far from being apologetic.

"Tell me why you can't do it," he said.

"Your order to her to vacate the house—I understand it means she has to leave the village. And that order applies to me, too, doesn't it?"

"Yes," he said. "In a way."

"Then you must know the reason why I won't accept that money for her."

"What reason?"

"I won't leave."

"But you are not welcome here any longer."

"What do you mean I am not welcome here?"

The old man frowned. He groped for words to say next, but he found it difficult to find the right ones which would make this conversation brief and final. "What you have done here so far . . .," he began. Then he began again, "Aren't you ashamed of what you're doing with the Western soldiers?"

"Ashamed? No," she said. "I am not ashamed. I used to be ashamed of many things, but not any more."

"Let's go inside," the old man said when he noticed that several women had gathered on the road to watch them. "We can discuss this matter more comfortably alone."

Without stepping aside, Ollye glanced at the old man, the cluster of villagers on the road, and Mansik and Nanhi down at the stream. "No," she said resolutely. "You won't set foot in my house. You said that yourself just a minute ago."

The old man gasped in astonishment and exasperation. Turning to the onlookers, he gestured for them to go away. Kijun's mother and the other women picked up their things from the ground, but stopped again after a few paces as soon as the old man turned back to Ollye.

Thrusting the bundle of money back into his sleeve, the old man said, "All right, since you deny my wishes outright in this way, I'd better be frank about my own feelings, too. I won't tolerate or forgive your behavior any longer. I want you either to stop what you're doing immediately or leave this county. Consider what has happened to us since the *bengkos* first came here. And consider what may still happen in the future. How could you do this to the village? I don't understand how you could do this with the foreign soldiers whom you should hate more than anybody else in the village because you were their first victim. I cannot allow it any longer. I won't sit back and watch my village trampled and disgraced by the soldiers and by you."

"You really want me out of this village," she said. It was a declaration, to convince herself, rather than a question addressed to the old man.

"I think this is best for both of us."

"For both of us, Master Hwang?" she said in a low voice, almost in a whisper. "How can it be desirable for both of us? I am to be expelled from this village. What benefit is there in that for me?"

"I don't want to hear any argument from you!" he flared up. "Just make your choice. The choice that is necessary to allow Kumsan to return to its peaceful past."

Ollye shook her head. "I can't," she said.

"You can't what?"

"I cannot make that choice."

Faced with Ollye's refusal, he felt the earth collapsing under his feet. Even Ollye was fighting him. Even Ollye.

"Why?" he said. He could not think of anything else to say.

"I cannot leave here because this is my home," she replied without any hesitation. It seemed she had all her answers ready now. "And I cannot stop bringing soldiers here because that is the only way I can make my living."

"Do you think that is the only way you can make your living?"

"What other way is there? What other way can I make my living, Master Hwang?"

"There are other decent ways for people to make their living," he said. The more belligerent Ollye's attitude grew the more his face stiffened, his complexion turning sickly pale. "Why do you have to bring shame to yourself as well as to my village by—"

"Decent ways, Master Hwang?" she cut in. Her voice sounded almost scornful. "Where can I find decent work in this village?" She turned to the villagers assembled on the road and asked them, "Is there anybody among you who would offer me a decent job?" Then back to the old man, "Who would give me work, any work, decent or not? If I ask you, would *you* give me any chore at your home?"

"I used to."

"You used to, yes," she said. "But not any more. I'm not talking about what you used to do. I'm asking what you would do now. What work did you give me after the—accident?"

"Are you accusing me?" he said, almost stuttering in irritation.

"I, accusing you? Do you think that's what I'm doing?" she said. "No. I am not accusing you. I am merely trying to explain what this village did to me. And what you did to me. Or what you did not do. After the accident, nobody in this village treated me as before, as you know perfectly well. Not even you, Master Hwang. You didn't even bother to wonder if I might by any chance starve to death with my children—"

"So you will keep bringing *bengko* soldiers to this village," the old man interrupted her, his mind made up. "Well, if you insist upon it, I will have to handle this matter my own way to keep this village clean."

Ollye suddenly laughed a hysterical laugh. "Oh, you're going to drive me out of here by force, is that it?" she said. She laughed again. "But that won't work, Master Hwang, I assure you. You can no longer tell me to do this and that. I have decided not to leave this place, and there is no way you can make me go. I will live here as long as I want, and if somebody burns this house down, I will bake mud bricks and cut trees to make roof beams and build the house again by myself and live and live and live on here until the last day of my life."

"Don't you care what will happen to the villagers on account of you?"

"The villagers? Why should I care about them? I feel sick to my stomach at the mere sight of these noble villagers who treated me like dirt. They held me in contempt and considered me a whore even before I actually became one. That's fine. You can despise me and laugh at me as much as you want. I don't care. But don't ever tell me what I am supposed to do for the sake of the villagers. I don't have any reason to be grateful to them or consider their welfare when I decide what I will do. I don't have any favor to return them. I don't think they have been fair to me. Think. I never wanted the soldiers to rape me. It was an accident. They happened to pick my house and violated me. If I had not been there, they must have done the same thing to some other woman. But people preferred to believe that I was a filthy slut who had chosen to be raped. Did any one of you decent folk come to see me to offer a word of consolation after my misfortune? No. Why not? Did anyone offer me even a gourdful of rice when I was suffering from hunger and misery? No one did. Did any one of you try to help me? Master Hwang, why do you think nobody did any of these things for me? I know why. They ceased to consider me as one of them. They thought I ceased to belong to this village, to exist. That is fine with me, too. I won't blame you. In return, you must not blame me for what I am doing—for what I had to do—because you cast me out of your world. Just don't ever tell me to leave. I will stay here as long as I live, hating every single one of you."

Old Hwang flushed again, his clenched fists trembling. "This can't be true," he said, his voice choking with anger and disbelief. "This can't really be happening. You must not do this to me, and to the villagers of Kumsan."

"Yes, this can be true," she said. "This is really happening. This has been happening among us all the time."

He turned back to go to his house, still muttering, "This can't be true. This can't be true."

To his back Ollye screamed, "And don't give that money to Yonghi either. She has also made up her mind to stay here for good. Even if all the villagers get killed in this war or by an earthquake, we will stay here and go on living, forever!"

THREE

Squatting in the dark, Mansik hated Yonghi. His bare feet felt cold, but he would not leave the walnut stump. He sat, staring at the Imugi House where Aunt Yonghi was turning his mother into a bad woman at this very moment. He used to hate the *bengkos* and then he hated his mother. Now he hated Yonghi.

Crusty patches of frost glistened in the moonlit field. Along the skyline of the hills in the west, leafless trees fringed the rising mass of dark earth. An orange rectangle of lamplight trickled out of the tiny windows of the lone mud house at the foot of General's Hill. Mansik heard a crooning male voice on the cold breeze, coming from the radio at Imugi House.

Nanhi was babbling something to herself. Mother had given her a yo-yo that afternoon and she was hitting it with a cloth whip to make it spin because she thought it was a top. Mansik would not bother to show her how to play with the *bengko* toy. He did not care about anything but hating Yonghi these days. He hated the very sight of her and he hated to call her "Aunt." She behaved as if she was proud to be a U.N. lady. She laughed too often and too loudly. She had a particular way of roaring with shrill laughter which he loathed.

Yonghi rarely came for breakfast but she had her lunch and supper at the Chestnut House every day. Sometimes she would make up her face there with Ollye's cosmetics, sitting carelessly before the mirror, exposing most of her breasts and thighs to Mansik's view. It was embarrassing for him to see the tangled patch of black hair in her armpits when she powdered under her arms to remove the musty odor of sweat. She looked messy and sleazy until she was finally made up and fully dressed for the night.

Without paying any attention to Mansik's presence, Yonghi said vile things often and openly. The boy could not help blushing at hearing her shameless bawdy jokes about sleeping with the *bengkos*. Then she would burst into laughter, saying, "Look at your boy blushing, Ollye! His face is as red as a monkey's ass."

Aunt Imugi had many bad habits and Ollye was learning those habits. Aunt Imugi not only drank beer and whiskey with men but smoked like a man, too. It was a matter of great shame for a woman to smoke; he had never seen a woman smoke before except for Old Lady Hwang, who had learned to smoke homemade tobacco as a child to get rid of roundworms and cure her frequent bellyaches. When she married, she could not drop the habit. She smoked secretly, in the privy, until her death. Old Hwang had been terribly ashamed of her on this account.

Mansik hoped that this serpent woman would go. But he knew she would not leave as long as the *bengkos* were stationed on Cucumber Island.

Bored with whipping the yo-yo, Nanhi began to call, "Mommy, sleepy, sleepy." Mansik went into the bedroom, spread the quilt, changed Nanhi's clothes, tucked her in and softly patted her on the chest to put her to sleep. He was responsible for looking after her when Ollye was not home, and she was not home most nights. When she did come, she was usually reeling and her breath stank of wine.

Nanhi fell asleep soon. Mansik lay down with his clothes still on to warm himself on the heated floor. He gazed at the ceiling. The scarlet patterns of the ceiling paper loomed faintly against the lamplight. The hazy patterns seemed to blur slowly and shake almost invisibly, the blurred patterns rippled and moved like flowing water. Mansik tried to put himself to sleep by imagining a small boat drifting down an endless river. The boat bobbed and drifted down and down the meandering river and through the lush hills and the sky was so blue and mild that the sun dazzled his eyes and the boat kept drifting down and down the river towards the V-shaped valley wedged between the ridges of Three Peak Mountain and the boat drifted into the silky afternoon mist and the boat vanished . . . down . . . down . . . . He was suddenly awakened by Aunt Imugi's shrill laughter, and he thought he heard her say, "You know how big their cocks are, don't you? Drooping like a horse's instrument!"

Mansik looked around to see that he was lying next to Nanhi, who was breathing peacefully in her sleep. He must have dozed off. He collected himself and listened to locate the source of Aunt Imugi's laughter. It was silent outside. He could not even hear music from the radio. He decided that he had heard the laughter in his dreams, too. He was wide awake now. He went out to the yard and stood for a while in the silence, feeling the chilly air against his knees and shins. He trudged over to the walnut stump and squatted on it.

The Imugi House glowed with a red light. The river and the field around the house were dark but it was almost as bright as day at Cucumber Island from the shanty town and the army camp's electric lights. Mansik tried to visualize what his mother might be doing with the *bengkos* at this moment. Sitting side by side with the *bengko* customers around the rickety plank table, drinking in the thick fog of cigarette smoke, jabbering strange words like "can do" and "no can do" and "hubba-hubba," laughing, drinking some more. . . .

Mansik wanted to run away. He wanted to run away from the Chestnut House, Aunt Imugi, Kumsan village, Cucumber Island and everything around him. He wanted to find the endless cave in General's Hill, jump on the silver stallion and gallop through the dark tunnel for days and nights to reach some place where nobody would recognize him as a U.N. lady's son. He wanted to steal a boat and drift down the river toward some unknown land.

Then Mansik noticed something move near the abandoned water mill up the stream. Someone was coming down the rice paddy dike alongside the stream. The prowler was too distant for Mansik to identify, but it was obvious that he did not want to be seen; he scuttled from one shadow to another, trying to conceal himself behind trees or stacks of threshed straw. Mansik was alerted. He recalled the night when the *bengkos* came to the Chestnut House to rape his mother. His heart beat fast. But this person was not a Yankee, he was coming from the wrong direction.

Mansik pressed himself against the chestnut tree and waited for the dark figure to come closer. He had to wait for quite a long time until the prowler reached the spot by the stream where Mansik went every morning to wash his face. Finally he could see that the dark figure was a boy. It was Kijun. Mansik was annoyed that he had been fooled by Jun of all people. But why was Toad prowling around in the dark at this hour of the night?

Kijun halted by the log bridge and looked around cautiously. Soon another boy emerged from the willow beside the bridge. Mansik could not see the second boy clearly because the long, drooping branches blocked his view, but his gestures were Chandol's. The two boys discussed something and began to move toward the Imugi House.

Mansik wondered what they were doing, heading for the river at this hour. He wondered if they were on their way to the dump on Cucumber Island. But they would not dare to swim across the river at this time of the year. Kijun was not much of a swimmer, and in the early winter cold his heart would stop pumping in the middle of the river and . . . Mansik concluded that they must be planning to take the boat moored in front of the Imugi House to cross the river.

He gripped the bark of the tree with trembling fingers. He vividly remembered the miserable afternoon when he had gone to the islet to join the boys at the dump. He would never forget what Toad had chanted while he was trudging across the sand toward the ferry, crestfallen:

Mansik mommy U.N. lady,
Mansik mommy Yankee whore,
Mansik mommy U.N. lady . . .

Mansik had no intention of letting them steal the boat. He hurried down to the road and ran along the stream in the same direction as the two boys. Finally he had a chance to get revenge, to get even with them for the way they had treated him.

When he reached the Imugi House, Mansik noticed something very strange, and very wrong. Everything seemed to be quite normal when it was not supposed to be. Inside the house they played music on the radio as usual; the two women laughed and chattered with the *bengkos* as usual; and the boat was there by the river, untouched. He looked around but the two boys were nowhere to be seen.

Walking on tiptoe, he circled the house twice but could not find any trace of the two boys. He checked the rice paddies, the river bank and the trees near the house. The boys were nowhere to be found.

"Is he gone?" asked Kijun, raising his head a little. He was lying on his stomach in the ditch.

Chandol peered toward the Chestnut House. "He's crossing the bridge," he said. "It's safe now."

"Boy, it was close," Kijun said. "He almost caught us."

"I wonder how he found out about us."

Kijun stood up, dusting his hands. "Maybe he's known for some time that we come here every night," he said.

"Do you really think so?" Chandol watched Mansik trudge up the footpath toward the Chestnut House.

"Well . . . I don't know."

Chandol answered his own question, "No, I don't think so. If he had been lying in ambush for us, he would have chosen a location closer to the Imugi House. Maybe Mansik happened to be outside tonight and spotted us coming here. We should be extra careful from now on. If Mansik finds out what we're doing, we won't be able to come to the Imugi House any more."

"If we can't come to the Imugi House, there won't be any more watching for us," said Kijun. "We can't go to Texas Town. The river is too cold at night."

"We've got to come up with something," Chandol said. "Let's go home."

"Aren't we going to watch them tonight?"

"No. Not tonight. It's dangerous. Mansik might come back."

"Oh."

"There're lots of other nights."

FOUR

It had been delayed too long to be called "The Autumn War," but the Castle village boys sent the youngest of them to Kumsan anyway to deliver the declaration of war. The challenge was most humiliating to the enemy when it was made by a little kid.

Chandol immediately summoned his gang. Only two of them, Kijun and Bong, went to the abandoned water mill located at the northern edge of Kumsan. When the boys first moved in, it had looked as devastated as a butchered ox; old Crow-Tit, the owner, had taken away the rigs and mortars and everything else he needed to open a new mill in North County. To make their headquarters snug, the boys brought their personal things to furnish it. It was decorated now with wooden swords and other weapons, an old crushed pot in which they made soup with the fish they caught, a clean tin bucket, sticks of different sizes and other playthings for games, straw mats and wooden crates to be used as seats, mud bombs and stone missiles and other war materials. The Kumsan boys were proud of the fact that they were the only ones who had a regular war headquarters in West County. Chandol even marked the creaking door in big white letters with chalk: Head Quarters.

At this headquarters the three boys waited, but Kangho did not show up.

"Maybe he's not coming," said Chandol, sitting astride the wooden apple crate, drawing meaningless lines on the dirt floor with his sword.

"Who's not coming?" asked Kijun inattentively, sitting side-by-side with Bong on a rolled straw mat, whittling an oak branch into a Y-shaped handle for a slingshot. But he knew whom Chandol was talking about and said promptly, "Oh. You mean Kangho. He isn't too crazy about playing with us these days, you know."

There was no disappointment in his voice; he seemed to be relieved that Kangho was not coming. He would automatically become the second in command then. He did not care if Kumsan lost the war to the Castle boys as long as he was honored by the post of second captain. Jun had been sure that Kangho would not come since Bong had reported that morning that Kangho had not responded when the little boy had gone to the rice mill to notify him of the captain's summons.

Kangho had begun gradually to estrange himself from the boys when they stopped playing with Mansik. Since Kangho had been a very close friend of Mansik's both at home and at school, it was only natural that Kangho would stand by Mansik when the other boys reached an unspoken agreement to exclude him. When Chandol drove Mansik away from the dump on Cucumber Island, Kangho almost punched Chandol but checked himself; Kangho knew he was no match for Chandol in a fistfight. But he did not have to check himself when he heard Toad chant, "Mansik mommy U.N. lady, Mansik mommy Yankee whore. . . ." Kangho punched him in the face and Toad bled a lot from both nostrils. When the Imugi House opened on this side of the river, Kangho had strongly objected to going there to watch Mansik's mother playing with *bengkos* at night; Chandol and Toad went since they could not go to Texas Town. Kangho eventually stopped playing with them and made new friends, the Eagle Rock boys of Hyonam village.

"I guess you'll have to go to fetch Kangho," Chandol said to Kijun.

"Me? No."

"What do you mean, "no"?"

"I don't want to talk to him. I hate him."

"This is not the time for me to argue with you. The war has been proclaimed, and we three have no chance of winning by ourselves against the seven boys of Castle village."

"I still don't want to talk to Kangho," Jun insisted. "Why don't you send Bong to fetch him?"

"Kangho won't come if I send Bong. He's got pride, you know. He won't come to fight for us unless you—or I myself—go and coax him with an apology."

"I won't go," Kijun said. "I don't want to play with Kangho. I'd prefer to lose the war to Castle village. You saw how he made me bleed at Cucumber Island, didn't you? If you really need him, you'd better go and talk to him yourself."

Chandol sprang to his feet and barked, "Do you mean it?"

Kijun winced. "Well, you know . . . I really didn't mean it, but I can't help hating him."

"I don't give a damn if you hate him or not. If we don't want to lose the dump to the Castle village boys, we have to win this war. And we need Kangho and Mansik if we want to win the fight."

"Mansik?" Bong asked, his eyes suddenly sparkling. "Are you going to call Mansik too, captain?"

"Mansik?" Kijun said. "What on earth are you going to call him for? You know what will happen to us if anybody finds out that we're playing with a whore's son."

"You don't have to worry about that," Chandol said in a friendlier voice, sitting on the crate again. "I have worked out the whole plan down to the last detail."

"I don't know what this plan of yours is like but I assure you that I will never go to fetch Mansik." Then Kijun made a concession. "I *could* go to fetch Kangho, though, if you really want me to."

"Good. If you get Kangho, he will get Mansik for us," Chandol said, grinning at Jun. "And once we have Mansik with us, all our problems will disappear like snow thawing in spring."

"But you can't be too sure that five of us will beat the Castle village boys even if we have Kangho and Mansik on our side," Kijun said skeptically. "Don't you remember what happened last year? They almost took the water mill when they attacked us with their peach medicine bombs."

"When I told you we won't have any problems any more, I didn't exactly have the Autumn War on my mind," Chandol said to Kijun with a wily smile.

"Oh," Kijun said. "I see."

"And we will win the war, too," Chandol said, glancing at Bong, who was puzzled by the double talk the older boys were exchanging. "We have new secret weapons of our own this year."

The white sun was pleasantly warm on the cold morning when Mansik heard the ox low in the Paulownia House stable. His mother was still asleep in her room and Nanhi was playing with her yo-yo. Sitting on the edge of the stoop, Mansik watched two farmers wash their hoes and shovels at the stream.

Then he heard it once again. This was the third time. A small stone hit the fence near the rabbit cage. There was no doubt that someone was throwing stones deliberately to signal him. Rising to his feet, he cautiously looked around. He went to the gate and looked outside. He could see nobody except the farmers at the stream. The stones must be coming from the hill behind the house.

When he went around the corner to the back of the house, Mansik saw Kangho hiding among the young alder trees. Kangho beckoned him.

"What are you doing here?" Mansik said.

"I brought a message for you," Kangho said in a whisper. "Is your mother home?"

"She's asleep in her room. Why?"

"It's all right if she's asleep. I don't want anybody to know that I am here."

"What do you want?"

"I want you to come with me to the water mill, to our headquarters."

"Is that the message you brought me?"

"Yes. Chandol is waiting for you."

"Chandol? Why does he want to see me all of a sudden?"

"He has something to discuss with you."

"Is inviting me to headquarters by any chance all your own idea? I don't want to be fooled like last time. I hated you for what happened to me at the dump that day."

"I know. I am sorry. But it's different this time. Chandol really wants to see you."

Mansik thought for a moment, watching the two farmers cross the log bridge. "Why does he want to see me?" he said.

"Well, the Castle village boys declared the Autumn War against us," Kangho said. "And we badly need you."

Kangho must be telling the truth, he thought, tempted by the invitation in spite of himself. "Did Chandol himself say that he needs me?"

Kangho nodded. "Yes. He did. And I believe he meant it," he said, and then added, "You see, I haven't played with them myself for a while." He did not elaborate. Nor did he tell Mansik that he had not agreed to help in the war until Chandol and Toad had sworn by their ancestors not to peek, ever again, at Mansik's mother playing with the *bengkos* at night. "I had an argument with Chandol and did not want to

play with the Kumsan boys any more. So I made friends with the Eagle
Rock kids and played with them until Toad came to the rice mill to see
me and delivered Chandol's message asking me to join them in the war.
At first I didn't want to go but I changed my mind when Chandol told me
he was going to call you as well. When I met him at headquarters,
Chandol seemed to be seriously worried. He has established a good war
plan and made some new weapons but still he needs as many soldiers as
he can get. He said he wanted you and asked me to pass the message
because he thought you might not like talking to him or Toad. They're
waiting for you at the headquarters."

As Mansik followed Kangho into the water mill, the three boys waiting
for him were illuminated by a pale shaft of sunlight which came in
through a hole in the ceiling. Chandol, who had been sitting on a
wooden crate, sprang to his feet.

"Hello, Mansik," Chandol said, placing a wooden sword in a
cardboard sheath at his waist. "I'm glad you came. I was worried that
you might not." He pointed at the crate next to his seat. "Sit down," he
said.

The invitation to sit on this wooden crate meant instant reinstate-
ment of Mansik as the second in command. Mansik did not take the
seat; he was wary of Chandol.

"I am glad to be back, too," Mansik said.

Mansik and the boys said hello like strangers who were introduced
to one another for the first time. Toad, trying to be inconspicuous, stole
furtive glances at Chandol's and Mansik's expressions. He avoided
Mansik's eyes. Kangho assumed a neutral attitude. Bong, sitting on a
rolled straw mat on the dirt floor, could not take his curious but
frightened eyes off Mansik. The little boy, not understanding exactly
what was happening around him, feared something unexpected might
trigger a fistfight among the older boys.

For a while they exchanged incoherent conversation interrupted by awkward pauses. Mansik took the offered seat but he wanted to speak as little as possible until he was sure of Chandol's true feelings. Chandol seemed too eager to talk to Mansik to have any secret evil intentions. Mansik decided that it was not wise for him to give the impression that he was not interested in playing with the boys again.

Mansik finally said, "I've been wondering about something. The night before last, I saw you and Toad going—" He faltered because he could not think of a suitable name for Dragon Lady Club, and then added vaguely, "Over there. I went after you but I couldn't find you anywhere."

Alarmed, Chandol turned and glanced at Kijun.

Kangho stared from one to the other and said, "Where did you go?"

"Well, you know," Chandol said evasively, stalling. "We went to the duck farm in Kamwa village to steal some eggs, but I'll tell you all about it later. Now that we're all here, we'd better go over our plans to defeat the Castle village boys. Don't you want to know what weapons we've secured so far, Mansik? The Castle boys gave us a hard time last year with their peach medicine bombs, but it'll be a whole different story this year."

Chandol was not bluffing. He proudly showed Mansik their secret armory. They had dug a new hole, resembling the foxholes soldiers had dug on the hillside during their battle, and used it to hide important weapons. The trap door of the hole was concealed by an empty manger. Mansik was stunned at the sight of the weapons Chandol showed him, one by one—a heavy chain soaked dark in grease, a bayonet, a metal box for storing machine-gun cartridges, steel clips that looked like miniature tricycles, a Communist rifle with a missing stock, used howitzer shells, a small dark green can containing DDT powder, cute little plastic spoons from C-rations, and one wooden box full of live ammunition.

"This cartridge is for the M-1 rifle and this for carbines," Chandol went on explaining elatedly.

"Where did you get all this stuff?" asked Mansik, feeling the shiny smooth M-1 rifle cartridge, fascinated.

"We found them on General's Hill and other places where the World Army had battles with the People's Army. These are the leftovers from those battles. We find lots of things to play with on the battleground. And they make wonderful weapons, too." Chandol grinned. "But you have to be very careful when you play with these things. You know what happened when some dumb kids got careless with this war stuff? There's a junk dealer at the foot of Phoenix Hill in town who buys every piece of scrap metal you bring to him. Brass, steel, copper—you name it, he buys it. Last week several town kids went to Kongji Creek to fish and found a large piece of metal that looked like a grinding stone. Naturally they brought it to the junk dealer. The old man looked it over, but he was not sure if there was any brass inside. So he told the boys he would buy the brass if they'd extract it from the disk. The kids took it to their school playground and tried to dismantle it with an axe. And then, wham! it exploded. Those poor kids had no idea that what they were trying to break open was an anti-tank mine."

"What is an anti-tank mine?" Mansik asked.

"It's a bomb buried in the ground to blow up tanks. You can imagine what happened to those boys."

"Do you have a mine?"

"No, we don't have anything as dangerous as that. But you have to be very careful when you handle any kind of explosives. If you find a strange object in the woods or anywhere, don't even touch it. You're supposed to come to me and report first, understand?"

The next thing Chandol showed him was gunpowder. He demonstrated to Mansik how to extract gunpowder from a live cartridge. "Hold the rear end of the cartridge fast with your two fingers, place it on a flat stone, and tap the bullet-tip with another stone or a hammer lightly until it is loosened enough to pull out by hand. Just twist the bullet a little and, look, it slips out like magic. Then you tip the cartridge shell and, there, you have the precious gunpowder on your palm." The gunpowder trickled out of the shell and formed a small pile like black millet grains on Mansik's palm.

"Now take a look at this," said Chandol, producing a small package and unwrapping it. In the package were little green sheets bound into tiny books. "This book gunpowder is used for the shells of big cannons. Taste it. Go on. It's a little sweet, isn't it? If you light it, it burns very fast. And there's another kind of gunpowder." He picked up a can stuffed with thin black sticks resembling pencils. "It's soft and you can bend it. See? When you light it, it burns very fiercely, shooting out blue flames and making a hissing sound."

Mansik was overwhelmed by the terrible and fascinating war playthings the boys had collected in the past two months. He said, "It must be exciting to play with gunpowder. What do you do with it?"

Chandol closely studied Mansik's face as if he was trying to find some hint. "All right," he said finally, "I'll show you what games you can play with gunpowder." He picked up the ammunition box, and stood. "Come."

The two boys went over to the corner where the boys kept their swords. Chandol took out a used machine-gun shell and placed it vertically on the dirt floor. He filled the empty shell halfway with the black millet gunpowder they had just extracted from the M-1 cartridge.

Handing a book of *bengko* matches to Mansik, Chandol said, "Strike the match and put the flame here."

Kangho and Kijun and Bong moved back toward the wall for safety, but Chandol did not. Mansik was afraid of the gunpowder too, but tried to conceal his fear as he struck the match and brought the flame to the open top of the machine-gun shell. There was a sudden puff of exploding gunpowder and a blue flame shot out of the shell. The flame vanished instantly. A sickly smell filled the headquarters.

"It was fantastic, wasn't it?" Chandol beamed.

"Well . . . yes," Mansik said in an absent sort of way. He was not sure if it had been fantastic. "It was."

"Now I'll show you a real gun we made," said Chandol, going over to the underground armory. He took out a pistol wrapped in a piece of torn army tent. "Kangho and I made it. You can touch it, if you want to."

Chandol handed him a pistol made of a pipe mounted on a piece of wood that served as its hilt. "Kangho found that pipe in the *bengko* dump," Chandol added, to flatter Kangho, too. Fixed at one end of the pipe was a nail sharpened by a whetstone; when a rubber band was pulled back and then released by the trigger the nail-tip would slam forward.

"The nail-tip is called the hammer," Chandol said. "When that hammer hits the snap cap, gunpowder explodes and the bullet is fired. Do you want to know how we make the bullets for this pistol?"

Mansik nodded.

"After you remove the bullet from a live cartridge, you mount in its place anything you want to shoot—a small stone or a barb or anything. You can mount it with kneaded candle wax. Then fit the cartridge's neck into this end of the pipe. And you're ready to shoot," Chandol said.

"It looks like a toy to me," said Mansik doubtfully. "I can't believe it really works."

"Oh, it works all right," Chandol said. "Tell him how we killed a magpie with it, Toad."

Kijun, who had been crouching by the door, could not remain inconspicuous any longer. "On the very day when we finished making this gun, we went to Eagle Rock to test its power. We snared a magpie with a horsehair, tied the bird on a tree branch and shot it at point-blank range. Ugh! You should've seen the mess."

"You can even kill a man with it," Chandol said proudly, "if you use a bullet made of lead."

"Are you planning to use this gun in the war against the Castle village boys?" Mansik asked. "Somebody might get hurt."

"We will bring this gun, the bayonet and the rifle with the missing stock to the battle. But we won't use them in the first phase of the war. Now that you're back with us, I think we can win even if we fight the old way. We'll take these weapons with us just in case. You never know what new weapons they'll surprise us with this year. You're coming with us, aren't you?"

Mansik nodded his head. "Yes."

An expression of relief flashed over Chandol's face.

The five Kumsan boys and the seven Castle boys fought like blind dogs on the sand around the dump, wielding their swords, tumbling, kicking, butting, clutching, hurling things, yelling, snarling.

"Surrender!"

"You're goners, pissing frogs!"

"Attaaaaaack!"

Mansik was happy. He was delighted even when he was hit by a Castle village boy. Even if he bled from his nose or broke his arm, he would not care. He was glad that Chandol had allowed him to fight Sinil, the enemy captain, who was one of the best fist-fighters in the county. He was afraid of nothing. He did not feel any pain from Sinil's punches. He did not even hate Sinil. He wanted to laugh and hug everybody around him.

"Beat 'em! Beat 'em!"

"Watch out! Someone behind you!"

"You dog-fucker!"

Jun, who had camouflaged himself like a real soldier with withered oak leaves and branches, brandished his sword at nobody in particular while Bong hid behind Mansik. Sinil tried to go after Chandol to avenge his nosebleed but his repeated attempts were blocked by Mansik. Mansik noticed Chandol was avoiding a confrontation with Sinil and was determined to fight with all his might to defeat the enemy captain on behalf of his own captain. Mansik did not care which village owned this miserable *bengko* dump. He did not care if his village won the war or not. He was just happy to yell and fight side by side with his old friends.

"Look out! Bombs!"

Several pebbles, missing their targets, fell on the sand around Chandol and Mansik. Mansik threw himself into a sunken hollow in the sand and let himself slide down feet first. Chandol jumped into the hollow immediately after and crawled to Mansik's side.

"Are you all right, Chandol?"

"Sure. I'm fine."

The boys were no longer grappling with one another. Hiding here and there on opposite sides of a sand dune, scattered boys hurled stone missiles and fired slingshots, uttering war cries and yelling.

"Surrender, you driveling bed-wetters!" Sinil hollered over the dune.

"*You* surrender, crap-licking dogs of Castle!" Chandol snarled back.

"Attaaaaaack!"

"Attaaaaaack!"

The boys from both villages charged out of their hiding places, waving their swords, and began to grapple with one another on the sand again. A Castle village boy with shaven head hit Kangho on the shoulder with a club and Kangho collapsed on the sand, groaning. Bong, frightened at seeing Kangho fall, whipped the air with his sword in all directions to keep everybody away from him.

"Attaaaaaack!"

"Beat the Castle sissies to pulp!"

Mansik fought joyfully, not bothering to find out which side was winning. Stones hit him on the knee and the shoulder, but nothing could hurt him now. The Castle village boys began to retreat to the ferry.

The Kumsan Army won the Autumn War. The new powerful weapons they had buried at secret spots in the sand remained buried. Laughing and shouting and swearing, Kijun and Kangho and Chandol and Mansik and Bong chased the fleeing boys over the dazzling golden sand.

Lying on the ground exhausted, his face stained with sand and blood and sweat, Mansik laughed. The other boys laughed too.

"You were just great," Chandol said with a big grin, kneeling beside Mansik. "You fought like hell and that Sinil certainly learned a good lesson."

"We won this war completely owing to you, Mansik," Kijun chimed in. "One boy was so scared that he leaped into the river and swam away."

"It was a good fight for both sides," said Kangho, cleaning his swollen lower lip with river water.

"Can we go to the dump now?" Bong asked Chandol. Dust covered the little boy's whole face and whitened his eyelashes but he was unhurt.

"Sure, you can. You don't have to worry about the Castle boys for some time because they won't dare to show up."

Kijun and Bong dashed to the dump and soon disappeared in the pit. Kangho massaged his shoulder and tentatively twisted his waist to the right and then to the left twice. When he decided he was all right, Kangho also went over to the pit. Mansik raised himself to join the garbage hunt. His left knee smarted very sharply but he would not have cared if every single joint in his body ached for a month.

"Wait, Mansik," said Chandol, who had been stalling. "I've got something to tell you."

Mansik felt his heart sink when he saw Chandol's expression. "What is it?"

"Well, you know, I'm really sorry to say this to you," said Chandol, stealing a quick sidelong glance at Mansik. "I hope you'll go home now. I mean, without joining us for the garbage raid."

"Why?" Mansik asked. Then he smiled, for he understood what Chandol had meant perfectly well, though belatedly. "Oh," he said. "You don't have to worry. I won't keep anything good I find. I'll give it all to you. There's lot of C-rations and stuff like that at my home, you know. *Bengkos* bring them to my mother. New ones. So I won't need anything I find."

Chandol hesitated a moment but decided he had better say it honestly. "You see, we'll be in a difficult spot if our parents find out that we're playing with you again. Sooner or later they'll have to know, but I don't think this is a good time. So I hope you'll go home now. If we return to the village by ourselves later, nobody'd notice that you've been with us here. It's all right for you to join us when we play in the woods or any place far from the village, but we should be careful not to be seen together near our homes." He stole another quick furtive glance at Mansik. "Do you mind?"

Mansik knew he was not in a position to argue. "I don't mind," he said in a faked, casual voice. "I'll go home now. It's okay."

"Thanks," Chandol said with a relieved expression. "I'll send Kangho for you when we go somewhere to play. See you soon."

Mansik trudged along the shore to get back to the Imugi House boat he had moored on the bank of the river. The shore looked like an endless desert. The river flowed noiselessly. Texas Town was also dormant because the people came alive at night and slept through the daytime there. The early winter sky was bleached pallid and there was not a patch of cloud in the brittle cold space of blue emptiness. He could no longer hear the laughter of the boys at the dump.

Mansik trudged across the desolate sand.

FIVE

Sokku came out of his room and sat cross-legged on the stoop to look over the low earthen fence of Paulownia House at the snow-covered village. Four boys were making a huge snowman under the old ginkgo tree and a playful dog hopped along the road to Hyonam. Then swirling snowflakes came down and covered everything in sight, erasing all the colors and shapes. The contours of the Inner Kumsan huts were blurred by the dizzy flurry of white moving spots and the hills in the distance had vanished. All human traces were hidden. The snow fluffed onto the branches of the paulownia tree like cotton flowers, and landed on the slushy mud by the sewer hole, on the plough leaning against the earthen wall, on the jar stand, on the stepping stones, on the worn-out rubber shoe abandoned in the yard, on the roads and rice paddy dikes, on the thatched roofs, and on the log bridge over the stream. The snow was making the world cleaner and cleaner, but Sokku was depressed.

Kumsan village, crouching in the gathering dusk, looked to him like a gentle cow peacefully waiting for its death.

Sokku could not understand exactly how the war was going. Some people said the Chinese Army had begun to infiltrate North Korea in October. The National Army was supposed to have advanced as far north as Wonsan, Pyongyang, and Hamhung. The *Migook* Yankees were supposed to have reached Hyesanjin by the Yalu River in early December but 750,000 Chinese volunteer troops were operating in wide areas south of the same river. Some town folks said that the World Army had begun to retreat. These rumors made him believe that the war was far from over. The Communists might come back to rule before this year was over. When the *Migook* Army first arrived, they brought battle to West County and raped women. Now another horde of foreign soldiers from China was surging south like a human sea. The war was growing bigger and bigger, and its irresistible wave would crash over this village soon. The villagers, who were only too well aware of what the friendly forces of the Liberators had done to them, shuddered in anticipation of what the enemy forces of China would do.

When his friends Moksu and Chiwan came from Hyonam village to encourage him to volunteer for military service because they would soon be drafted, without any volunteer privileges, anyway, Sokku told his father that he wanted to enlist. Old Hwang's reaction was far from what Sokku had expected.

"You mean you're going to the war to try to end it?" the old man said. "Are you out of your mind? Now even the Chinese are in the war. If people keep joining the army this way, we will have so many soldiers on both sides that it will take decades for them all to get killed and for the war to end. The bigger armies you have, the longer a war will continue. It's human nature. One wants to stab someone when he has a sword in his hand, so the killing will continue as long as someone has a weapon. If you join the army, it's to continue the war, not to end it. I will order Moksu and Chiwan not to go to the war. And you, do not dream, ever, of enlisting."

Moksu and Chiwan listened to the old man's lecture out of courtesy, but they left the village early next morning and joined the National Army anyway. Sokku knew there was another reason, a very practical one, for his father to stop *him* from going to the war. The old man did not want to lose his only son.

Sokku glanced over at his father's room. Through the whirling snow he saw the rice paper on the latticed door glow a warm orange color; the old man had lit the lamp early in the afternoon, perhaps to spend some winter hours reading a Confucian classic. Old Hwang had been ailing on and off since the cold season had set in, and Sokku believed his failing health was aggravated by his gradual but steady loss of will. He's running short of breath, Sokku thought.

Young Hwang often had the impression that his father was sinking into a mire of despondency. Everything around his father, the old man's whole world, was crumbling. Sokku had felt this same sense of distress when he had returned home from the town and heard from the miller that his father had gone to the Chestnut House to buy back the snake hunter's shack but had been ridiculed by Mansik's mother in the presence of many amused onlookers. Sokku pitied his helpless father and loathed that ungrateful insolent woman, Ollye, but he could not do anything either. It was his father who was supposed to do the talking. Sokku was not entitled to speak with Ollye or anybody about anything concerning his father. Like a shadow, he always followed his father. Old Hwang never encouraged him to do or say anything of his own, and Young Hwang had never demanded an opportunity to make his thoughts known. It often occurred to Young Hwang that his father simply wanted his son to be with him wherever he went as a symbol. For Old Hwang his son existed only conceptually, as his *potential* successor. Perhaps Old Hwang hated to admit that Sokku was an independent individual. Or perhaps the father was aware of his own emasculation but hated to expose it to his son.

The wealth and authority of the Hwangs had begun to decline under his father. Sokku wondered if the Hwangs no longer maintained geomantic harmony with this land. Should they have moved, taking the remains of all the ancestors buried here with them, to a new place before the family fortune had been dissipated?

Old Hwang had secretly invested virtually all the family fortune in a gold mine in the Hwachon area. The old man had not said anything about this investment to anyone in the village, not even his own son, until he realized that he had committed a fatal and irrevocable mistake. Maybe it had been the last attempt on the part of the old man to save the declining family, but this mining investment only hastened the fall of the Hwangs. The other three partners were acute businessmen from Kapyong and they quickly pulled out, but Hwang Sunggak held on to the very last minute, until he lost all his land including the fertile rice paddies at the foot of General's Hill.

When he had to give up his land to pay his accumulating debts, Sunggak decided not to sell to a wealthy family in town lest scornful gossip spread that the Hwang family had turned to paupers thanks to the senile old man's stupid investment. Shame was more unbearable than poverty to the old man. After many agonizing nights, the old man finally decided to sell all his land to Kangho's father. Although he never admitted much less bragged about it, the miller was the richest man in the whole county. He had worked diligently all his life, purchasing land bit by bit until he owned the largest farm on this side of the river as well as a wholesale grain shop at the Market, and the biggest rice mill in West County. Old Hwang was aware that the miller, the only person around who had the ready cash to buy his land, was also very loyal to the Hwang family, as his parents and grandparents had been their sharecroppers. Hwang Sunggak summoned the miller and explained his embarrassing situation. The miller promised to keep the transaction a secret until the old man's death. Kangho's father was a man of his word, and he never told anybody, not even his own wife, that he owned most of the Hwangs' properties. But Sokku knew this secret would be revealed to the villagers after his father's death. Before that shameful revelation, Sokku had to find a new home somewhere far away.

The crust of the frozen snow crunched under their feet as Chandol and
Kijun slunk across the rice paddies. The village was asleep in the dark.
The hills, the trees and the houses loomed grey, barely recognizable in
the pale moonlight. Mansik must have been in bed, for the Chestnut
House was in complete darkness.

Kijun had put on a woolen hood over his head, but nonetheless his
bulging eyelids and nose-tip felt cold. "The river will freeze over in a
week or two," he said, breathing through his mouth. "We can go to
Texas Town then. We can sled across the river on the ice."

Chandol started to rub his frozen ears with his palms. "You sled
across the river and go to Texas Town," he said. "I don't see any reason
why *I* should go to that trouble. At the Imugi House here you can see
everything you can see at Texas Town."

"But there isn't as much to watch here. Lots of things are going on
over there because there're more whores and Yankees. And it's easier to
watch them, too. This Imugi place is different. There's only two rooms,
and when they fuck in only one room, you always take that room and I
don't have anything to watch."

"If you resent it so much, you can watch the room with me from now
on. Or you can go to the island, if you really want to. I don't mind."

"I've hardly seen anything lately."

"I said you can watch the main room with me if there's no action in
the other room."

The two boys quietly moved in the dark across the snow-covered
field toward the Imugi House.

The previous night Mansik had once again spotted Chandol and Kijun
going somewhere in the middle of the night. The next morning he had
followed their footprints in the snow to find out where the two boys had
been. He went down to the stream and followed their tracks across the

rice paddies straight to the Imugi House. The telltale footsteps stopped behind the house. They must have been snooping, he thought. But why? It occurred to Mansik that the two boys might have not gone that first night to steal eggs at the duck farm in Kamwa village. Had they been coming here every night for some purpose?

Mansik brooded over this matter all morning and then it began to dawn upon him. He had wondered lately what had made Chandol suddenly change his mind and invite him to the Autumn War after his total exclusion for over two months. Now he began to suspect that there might be some connection between the secret trips to the Imugi House and Chandol's invitation to him to join the war. Was it, then, by any chance Dragon Lady Club that somehow caused the boys to want him back in the gang?

Since the Autumn War Mansik had joined the boys' adventures four times. Although he came home separately each time, he had been allowed to join a *bengko* garbage raid and participated in an expedition to the grave-keeper's spooky hearse shed near General's Hill. Mansik had also made two more visits to the water mill headquarters and was encouraged by Chandol on one of those visits to extract the millet gunpowder from carbine rifle cartridges and make a glass bomb: a small glass bottle stuffed with gunpowder to be exploded by a cloth fuse attached to the cork stopper. Although he could not play with them openly in the village yet, Mansik was so happy to be back with the boys that, whenever they got together, he brought the boys nice gifts like C-rations, chewing gum, jelly candies and other American goodies that the Yankees had brought to his mother at the Club.

Now Mansik wondered if he had been wrong all the time about the boys—at least about Chandol and Kijun. On several occasions Mansik had noticed Toad's frightened squints; this boy was obviously afraid of Mansik. Chandol's behavior had been strange, too. His expression and attitude changed abruptly every so often and he seemed to be telling only half of what he had on his mind.

When night finally came, he put out all the lights at home, pretending he and Nanhi had gone to bed early, and, perching motionlessly before the latticed door in his room, watched the field and the stream through a hole he had poked in the paper. Mansik waited and waited, but the two boys did not show up until the *bengkos* at the Club returned to Omaha and his mother came home reeking of whiskey and vomit.

This evening again Mansik sat in his dark room, watching the stream and the rice paddies, waiting. When he finally spotted Chandol and Kijun crossing the rice paddies, Mansik quietly sneaked out of his room and began to shadow them.

A white massive bulk of a *bengko*, mumbling something in a monotone, climbed onto her stomach and the Serpent Woman, giggling, her legs wide open waiting for the soldier's thrust, babbled, "Darring haany, I rub yore cock. Wassa merra? Wassa merra? Ma cunt namba teng?"

Peeping in through a knothole in the wooden window frame, Chandol had to move his head up and down, to have a better view of the whore and the Yankee, who were rolling on the floor, their groins stuck together. Toad was anxiously waiting for his turn to watch. There was nothing much to see in the other room; Mansik's mother had put out the lamp, as she always did, before starting her play with her soldier, and the play itself did not last too long.

The whore bent over the giant *bengko* sprawling on the floor and pecked at his nose-tip and eyelids and then nibbled at his earlobe. With both hands the *bengko* kneaded her breasts which drooped over his face like two dangling lumps of dough. They sucked each other's spittle for a long while. Toad and Chandol took turns and by the time Chandol returned again to the peephole, the soldier was on top of the woman, pumping. The soldier gasped and the whore moaned. Soon the whore's moan changed to pleasure, the woman apparently enjoying her pain, and their groans and pantings quickened. Chandol trembled in violent arousal as he watched the two entangled naked bodies writhing in the room.

Then someone tapped his shoulder.

He instinctively knew it was not Kijun. Chandol quickly stepped away from the window.

Mansik stood glaring at him. He pointed at Chandol and Kijun one by one. He gestured for them to follow him. They headed for a lone tree by Mudfish Pond. Lagging behind Mansik, Chandol and Kijun glanced at each other. Kijun pointed at the stream with his head to suggest they should run away. Chandol thought for a moment and shook his head. Kijun, crestfallen, followed Mansik across the ankle-deep snow. Chandol did not seem to be worried but Jun believed he should be. Mansik was a good fist-fighter and could punish Chandol if he made up his mind to.

Mansik stopped by a stack of hay. They were far away enough from the Club now; he did not want anyone to overhear.

Kijun was terrified. "I think he's going to beat us up."

"Shut up," Chandol said in a hoarse voice.

Kijun tried to make up with Mansik. "I'm sorry, Mansik," he bleated. "I'm sorry, Mansik, I'm sorry. I mean it. You have it all wrong. The truth is. . . ."

"I told you to shut up," Chandol barked.

Kijun flinched.

Mansik stared at the two boys. "What were you doing there?" he asked in a tone that showed he already knew the answer.

Kijun blubbered, "We didn't watch anything. I swear. We didn't, did we, Chandol? We didn't see anything, did we?"

"So you came to watch something, huh?" said Mansik, pulling his clenched fist back to punch Jun. "That's what I guessed."

Kijun ran to Chandol's side to seek shelter. "Don't let him hit me!"

"If you don't keep your trap shut, *I* will hit you," said Chandol. Then he faced Mansik. "You've got something to say to us, I guess."

"What were you doing there?"

"You already know. We came to watch what's happening in that house."

"How often have you come here?" Mansik asked.

"This is the first time we've ever been here," Jun said.

"How often?" Mansik asked Chandol.

"I don't think it matters too much how often we came here."

"Every night?"

Chandol stared at Mansik for a while. "Almost," he said. "Almost every night."

"What exactly did you watch?"

"We'd better not talk about it. You wouldn't like it."

"And exactly what did you see?"

"All right, if you insist. We watched them play in the room, you know, the *bengkos* and. . . . Do I really have to tell you?"

"Watched them play what?"

Chandol glanced at Kijun and said, "Maybe we can let Toad go home and settle this matter between you and me."

"I can fight you both," Mansik said, clenching his fists and getting ready.

"I didn't say anything about fighting. I just meant that we'd better talk in private."

When he saw Mansik wavering, Chandol pressed on, "If a fight is what you really want, you can fight me now. You can take on Toad and beat him up any time you want later. If you can't get hold of him, just tell me when you want him. I promise I'll personally bring him to the water mill exactly when you want him there. But I don't believe you'd bother about a miserable fat boy like him."

Mansik stared at Toad for a while, thinking. "All right," he said finally. "I'll let him go."

"Can I really go?" Kijun asked Chandol. "Does he really mean that I can go home now?"

"Yeah. Go home. But come to headquarters tomorrow morning. I will have something to say to you."

Kijun did not wait for another word. He scurried away across the rice paddies like a startled mouse, finally slowing down and looking back twice when he reached the log bridge. Then he started to run again.

After Kijun had disappeared beyond the bridge, Chandol turned to Mansik and said in an unexpectedly soft voice, "I had to send Toad home because I didn't want him around when I talked with you."

Mansik, who had anticipated a fight, could not make out Chandol's intentions. He kept quiet, unsure of what he was supposed to say now.

"Honestly speaking, I feel a little sorry for what we've done," Chandol said.

"A *little* sorry?"

Ignoring Mansik's accusation, Chandol went on, "But you might have noticed that we did not peep in your mother's room. We were both watching Imugi playing with her soldier. Well, you know, I don't have anything to apologize for as a matter of fact and we don't have any reason to fight because I haven't done anything wrong to *you*. Tell me, what did I do wrong to you?"

Mansik was at a loss at this sudden twist. Too many things were going on at once in his head.

"What did I do wrong?" Chandol repeated.

Mansik was confused. What had Chandol done wrong indeed? If it was a fact that the boys had not peeped in his mother's room . . . "How can I know for sure if you're telling the truth?"

"You'd better take my word because that's the honest truth," Chandol lied nonchalantly.

Watching only one out of the two adjoining rooms—any idiot could tell it was a lie. Mansik knew it was a lie but he wanted to believe it to be true. There certainly existed a possibility, however feeble it might be, that Chandol was telling him the truth. For one thing, this evening the two boys had been both peeping into Imugi's room. Why should he care about that? It was none of his business as long as they stayed away from his mother's room. But they might have watched his mother doing some strange things with the *bengkos*, at least once, or several times, other nights at Dragon Lady Club or at Texas Town. No, Mansik thought, no, he could not believe Chandol's lies. If they had been prowling around the Club at night, it was virtually impossible for them not to see, purposefully or by accident, his mother drinking or playing naked with the Yankees or. . . . Why did he argue with himself about whether the boys' behavior was right or wrong? They were wrong, absolutely wrong, and they should never have come near the Club. He could not let them watch his mother at night. But he realized he was thinking one way, but speaking another.

"All right," Mansik said. "I'd like to believe you. I'll forget what has happened this evening and let you go home." But this is all wrong, he thought. He should not let Chandol go unpunished. He had to give him a warning, at least. A strict warning so that he would not even dare to think of coming near the Club ever again. "I will let you go tonight but you should be prepared for the consequences if I catch you again snooping around the Club."

Chandol said nothing.

"Promise me you will never come again," Mansik said.

After a short silence, Chandol said in a calm cold voice, "I can't promise that."

Mansik was stunned. With a gasp, he asked, "What do you mean you can't promise?"

"I want to come to the Imugi House and watch things," said Chandol, showing no sign of giving in. "So I will come and watch things."

"Then I will have to stop you."

"You may try to stop me but I will keep coming all the same," Chandol said. "It won't be easy to stop me. And think. I'm coming to watch Imugi, not your mother. I'm not so hot on watching your mother. Watching your mother isn't as much fun as. . . ." He realized his tongue had slipped and quickly corrected himself, "I mean, it won't be any fun to watch a friend's mother playing with the *bengkos*. When watching is concerned. . . ."

"I don't want to hear any more of this crap."

"Fine. That's fine with me. I'll go home now because I don't have anything more to say. But you think hard. Because, if you try to stop me from watching Imugi, you will never play with us again. And you may get hurt if you try to stop me."

Mansik was speechless.

"One more thing, Mansik," Chandol added. "If you let me watch Imugi, I promise I won't let anybody else come near that house. Not Toad, not anybody. You think it over and you'll realize that this is the best deal you can hope for."

Blankly, Mansik watched Chandol amble away toward the rice mill. Mansik could hear distinctly the sound of the frozen snow crumbling under Chandol's feet, *crunch-crunch*, as he disappeared into the moonlit landscape.

SIX

"**P**eck! Peck him! Kill him!"

Gripping the base of the scarecrow with both hands like the hilt of a wooden sword, Mansik thrust the flat painted face of the dummy toward the rooster again and again. The frightened rooster, one leg tied to the rice mortar, desperately fluttered, trying to get away.

"Peck here!" he hissed furiously, pointing at the scarecrow's exaggerated large eyes. Mansik was trying to train the rooster to attack human beings. "Peck here! Here! Right here!"

The rooster fluttered away frantically to the left and then to the right, hopping on one leg, the other leg pulled back taut by the hemp string, shrieking.

Mansik gave up. He leaned the scarecrow against the rabbit's cage and went over to the sunny stoop. He sat on the edge of the stoop and gazed over the fence at Chandol and Toad and Bong making three snow babies to place around the papa snowman under the ginkgo tree. In the room behind him, Nanhi was playing alone with a spoon and an empty can, beating them together to make noisy music, *clack-clack-clack.*

Lolling against the stoop, Mansik recalled the short happy days he had enjoyed with the boys after the Autumn War. A treasure hunt for used cartridge shells among the trees and the rocks on General's Hill on their way to the grave-keeper's hearse shed, the birds warbling in the groves and the mild late autumn sky high above, the fresh cool breeze on the hill, wild chrysanthemums and mountain lilies blooming along the faint path through the oaks and pines, the excitement of chasing the Castle village boys on the sand, yelling and laughing, yellow and white dust rising on the shore of Cucumber Island, the cheerful jabbering boys. . . . The old days had returned to him; everything of the old days, and his friends, had all come back to him. He was no longer alone, no longer desolate. Everything was like a dream and that dream instantly shattered when he recalled what Chandol had told him. . . . *But you think hard. Because if you try to stop me from watching Imugi, you will never play with us again. . . .*

Everything was about to change once more. If he tried to stop Chandol, his winter would be solitary. The two months of isolation, of silent tedium, of endless monotony, would return, and loneliness would resume its dominion. He would have nothing to do, nothing at all, except for shuffling back and forth, back and forth in the yard, or squatting on the walnut stump and watching the empty world before him.

Again and again he tried to convince himself that it was all right, it had nothing to do with him if Chandol peeped into Imugi's room, but hardly had he started to lean toward the decision to let him watch the room, when he would be seized by an overwhelming suspicion that Toad and Chandol must have watched his mother too. Then he felt like a criminal.

Mansik was appalled when he visualized Chandol and Toad spying on his mother. He knew perfectly well what his mother was doing at the Club. He had actually seen it with his own eyes one night when he ran to the Club, carrying Nanhi on his back, to ask Mother what he was supposed to do because his sister had diarrhea and kept crying. When he arrived at Dragon Lady, he heard laughter and music coming through the closed door. Nanhi was still crying but his mother did not come out; nobody inside heard her cry, maybe because the music was too loud or because they were too busy drinking. He pushed open the door and saw his mother taking her lace underwear off, dancing on the plank table to music from the radio, while two *bengkos* and Imugi watched her, laughing and applauding wildly. They were so engrossed that they did not notice the door open and then close again. Trudging back home, Mansik kept asking himself how it was possible for his mother not to hear her own daughter cry so close at hand, just outside the door.

Mansik was aware of precisely what was going on every night at Dragon Lady Club from Imugi's casual talk and it was unbearable for him to imagine the boys watching his mother at such embarrassing moments. But he could not stand guard behind the Imugi House forever, night after night in the cold as he had done in the past four days, to keep the snoopers away.

He had asked his mother to buy a dog "as big as a horse."

"Why do we need a dog?" Mother said. "Are you afraid to be home alone with Nanhi at night?"

"I didn't mean to keep a dog here," he said. "I think you'd better have a dog at the Club."

"What for?"

Mansik could not tell her the real reason. "Well, you have many expensive things over there," he said. "Aunt Yonghi's camera, the radio, PX stuff. A burglar may break in to steal them some day."

"We don't have any burglars in this village."

"There have been no burglars because there was nothing worth stealing. But you have valuable things at the Club that might attract burglars."

For no other reason than to please her son and relieve herself from the pangs of a guilty conscience, she agreed to keep a dog at Dragon Lady Club. Mansik immediately went to the town and bought the biggest and fiercest dog he could find. He drove a stake into the ground behind the Club to tie the dog's leash to. He used a very long leash to allow room for the dog to attack anybody skulking around the back of the house. He concealed himself every night and watched. Chandol and Kijun never showed up; maybe they were aware of the presence of the savage dog, or they had decided to wait until Mansik cooled down and relaxed his vigilance before they came to watch the rooms again. But the dog scared the *bengkos* coming to the Club. Ollye complained that the dog was driving her customers away and told Mansik to get rid of it. Mansik sold the dog in town and bought the fierce-looking rooster instead. He had planned to train it to attack. Maybe a trained rooster could guard the house, he thought. But he soon realized that he would never succeed in making the cowardly rooster attack anybody.

Now Mansik had no plan. And he had to see Chandol sooner or later to let him know his decision, if he could reach one. Chandol might have interpreted his silence in the past four days as a refusal. But was it indeed a refusal? Mansik was not sure.

Mansik glanced over at the three boys making snow babies under the ginkgo tree. Kangho was not with them.

Mansik thought this winter would be even longer than the summer.

"You surely made the right decision, Mansik," said Chandol. He had finally come to the Chestnut House to ask in person whether or not Mansik agreed to his proposition. "I promise I will not fail in my part of the deal."

"You're going to watch only Imugi's room. No matter what. And you will go to Texas Town and never come to the Club when the river freezes over. You promise."

"Sure."

"And you also promise to keep Toad away from the Club."

"You don't have to worry about him. When I tell him not to come near the Club, he won't come near the Club. He knows perfectly well what he'll get if he goes against me."

"This deal will be immediately called off if you ever go near my mother's room or Toad shows up anywhere around the Club."

"I know. You can rest assured." Chandol was in a hurry to finish talking and go home before Mansik had time to change his mind. "By the way, we're going to the woods for a weasel hunt. I want you to come, okay? We leave the village one hour after noon. We will be waiting for you at Eagle Rock."

The five boys of Kumsan village, hiding among the rocks on the ridge, waited for the weasel to come out of its hole. Nobody knew for sure if the hole was a weasel's, but they liked to believe it was. They would not mind if the hole belonged to a bobcat or a fox; they were ready to kill any animal that came out of the den with their magnificent pistol. Lying on their stomachs in the snow, they waited.

Mansik's clothes were soaking wet. His skin was slowly freezing; he had not put on enough warm clothes, for he had not expected to be lying in hiding this long. He felt exposed and abandoned. He felt there was nothing but cold emptiness in his heart. He was with the boys and he was out on the weasel hunt, but he felt sad and desolate.

The color of the sun was white. The winter sun had lost its heat and glow, blending into the pale sky. Even the scanty patches of cloud looked colder in its whiteness. The field and the village at the foot of the hill, the pile of fallen leaves in the gulch, the dead ivy leaves clinging to the rocky cliff opposite the ridge, the rice paddies and the hilltops— everything in sight was shrouded.

Looking at the undulation of snow-capped mountains in the distance, he felt empty inside. Whatever he did Mansik felt empty inside, as if he had left something very important unfinished, as if he was suspended, lost, in the air. He felt he should be somewhere else, doing something totally different from whatever he was doing.

Mansik looked around at the other boys. Prostrate under an oak tree like a resting turtle, Bong shivered with cold. The little boy was too young and innocent to notice what was going on in the minds of the older boys around him. Chandol pretended to be casual, but he was either too dramatically flattering or too consciously aloof toward Mansik. Kijun was spiteful and irritable, hating everybody in sight; he jumped at any slight, real or fancied. Kangho was a reticent boy by nature, but he was too quiet today. Kangho had probably noticed something fishy was going on, Mansik thought. On their way up to this ridge, Kangho had not said a single word to him, and Mansik did not venture to talk to Kangho either.

Mansik thought this was not right—his lying side by side with the culprits. But everything was over and done with him anyway. The deal had been made and he could do nothing about it. It was all over, all over.

The boys waited, lying in the snow, but the weasel never came out of the hole.

Opening the door to let the fresh air in—the room was always foggy with cigarette smoke when Yonghi had been there for longer than an hour— Ollye looked up at the little icicles dangling closely in a row along the eaves. The icicles, yellow against the straw thatch, slowly melted in the warm sun and dripped in shining beads into the tiny puddles on the ground.

"Is the tingling pain gone now?" Sister Serpent said, leaning against the papered wall and stirring the coffee in her china cup with a plastic spoon.

Ollye glanced at Nanhi, who was rolling her yo-yo around the floor, babbling something to herself. Mansik was not home and Nanhi was too young to understand what they were talking about but Ollye was selfconscious about discussing anything related to her profession in the presence of her children.

"The shots must be working fine," Ollye said, returning to the mirror stand to continue making up her puffy face. "I think I am clean now. No more pus, you know."

Ollye had been terrified when green pus had started to ooze out of her down there one afternoon. She rushed to the Club and asked Yonghi what was happening to her. "Am I going to be a leper?" she said in breathless fear, for leprosy was the only disease she knew of that was supposed to produce oozing pus.

"That's the social disease I told you about," Yonghi replied casually as if it was the most common thing in the world.

So she finally had contracted a social disease, the dirtiest and most shameful disease in the world, Ollye thought in consternation. She was appalled and terrified at first, but soon began to wonder, in anger and indignation, which Yankee had given this dirty disease to her. She recalled the soldiers she had slept with recently and mentally examined them one by one. She concluded that the stumpy *bengko* called Herman was the culprit. Every *bengko* carried the nauseating body odor of burning fur, but Herman had the most disgusting stench of them all. Ollye remembered what his crotch had smelled like when she had had to lick his thing. Now that her own crotch had begun to give off a similar stench, Ollye was sure that Sarging Herman had had the disease.

It would not help a bit to locate the soldier who had given her syphilis. She had to cure this smelly oozing complaint immediately. She asked about the town doctor who specialized in this kind of trouble. "I don't want to die of this sickness," Ollye said. "What would people say about me?"

Sister Serpent was outrageously relaxed and careless. "Don't worry too much, Sis," she said. "Lots of people died of pox in the old days, but there're very good medicines these days and I assure you, you'll be clean again in no time. And you can't call yourself a pro in this business until you experience both clap and pox at least once."

Ollye went to town with the map Sister Serpent had drawn for her to find the doctor who had treated many Texas Town girls. It did not take much time for her to locate the old tiled house with a shabby plank sign saying "General Gurinick" in the alley behind Central Market, but she found herself unable to open its gate and step into the house. She feared she would never come out of the clinic alive again once she entered it. It occurred to her that nobody would care if she was killed in that seedy clinic. And she was too ashamed of her illness to walk in and tell somebody, some stranger inside General Clinic, the reason why she was there. She paced up and down the alley for some time to summon enough courage to face the doctor but finally gave up and returned to Dragon Lady Club. She asked Sister Serpent to accompany her to the clinic.

"You are really impossible, Sis," Yonghi said, chuckling. "What face do you think we have to save in this business? You have been a U.N. lady long enough to become brazen about these things. And you say you're afraid to see a doctor for syphilis treatment!"

The fat doctor and Yonghi seemed to be on intimate terms and exchanged bawdy jokes about the bed manners of some Yankees and Korean Army officers they knew in common while he was taking a sample of her pus and examining the slide with his microscope. Yonghi's presence made Ollye feel worse. Although she had exposed her naked body to many soldiers so far, it was still humiliating and exasperating to expose her smelly secret part to the gloating doctor who had a sly knowing look in his cynical eyes behind the thick glasses he wore. Ollye was not sure if some of his questions were really necessary for curing her: "How many soldiers have you slept with this week?" "Which soldier did you like best among them and why?" "Did you suck his thing?" and so on and on and on — while Sister Serpent was listening in the waiting room. Whenever she went to the clinic, there were one or two U.N. ladies from Texas Town in the waiting room. Even if there was nobody else in the clinic, Ollye felt like dying whenever she had to display her body to the doctor, who ordered her to undress on every visit. She came to believe that he enjoyed his work too much and that was the reason he had not hired a nurse.

The most distressing fact was that she had to keep entertaining the soldiers while undergoing the treatment. She wanted to rest until she was completely cured but she had to make as much money as possible quickly; the Texas Town U.N. ladies said the Allied Forces would retreat soon. Besides, Sister Serpent could see no reason at all why Ollye should care if every Yankee in the world got syphilis from her.

"You got it from *them*, after all, didn't you?" Yonghi said. "Do you think other girls stop working when they contract V.D.? No. They don't give a hoot. If you stop working every time you get V.D., you will starve to death. It'll take at least two months until you're completely cured, and the whole war may be over by the time you start working again! Keep working, but play it smart. When a steady customer comes to sleep with you, tell him you have the disease. Say 'I got bee dee' and he will understand. Some *bengkos* appreciate it a lot if you tell him you have the disease and stay with you all night anyway. If he wants a fuck with a condom on, let him do it. If he doesn't want to do it, give him a nice suck or other services so that he won't go to Texas Town for another girl. Remember—the steady customers are the best capital you have."

There was something that tortured Ollye even more than the disease did. She had to drink every night. It made her sick to her stomach at night and even in the morning, day after day. If she sneaked out of the drinking party and puked everything she had inside her, beer or whiskey and sausages and carrots and everything, she felt her guts were being scraped out with sharp razors. After vomiting like that for a while, squatting in the dark rice paddies behind the house, shedding tears of pain and anger, she would wash her face with a handful of snow and shamble back to the party for some more drinking.

To please all sorts of perverted customers was not easy either. She was expected to satisfy every demand the *bengkos* made; the soldiers came and paid her, as Sister Serpent once said, because they wanted to have her fulfill their most impossible whims. "You still have a lot to learn, Sis," Yonghi said. "How can a whore *choose* her customers? Some *bengkos* are beasts who want to try the weirdest things with their women. If you happen to have that kind of a customer, think this way — at least this is an easier way to make a living than toiling all day long under the scorching sun on a farm owned by some fat neighbor. I told you, you'll get used to everything in time, didn't I?" But Ollye suspected she would never get used to the requests made by some soldiers. There was a *bengko* who liked to put various strange things inside her. Another *bengko* enjoyed watching Yonghi and Ollye perform sexual acts with each other. There was a soldier who ordered her to sit upright with her legs wide open, took lots of close-up photographs of her crotch, collected a sample of her dark pubic hair in an envelope and went back to Omaha without any actual sex. One *bengko*, whom she had never seen before nor since, asked her to do various humiliating things for two hours, constantly swearing, and then did not pay her anything, saying he had left his wallet back at the camp. After this soldier, she lay in her room for a long while, naked, blankly looking up at the ceiling with an odd feeling that she was falling into a bottomless dark well. When she told Yonghi about this incident the next morning, Sister Serpent laughed and said, "Tough luck." That was all.

But all this might be over soon. Texas Town was stirring because of the rumor that a total retreat of the U.N. Forces had begun. The departure of the Yankee soldiers would mean the conclusion of a phase for Ollye. She could not see what her future would be like after this. As the time for the retreat neared, Sister Serpent asked every Yankee she knew when and where Camp Omaha would move but the *bengkos* themselves did not seem to know anything definite. Yonghi suspected General Megado's Army was losing badly to the Chinese and considered moving to safety as far south as Pusan. She hoped to open a big club like Bichuku somewhere on Haeundae Beach and asked Ollye more than once if she would go with her. Sundok had already agreed to work there if Sister Serpent opened a club, but Ollye was not sure if she wanted to work for her any more.

On many occasions Ollye had resented Yonghi. As the days passed she began to wonder why Yonghi took half of the money Ollye earned by entertaining *bengkos*, when she was providing so many services to Sister Serpent such as cooking, washing her clothes and disposing of the Yankee goods on the black market. But what would happen to her and her children if the World Army moved away? When the *bengkos* and Sister Serpent along with the Texas Town girls were gone, what actions would Old Hwang and the villagers take to avenge themselves? They would surely do something to release their pent-up animosity against her. What would she do then?

Ollye briefly considered going south with Sister Serpent as an escape. She saw nothing but despair in her future if she travelled with Mansik and Nanhi across the country following the horde of *bengkos* and U.N. ladies. What weighed most on her mind was Mansik. And Nanhi, too. Whatever she might choose to do from now on should not bring any more suffering to her children.

Nanhi chortled, chasing after the yo-yo rolling toward the C-rations basket. Gazing at her daughter, Ollye swore to herself that she would never go anywhere with her children to continue prostitution. She had saved some money in her secret jar buried in the corner of her kitchen, though Yonghi had taken so much from her earnings. Perhaps she could start a new life somewhere with that money. Then Mansik and Nanhi would no longer be ashamed of her. Where was Mansik, she wondered. She had not seen him all morning.

"I wonder where he's gone," Ollye said to herself, looking for the lipstick in the drawer of her mirror stand.

"Were you talking to me?" asked Yonghi, closing the door before changing her underwear.

"I wonder where Mansik has gone. I haven't seen him all morning. Do you know where he is?"

"He went out when you were still sleeping."

"Where did he say he was going?"

"He didn't tell me. He doesn't speak to me much, you know. And I didn't ask him either."

"I wonder where he's gone," she mumbled again.

"You look worried. Anything wrong?"

"Don't you think he goes out too often these days? I wonder why he goes out so much."

"Maybe he's going out to play with his friends."

"He doesn't have any friends."

"Oh."

"The village kids stopped playing with him ever since—you know."

"You told me so."

"So he must have gone out for some other reason."

"Now I remember that Mansik looked rather grumpy when he left home."

"He's always grumpy lately."

Ollye gazed at herself in the mirror for a while and then began to paint her lips.

SEVEN

Mansik had been hiding among the stacked sheaves of straw about a hundred yards away from Dragon Lady Club; after dark his mind was never at peace unless he kept his vigil over the house himself. Since the agreement had been made with Chandol, Mansik found himself unable to sleep comfortably at home, troubled by the vivid image of the boy slinking around the Club in the dark. He knew he was partly responsible for what was going on behind the Club every night, for connivance was another face of conspiracy. He had to do something, though within limits, to mend matters. He had to do at least this much—keep surveillance over the Club to make sure that Chandol was faithful to his bargain.

Dressed in a thick army field jacket and a woolen cap with large furred side flaps and heavy Yankee boots, Mansik crouched in the nest he had made, a blanket draped across his shoulders. A drop of cold snot dangled at his nose-tip. He wriggled his toes and massaged his knees to warm himself. Still wriggling his toes, he looked around the Club, the field, the village and at the brittle stars in the icy sky.

The muffled sound of laughter and voices occasionally trickled out of the tightly-closed windows of Dragon Lady Club. "Hey you goddamn! No touch there!" Giggling. A beer bottle clinking against a glass. The music from the radio. Imugi started singing, "*Arirang arirang arario.*" The *bengkos* awkwardly repeated the line. "Wondopul, wondopul," Yonghi said, "you song namba wang."

Mansik felt drowsy from the cold; he had been crouching in the straw nest for twenty minutes. Gradually his vision blurred and he could not resist his overwhelming sleepiness. In the sky the moon grew brighter and brighter and brighter until it turned to a blazing summer sun and the warm sun rays poured over the green field and a white origami paper boat drifted down the stream toward the river, bobbing, bobbing, bobbing, and somebody threshed bean pods with a long bamboo flail somewhere, *whack-thud-whack-thud-whack-thud*, and twelve farmers were building a bonfire in front of the rice mill although it was broad daylight and the five boys sat around in a circle under the old ginkgo tree and each boy told ancient tales in turn about ghouls and foxes governed by evil spirits and a woman spread red peppers on the thatched roof to dry them in the autumn sun and then suddenly the whole world was covered with snow and Mansik was walking along a mountain path and he missed a step and fell down into the *bengko* dump pit and he woke up, startled.

Pulling himself together, Mansik looked over at the Club. The music from the radio had stopped but the drinking party was still going on. He rubbed his gloved hands together and exercised his shoulders under the blanket. He took a more comfortable position in the nest to continue his surveillance.

This was his third night on lookout. On the first night neither Chandol nor Kijun showed up. He searched around the Club twice during the night but found no evidence of the boys' presence among the frozen grains of vomited rice and the poked holes in the snow where the soldiers had urinated.

Last night, Chandol came. He had to pass by Mansik's hiding place because the straw stack was located next to the shortcut across the rice paddies from the log bridge to the Club. Chandol was startled to see Mansik scramble up to his feet among the sheaves of straw.

"Oh, it's you," Chandol said. "You scared me out of my wits, rising out of nowhere like that. What on earth are you doing here anyway?"

Mansik was at a loss momentarily. He had nothing to say but, "You'd better not forget what you promised me."

Chandol slouched over to the rear window of the Club. While he was peeping in Imugi's room, clinging to the wall like a giant bat, Mansik nervously watched him, hoping Imugi and her soldier would quickly finish whatever they were doing inside so that Chandol would leave soon. After what seemed to be an eternity for Mansik, Chandol was at last sated and came back to Mansik. "I'm going home," he said. "See you tomorrow at the headquarters. And thanks."

After he had disappeared beyond the log bridge, Mansik picked up the rolled blanket and returned to the Chestnut House, shivering like an abandoned dog.

Tonight Chandol had not yet showed up. Mansik had no other choice but to wait until all the activities in the Club were over and the *bengkos* returned to Omaha.

Dozing despite himself, faintly, in his hazy consciousness, Mansik heard somebody, a *bengko*, burst into laughter. His calves were numb and he waited and waited and he was trudging somewhere across an open field pure white with snow and he had no idea where he was going or where he was now but the river was flowing to his left and he was now sauntering along a sandy shore and the summer sun rays were pouring over the clear blue water but the white snow had drifted ankle deep on the riverbank and he could not see the Three Peaks or anything in that direction because of the whirling snowflakes as big as his fists and two boats with yellow cotton sails sailed up and down the river, up and down, up and down, and he just kept trudging and when he reached a rice paddy dike he trudged on and on along the dike that kept extending by itself in the snowstorm and he crossed a narrow stream and when he reached a vast open field without any house or human trace the snow suddenly stopped and he saw vegetable patches and rice paddies and trees basking in the warm spring sun and he wondered why no human beings lived there. . . .

He had no idea how long he had been asleep, but he woke up when his hips felt the cold of the frozen ground through the straw. He saw the moon hanging low in the western sky. The white field looked barren. Nothing in sight moved. The laughing noise had stopped in the Club and the night was silent and empty. It must be very late now, he thought. Tucking the blanket around his waist, he glanced over at the Club.

Somebody was there.

Suddenly alerted, Mansik looked more closely. A boy was pressing himself against the wall in the shadow under the eaves, peeping into Imugi's room. That bastard Chandol is here again, Mansik thought flushing with a sudden burst of anger, but he tried to cool himself down. As long as he could not do anything to remove him, it was best to simply ignore Chandol's presence. Anger would not help. Let him enjoy himself, he thought.

The light went out in Imugi's room. Mansik noticed the peeping boy hesitate for a moment by the dark window. Then the boy moved on his tiptoes over to the other room where Mansik's mother's light was still on. Chandol peeped in Mother's room through a chink in the window. That son of a bitch! Mansik sprang to his feet. Chandol was well aware that Mansik was out here and he still went over to the other window to watch his mother. His words were good apparently for only one night! I will kill that son of a bitch, Mansik screamed in his heart, picking up the broken handle of a sickle which had been abandoned by the straw stack. He ran to the boy, gripping the stick firmly in his clenched fist.

Mansik stopped short. The boy who was peeping in Mother's room was not Chandol. It was Toad.

Kijun flinched, startled, when Mansik poked his side with the stick. He sidled to the wall, staring at Mansik. Mansik gestured for Jun to go over to the pile of straw. Kijun faltered for a moment, glancing at the stick in Mansik's hand, probably wondering if he should run away. Then he headed for the straw stack, giving up. Mansik followed him close behind.

"Stop," Mansik said.

The two boys faced each other before the straw pile. Mansik glared at Jun without any word. He could not see Jun's expression clearly in the dark but strangely Toad did not seem to be scared.

"Hasn't Chandol told you something?" Mansik asked.

"Told me what?" Jun said nonchalantly. "Oh, that. Sure, he told me not to come here."

"Then you must be prepared for what I'm going to do to you."

"Well, what exactly is it that you're going to do to me?" Jun said, stepping back to stay out of Mansik's reach in case of a sudden unexpected blow. "Are you going to beat me?"

Mansik poked Jun in the stomach with his stick. "What do you think I'll use this for?" he said.

"You'd better not beat me," said Jun, somewhat frightened but nonetheless challenging.

Mansik raised the stick to hit him.

"Wait, Mansik. Listen to me before you start something you'll regret."

"There's nothing I want to hear from you."

Toad said quickly, "I'll tell your mother if you hit me."

"Tell my mother what?"

"About the deal you made with Chandol. You're showing him what's going on in the Imugi House at night, aren't you? I'll tell your mother everything about that if you beat me."

Mansik halted. Jun was not retreating any more. It seemed Toad had anticipated and been fully prepared for this situation. He was sure of himself.

"As long as you're showing the rooms to Chandol, why don't you show them to me as well?" said Jun, stealing a sidelong glance at Mansik's troubled expression. "I think I will come back to watch the room tomorrow night whether you like it or not. If you refuse to let me, I'll tell everybody about the deal you made with Chandol. Your mother will hear about it, and Rich Hwang will hear about it, and everybody in the village will hear about it. What do you think will happen to you then?"

Mansik slashed Jun's shoulder with his stick. Jun staggered, gasping.

"All right, Toad, tell them! Tell them if you want to. You tell anybody about it and I will break every little bone in your fat body."

Dodging from the lashing stick, Kijun ran away toward the stream. Mansik chased him, beating him, swearing at him, hating him, hating Chandol, hating the world.

When Chandol came to the Imugi House in the early evening of the next day, Mansik was waiting for him, pacing among the scattered sheaves of straw. "On guard duty again?" Chandol joked.

Blocking his way, Mansik said nothing.

"What's the matter, Mansik? You got something to say to me?"

"Yes."

"Well, what is it?"

"Toad was here. Last night."

"He was?" said Chandol. He sounded a little offended but not very much surprised.

"You promised me you'd stop him from coming here. But he came."

"I told him not to."

"I know you did. Toad told me. What went wrong?"

Chandol said nothing for a while, annoyed. He glanced over at the lights of Texas Town as if he was looking for an easy answer there to justify his awkward situation. But instead of giving an answer, he asked, "So what did you do?" Somehow Mansik received the impression Chandol knew precisely what had happened between him and Jun last night. "Did you have a fight?"

"Fight?" Mansik scoffed. "I don't fight a fat, slow boy like him. I just beat him up."

"I see."

"Toad seems to know everything about our agreement."

"I guess he does."

"How did he find it out?"

"I told him."

"You told him?"

"Sure. I had to. He demanded an explanation when I told him to stop coming to the Imugi House." Then he added brusquely, "Anything wrong about that?"

"That bastard Toad dared to threaten me," Mansik said. "He warned me he'd tell people about the deal I made with you unless I let him watch the room too."

Chandol said nothing, reflecting.

"We must stop him from telling it to anybody. What should we do?"

"I'll leave the matter to you," Chandol said in a casual voice as if this was none of his business.

This time Mansik could not think of anything to say.

Chandol said, "What did you tell him, anyway, when he made that proposition to you?"

"I didn't tell him much of anything," Mansik said irritably. "I just beat him up. I told you."

"Yes. You did."

"I think he meant it when he said he would come here again to watch the room whether I like it or not."

"What are you going to do about it? Are you going to beat him up again?"

"Of course. I'll beat him up every time I catch him snooping around the Club. Until he gives up. And I want you to talk to him once more. Do something to stop him."

Chandol said quickly. "Maybe you'd better let him watch the room."

"What?" Mansik said, disbelieving.

"Maybe you'd better let him watch the room," Chandol repeated.

"Are you serious?"

"Yes, I'm serious, and I want you to give some thought to it. I believe that's the best and easiest way to settle this whole matter. What difference does it make if you show the room to one more boy, anyway? There won't be any more trouble if you let him watch Imugi's room."

"That filthy scum peeped in my mother's room too last night," Mansik said.

"I will make him never watch your mother again. That much I can do for sure. And he knows that you're coming out here every night to keep an eye on us. He will be careful from now on."

"I can't let him come. I don't want him anywhere around me."

"But I don't think you have much choice. What do you think will happen to us if Toad starts talking and people find out about our deal? My mother will kill me if she finds out."

"So you'd better start thinking, fast, how to take care of Toad."

"You have to do your own share of worrying, too. After all, you will be in the biggest trouble among us all if this mess blows up. Consider what will happen to you when people find out that you invited us to watch your mother fucking with the *bengkos,* hoping we'd let you play with us."

"That's not true," Mansik protested angrily. "I never invited you. You started this whole thing."

"No, Mansik, people won't think that way. They will believe what Jun and I tell them."

"What are you talking about?"

"If anything goes wrong, that's the story Jun and I will tell our parents and the villagers. That you came to us and offered to show your mother's room if we let you play with us again."

"But that's a lie."

"The villagers will think differently."

Mansik was frightened, sensing something terrible going on. "You're not going to tell that lie to anybody," he said uncertainly.

"Don't be too sure about that."

Confused, Mansik tried to decide what he had to do. "Why are you doing this to me, anyway? You sound as if you are siding with Toad," he blurted out.

Chandol stole a glance at Mansik. "To tell you the truth, I cannot help siding with him. Well, you know, he sort of threatened me, too. He said he'd tell my parents that I'm coming here to watch the whores if I don't let him come with me."

"And what did you do?"

"Nothing."

"Why didn't you beat him up half to death so that he couldn't even dream of telling anybody?"

"Well, I did think of punishing him but thought better of it."

"And what did you think was the better way?"

"As I told you, it won't make much difference if you allow one more boy to watch."

"Please, Chandol." Mansik's voice suddenly took on a pleading tone. "Don't make me do that. I will give you chocolates, chewing gum and other Yankee candies if you want them. I will give you anything I have. Just make him stay away from the Club. I can't let him come here."

"Don't ask me to do what I cannot do for you," Chandol said. It was obvious that his mind was made up. "Rather, you have to do what we want."

Mansik stared at him, taking a deep breath; now his mind was made up, too. "All right," he said. "If you insist, I'd better make my stand clear. I want you to stop coming here as well. I can't let you come here if you can't stop Toad."

"You may get hurt if you try to stop us."

"I don't care," Mansik said. His determination was growing as he talked. "I don't care what you or anybody in the world may do to me. And I know I can stop you. Somehow."

Chandol stared at Mansik, thinking. He sighed. "All right," he said. "I'll go home and think about this whole thing tonight. You will hear from me soon."

Chandol turned back and wandered toward the stream, whistling. He's whistling because he's afraid but doesn't want to show it, Mansik thought. Suddenly relieved, he felt the night air cold against his cheeks.

As if to make his point very clear, Chandol brought Kijun with him the next evening. The two boys came directly to where Mansik was on lookout. Mansik understood instantly that a confrontation was inevitable and slowly raised himself, shedding the blanket and grabbing the stick. Chandol stopped before Mansik. Kijun, standing a few paces away, excitedly watched them.

"We came to look into the room," Chandol said point-blank. "Now, are you going to stop us?"

Mansik attacked him with his stick. Chandol was much faster than Mansik; he dodged the blow and kicked Mansik in the abdomen with both feet at the same time. Mansik fell, covering his groin with his hands. Without giving him a chance, Chandol snatched the stick from Mansik and started beating him on his back and shoulders.

"I told you I'd hurt you," Chandol said between his clenched teeth.

"I want to beat him, too," Mansik heard Toad hiss.

"You stay there, Toad, and shut up," Chandol said, still striking. "I told you I'd hurt you! I told you I'd hurt you!" he repeated to Mansik.

"Kill him!" Jun urged. "Kill that son of a bitch! Let me beat him, too! He beat me the other night! Let me beat him, too!"

Chandol's attack was ruthless and overpowering. Shrinking into a ball like a porcupine, Mansik sustained the blows until Chandol, tired of fighting an unresisting opponent, decided that this was enough to teach Mansik a lesson. He finally threw away the stick and dusted the snow off his hands and knees.

"You listen to me and listen well, boy," Chandol said. "Now you *know* what I will do to you if you go against my wishes."

Mansik moaned; he had no strength left with which to say anything.

"From tomorrow night on, you will not come out here to watch us either, Mansik, because I don't like it," Chandol went on. "We're going home now, but you better not be around here when we come next time. Okay, Toad, let's go home."

Although he had gotten a sound thrashing without having a chance to return a single blow, Mansik felt strangely happy. The snow melted against his cheek and hands, but he remained sprawling on the snow for another full minute. When he recovered enough strength to raise himself, he realized he should go home right away to wash up so that his mother would not notice his bruises. Yet he did not rise from the rice paddy. Just lying there, his shoulders and ribs smarting and burning all over, he felt his heart overflowing with satisfaction. That nagging sense of guilt was completely gone, totally wiped out by Chandol's beating. He was neither sad nor worried by the first thought that occurred to him — the fact that he had made his choice, had become an outcast forever.

Mansik breathed slowly and deeply through his mouth. It tasted salty and he spat spittle mixed with blood. Pain began to leave his body slowly. Very slowly. And he began to cry although he was happy. He began to cry *because* he was happy. Sprawling on the snow, he wept peacefully.

EIGHT

As Sokku entered the room, Old Hwang raised the wick of the kerosene lamp a little higher and sat up, his shadow, silhouetted distinctly against the illuminated halo on the wall, like a sitting Buddha. "Sit down, son," he said.

Kneeling next to the door, Sokku wondered why he had been summoned by his father in the middle of the night. "Is there anything wrong, Father?" he said.

Old Hwang cleared his throat and said, "Han, the miller, came to see me early in the evening."

"I know, Father."

As the old man kept quiet without giving any further explanation, Sokku suspected his father was waiting for him to pose a question so that he would be politely forced to state what he was reluctant to say.

"What did the miller come to see you for, Father?" the son asked.

"He said he wants to leave," the old man said.

Kangho's family was going to be the first to leave Kumsan to seek refuge. Several families of Charcoal village had already left for the south but the Kumsan villagers had been delaying, for nobody liked to be conspicuously remembered, possibly for generations to come, as the first to flee in wartime. Now somebody had volunteered to be the cowardly first, and others would follow promptly.

"When did the miller say his family would leave?" Sokku asked.

"They'll pack their valuables tonight and depart before sunrise without saying goodbye to anybody. The miller seemed to be very ashamed of running away."

The old man and the son kept quiet for a while, avoiding each other's eyes. The father blankly gazed at the rice paper of the door which vibrated with the passing gusts of cold wind while the son stared at the flame flickering in the smudged glass ball of the lamp.

"The villagers are restless because the war is going unfavorably to the South," Young Hwang said to prompt their conversation.

The old man did not reply. Sokku believed his father kept silent because he had something serious to tell him which was too embarrassing to put into words. What matter could have been so urgent as to make his father wake and summon him to this room in the middle of the night?

At long last the old man opened his mouth and said enigmatically, "They have no other choice."

"About what, Father?"

"Taking refuge."

"Are you talking about the miller's family?"

The old man reflected briefly before he said, "And about others."

Sokku could not comprehend what his father meant. Maybe Father was simply telling him that he approved the villagers' wish to leave this land. Or—was it possible that Father also considered abandoning this place, the home of the Hwangs for generations, to take refuge? Sokku did not have a ready response and in the ensuing silence they avoided each other's eyes.

Sokku could understand as well as his father did the reason why

Kangho's father and some farmers, perhaps many of them, wanted to leave now. When the North first invaded the South in June they had felt no sense of danger and also the Communists had swept down too fast to allow them to escape. The whole situation was different this time. Even North Koreans, hundreds of thousands of them, were taking refuge in the south. The villagers worried about what harm might befall them if this land changed hands once more. They knew now that this side of the river was not a sanctuary. Like a herd of cattle, they might all stampede if someone started to run.

Considering what he had heard from the townspeople, Sokku was sure that the National Army and the U.N. Forces were losing the war very fast. A large-scale air raid had taken place over the northernmost Siniju area in early October to wipe out a massive force of Chinese troops concentrating there, but they said that the Chinese commanders had decided to deploy more troops along the Korea-Manchurian border after the American air attack on the bridge over the Yalu River to defend against an imminent American invasion of China. The most generally accepted conclusion was that the Yankees had a lot more cannons and airplanes and tanks than the Communists did, but the Chinese were overpowering them with awesome "Human Sea" tactics. There were simply too many Chinese soldiers to kill. Endless waves of Chinese troops had already recaptured the North Korean capital of Pyongyang. The National Army had retreated as far south as Hwanghae and Kangwon Provinces. And a detachment of North Korean soldiers, which had been isolated in the south during the fast advance north by General Megado's Army after the Inchon landing, were actively operating as guerrilla forces in the Taebaek Mountains. It was rumored that a detachment of these guerrillas from Hwachon had infiltrated the town to secure a foothold for an all-out future assault by the main Communist Allied Forces. Sokku knew, as most well-informed townspeople did, that they had to seek refuge before this year ended, if they were ever going to leave, for the Communists were planning a coordinated offensive for the New Year season. If Chunchon had really been designated by the Communists as one of the launching points of the New Year offensive, there was no doubt that the Chinese would be here in a matter of days.

The old man lit his bamboo pipe and said between slow puffs, "Village Chief Pae said the foreign soldiers will leave Cucumber Island soon."

"So I heard, Father," Young Hwang said. "They'll be all gone by the end of next week. About half of the prostitutes at Texas Town have already left for Osan and the rest of them will scatter to the southern towns where the Yankees are stationed."

"I guessed that was the reason why," Old Hwang murmured.

"What reason, Father?"

"That strange woman called Imugi came to see me the day before yesterday and asked me to buy the snake hunter's hut. She plans to move to Pusan, she said, and thought it was only proper to return the house to this village. She is a sly woman. We know she cannot stay here any longer but she pretended she is going away to do us a great favor, and she believed she deserved to be compensated for the hut."

"I hope you did not pay her."

"No. She begged for only half of the money she had paid. She even tried to flatter me. I couldn't believe this was the same impudent woman who insulted me so much."

Sokku was sure that his father had summoned him for something more important than exchanging this kind of small talk. "Do you have anything in particular to speak to me about, Father?" Sokku prompted.

The old man sat up erect, resting the brass bowl of the pipe on the stone ashtray. Staring at his son, the old man said, "We are leaving here, too."

"Leaving?"

Old Hwang nodded his head slowly.

"But do we have to? You are not healthy enough to travel in this cold weather, and I don't expect the Communists would harm us even if they come." In fact Sokku was not saying what he truly believed. He wanted to take refuge, and he was not sure if his family would be safe when the Communists arrived. "I believe the Hwangs should stay here to the last," he added.

"We have to go. We have a very good reason to."

"What reason, Father?"

"You know perfectly well the reason why we cannot live in this village any longer."

Sokku tried to guess what his father meant, but could not.

Finally, Old Hwang forced himself to say the words: "This house is no longer ours."

"What do you mean?" Sokku asked, surprised.

"I asked the miller to buy this house and he agreed. He made full payment."

Sokku had anticipated that this final blow would fall upon his family sooner or later but the sudden revelation shocked him. Although he did not want to acknowledge reality, he could now see the fall in plain sight. "Was Kangho's father willing to buy this house despite the fact that he has no idea when or whether he will return here?"

The old man said with a distressed sigh, "He was doing a favor for me. He did not even take the deed papers, saying I could reclaim the house any time I want in the future." He paused. "But I don't think we will ever come back here."

"Your determination to leave this village is final?"

Old Hwang nodded. "I think now is a very convenient time for us to leave," he said. "The villagers will never guess we're leaving for any other reason than the war."

"But you have to consider. . . ."

"There is nothing else to consider, son. The longer we stay here, the more shame we will have to endure."

The son kept silent.

"You'd better start packing secretly tomorrow," the father went on. "Pack only the most valuable things we will need for our future life in a strange land. We cannot take anything more than what we can carry on the oxen's back."

"Where do you plan to go when we leave here?"

"We should go as far south as we can."

"Even if we reach some safe place like Pusan or Mokpo, how can we earn our living?"

"We will manage somehow because I have some money. Besides the money I received from Han for this house, I also have the money I raised to buy back the snake hunter's hut after the harvest. Maybe we can open a small shop on a busy street somewhere."

Sokku was sad when he imagined his father selling candies or vegetables in a shop. The most humiliating degradation for a man of knowledge was to become a merchant. "When do you think we should leave, Father?" he said.

"Get ready as soon as possible. We will stay here no longer than five more days."

"I see."

"Now go back to your room and get some sleep."

Sokku raised himself. "Have a peaceful sleep, Father. You have to rest well before departing for the long journey."

"I know," the old man said.

When Sokku turned back to open the door, Old Hwang murmured in a low voice behind him, "I have a premonition that I will die in a strange land as a refugee. I hope you will move my remains to our family grave site when the war is over and bury me just below my father."

The small hill for the family graves was the last and only land left to the Hwangs in Kumsan.

Mansik fumbled in the abandoned water mill and lit the candle he had brought with him from home. He stood the candle on a wooden crate and pulled up the trap door of the secret armory. Dragging out the ammunition box he thought, I will stop them, I will stop them even if I have to kill them both. He opened the ammunition box and took out the pistol. The pipe, fixed tight on the wooden hilt with silk threads and rubber bands, glinted bluish in the candlelight.

Mansik did not hesitate. His mind was made up. Chandol and Toad were already at Dragon Lady Club to watch the rooms and Mansik knew this was the only way to drive them away.

He cocked the hammer of the pistol and loaded an empty M-1 cartridge shell with a live percussion cap into the pipe barrel. Turning his face away, he stretched his arm to thrust the pistol into the pile of straw to muffle the sound, and pulled the trigger. The percussion made a cracking sound. The pistol was working fine.

Mansik took a new empty M-1 cartridge shell, filled it with millet gunpowder, kneaded several pieces of snipped wire into the ball of molten candle wax, and mounted the wax ball on the open tip of the cartridge. He loaded the pistol with the cartridge. He put several live cartridges, a handful of gunpowder and the wire scraps into his pocket for possible future use, blew out the candle and left the water mill.

"It's killing me, oh, oh, it's just killing me," Chandol whispered between gasps, peering into Imugi's room.

"It's exciting over here, too," Kijun said in a choking voice, watching Mansik's mother playing with her *bengko*'s huge erection.

The boys watched both rooms since Mansik was not out on guard tonight. Holding his breath, Chandol peeked in at the naked *bengko*, mumbling something in a drunken voice, fondling the flattened breasts of Imugi, who kept kicking the air at his touch, as she sprawled on the floor displaying her wide open black hairy crotch. After several minutes of touching and sucking each other, she pulled the soldier onto her stomach and the Yankee began to pump his groin into hers. The woman began to moan.

Something poked Chandol in his back. He did not have to turn to know it was Mansik, but when he did Mansik was pointing the pistol at him. Kijun stood by the chimney, terrified. Although Mansik did not make any gesture this time, the three boys automatically headed for the hay stack.

When they stopped and stood facing one another, Chandol said, "I guess you need an extra lesson."

Aiming the pistol at the two boys alternately, Mansik stayed far enough from Chandol to avoid being attacked by a flying kick. "It's you who needs to learn a lesson," he said. "This is my last warning. If either of you come here ever, ever again, I won't hesitate one single moment to shoot you."

"Give me that pistol," Chandol said. "I knew you were a whore's son, but I didn't know you were a thief, too. Sneaking into our headquarters and stealing our weapon, you deserve to . . ."

"Stay there. Stay back! I'll shoot if you come any closer."

"Let's go home, Chandol," Kijun said. "Looks like he's gone crazy. He may really shoot us."

"Shoot us? You wouldn't dare, would you? Give me that pistol back if you don't want to be hurt really bad."

"No, you're not going to hurt me. Not ever again. I will keep this pistol and use it, too, when I have to. I have enough gunpowder and cartridge shells to kill both of you."

"Hand over the gun, I said."

"Stay away. Don't come closer!"

"Give me that pistol."

"Don't come closer!"

"You wouldn't fight me, would you?"

"Stay away!"

"Are you really going to fight me?"

Mansik pulled the trigger.

. . .

Mike and Fist Nose had come early in the evening, bringing strong Yankee liquor and juicy boiled meat for an advance Christmas party because they knew Camp Omaha would not remain on the islet until the holiday. A little while after the soldiers had gone into their rooms with Ollye and Sister Serpent, they heard the pistol shot. Fist Nose instantly stopped, and sprang to his feet. He snatched his helmet and underwear from the nail on the wall and dashed out to the hall to grab his carbine. Pulling on his shirt and shorts he charged out of the house and saw two dark figures fleeing toward the log bridge.

Sergeant Mike, still quite drunk, stumbled out of the other room with nothing on his naked body except the dog tag dangling on his hairy chest. He seemed to suddenly turn sober when he saw Fist Nose charge out of the Club with his rifle. He went back to the room and hastily put on his fatigues. He could not find his helmet anywhere and went out to the hall to get his rifle. In the confusion Ollye was still calm enough to gather her soldier's trousers and boots and hand them to Mike, saying, "Hubba-hubba, hubba-hubba." What she meant to say was that she wanted Mike to promptly take these things to Fist Nose, who was out in the snow barefoot with nothing on below the waist but his shorts.

When Sergeant Mike went out, Fist Nose was firing warning shots in the air. The rifle shots rang out against the silent sky and echoed somewhere in the distance. Yelling "Halt! Halt!" in *Migook* language, Fist Nose kept firing. The two fleeing persons apparently did not understand English, but one of them suddenly stopped in the middle of a rice paddy, raising his hands high, frightened by the rifle shots. Waving his hands wildly to show the soldier that he was surrendering, he shouted, "Help! Help! A *bengko* is shooting at me! A *bengko* is trying to kill me! Help!" The other one continued to run and vanished down the bank of the stream. When they heard Kijun shout for help, the soldiers realized the two fleeing persons were mere boys.

When Sergeant Mike handed the trousers and boots over to him, Fist Nose leaned his rifle on the wall of the Club and hurriedly put them on. Mike glanced over at the boy in the paddy, blubbering, with his hands high in the air. Then he began to run toward him.

Lights went on here and there in Hyonam, Kumsan and Castle villages, as the villagers woke up startled by the gunshots. Light also went on in the Paulownia House and the papered door opened. Old Hwang leaned out and looked around the village to see what was going on.

By the time Ollye and Yonghi dressed hastily and came outside, Fist Nose, shivering in the cold, was about to go back to get his field jacket when Mike, who was going after Kijun, found someone lying in the snow. He urgently beckoned the two women over.

"Your son Mansik!" Mike shouted. "Your son is here! He's hurt bad!"

Then he rushed across the rice paddies to grab Jun. Ollye, startled to hear her son's name, ran to him. Mansik was groaning painfully, and screaming briefly, jerkily.

"Mansik!" Ollye shrieked. "Mansik! What are you doing here? What happened? Mansik! Mansik! Who did this to you?" Embracing her son in a confused panic, she saw his right hand was mangled and bloody. "You're bleeding, Mansik. You're bleeding! What happened? What happened to your hand?"

Mansik kept groaning and weeping. Ollye lifted his hand and examined it by the moonlight. Mansik screamed again. He had only three fingers left. She felt his fingers one by one to make sure. There was no doubt; the index and the middle fingers were completely gone.

"What happened to your hand, Mansik? Where are your fingers? What happened?"

Fist Nose came out of the Club again and hurried over to take a look at the boy.

"Zippo!" Ollye asked him urgently. "Zippo! Give Zippo me! I wanna see hand my son."

Fist Nose fished the lighter out of his pocket. Either because her hands were trembling too much or because they were slippery with blood, she had to try five or six times until the lighter finally worked. She looked around for Mansik's lost fingers, holding the lighter over her head, but there were nothing but bloodstains in the snow. Fist Nose also searched around with his flashlight. He found a broken pistol on the ground nearby. He showed the crude handmade weapon to Ollye and she saw the pipe, bent from the explosion.

Mike came back dragging Kijun by the collar. When he saw Mansik's mother, the boy burst out with incoherent apologies and babbling excuses. "Honest, Mansik's mother, I was not watching alone. Chandol was with me, I swear, and it's Chandol who suggested coming here in the first place. I just came because he told me to come with him. And I never watched the real thing. I wouldn't have come to watch if Chandol hadn't told me to."

"What are you talking about?" Ollye said, puzzled. "What did you watch, anyway?"

Fist Nose examined the pistol and put it in his pocket. He checked Mansik's bloody hand and called Yonghi to tell her something very fast.

"It was all Chandol's idea," Jun went on. "I just followed him here, not knowing what he had in mind."

"Fist Nose says to take Mansik immediately to Cucumber Island and show his hand to the medic at the camp. Mansik needs emergency treatment, he says," Yonghi told Ollye.

Fist Nose slung Mansik over his shoulder and hurried down the bank to the frozen river.

"What did you watch?" Ollye asked suspiciously.

"You must go with the sarging, Sis. Hurry! You can talk to that fat boy later. Mansik is bleeding seriously. Come on. I said, hurry!"

"All right, Jun, you go home and wait for me. I want to talk to you when I come back."

"I swear, Mansik's mother, I haven't done anything wrong! I haven't watched anything."

"Hurry, Sis! The sargings are waiting!"

They went straight to Camp Omaha. Fist Nose and Mike explained to the MP guarding the main gate, showing him Mansik's bleeding hand. The MP called someone on the telephone and had a long discussion. Then he said something to Mike, shaking his head. Yonghi explained to Ollye that the two sergeants were trying to get emergency treatment for Mansik at the camp clinic but the MP would not let them pass.

"I think we should go to the town, Sis. The MP says no Korean civilian is permitted to enter the camp because of reports that some Communist guerrillas have infiltrated town."

Mike said, "I'm sorry," and disappeared into the camp, but Fist Nose, carrying Mansik on his back, went to Chunchon with the two women. Mansik's hand was wrapped completely in towels and clothes but blood still flowed from it, soaking the soldier's chest. Mansik did not groan any longer, but he wept on and off.

"Tell me what happened, Mansik," Ollye asked again as they crossed the bridge to the town. "Why was your hand injured? What did Kijun and Chandol come to watch? Did you have some trouble with them?"

Ollye kept asking the same questions over and over again but Mansik would not give any answers.

The doctor Yonghi took them to was none other than the gloating bespectacled man who specialized in curing the shameful diseases of the Texas Town girls. The fat doctor came out to meet them, frightened by the loud noise as the *bengko* soldier pounded the door fiercely with the stock of his rifle. When he saw the boy's hand, the doctor was infuriated; his sleep had been disturbed for nothing. "I don't handle this kind of patient," he said impatiently to Yonghi. "You know perfectly well what I handle, don't you!"

"But no other doctor is available," Yonghi said. "You're the only one who hasn't fled south yet."

"I am leaving here first thing in the morning," he said. "So, why don't you go to a horse doctor?"

249

Reluctantly, the doctor started dressing Mansik's hand, apparently intimidated by the ferocious frown of the armed *bengko*. The bloody stubs of the torn fingers looked more gruesome in the bright electric light. Terrified at the sight of his own destroyed hand, Mansik started to cry louder. Ollye's heart burned with rage.

"Tell me, Mansik, who did this to you? Why did this happen to your fingers?"

Shocked by the gory sight of his ruined hand, Mansik finally began to talk in snatches between sobs, "I wanted to kill that son of a bitch Chandol and I shot him. I shot him with the pistol because I wanted to kill him."

"Go on, tell me."

"I think the pistol was jammed. There was an explosion. The whole thing blew up in my hand."

"You mean the pistol burst in your hand? How come?"

"I don't know. It just happened."

"Why did you want to shoot and kill Chandol, anyway? What did he do wrong?" Ollye asked. "Kijun said he had come to the Club with Chandol to watch something. What is he talking about? Mansik, don't faint! Pull yourself together and tell me everything!"

Ollye kept quiet while the V.D. doctor was adjusting the sling for Mansik. She kept quiet while they were crossing the frozen river, Fist Nose carrying the boy on his back. Back at the Chestnut House, she kept quiet for a long time after the Yankee had returned to Camp Omaha, brooding and watching her son who tossed in his bed and groaned intermittently in his troubled sleep. Then she said to Yonghi in a very calm and collected voice, "Please stay here with Mansik tonight and look after him if he wakes up in pain. I have to go to see someone."

"You want to talk to that fat boy the *bengkos* caught at the Club?" Yonghi said.

"No," Ollye said. "I want to talk to the other boy."

"Why don't you see him in the morning? You already know the whole story now."

"I can't wait till morning."

When Ollye came outside, she saw the windows of the rice mill glowing with lamplight. She vaguely guessed that Kangho's family were still awake. She passed two more huts with glowing windows on her way to Chandol's house.

Ollye took a deep breath to compose herself at the gate and called out, "Chandol!"

There was no answer. When she called twice more, Chandol's mother asked, "Who is it?"

"It's me. Mansik's mother."

Somebody else, Chandol's father, grumbled in an annoyed voice, "What is that woman doing out there?"

"You get back to sleep, dear. I'll go out and see what's up this time."

It took a very long time for Chandol's mother to get dressed. Finally the door opened. She came out to the gate in her thick shabby sweater. She said, "Glad to see you."

This was a rather awkward greeting on the occasion of this strange, unexpected reunion of the two women, but neither minded such trivial deviations from decorum.

"Well, I guess. . . .," Ollye mumbled.

"I heard some noise and gunshots coming from—your shop over there," Chandol's mother went on. "Some of us went to the snake hunter's house to find out what was going on, but nobody was there when we got there. Was there anything up?"

"Nothing serious," said Ollye, peering into the house over Chandol's mother's shoulder. "By the way, is your boy in?"

"Of course he is. He's asleep in his room. Why?"

"I just wanted to make sure," said Ollye. "Was he home when you heard the shots?"

"Why do you ask me these questions?" Chandol's mother said, offended.

"Because I have a good reason to. And I want you to wake him up. I have to talk to your boy."

"Why do you want to see him at this hour?"

"Just let me talk to him. I want to ask him some questions."

"Can't you come back again in the morning?"

"No. I can't wait."

"I see," Chandol's mother said, hesitating. "Wait here." She went over to her son's room. She opened the door and fumbled in the darkness. "Chandol. Wake up, Chandol. Wake up." She shook the boy.

"Uh? Who is this?" Chandol said in an extremely sleepy voice. "What's up, Mom?"

"Wake up and come out to the gate. Mansik's mother came to see you."

"Who came to see me?"

"Mansik's mother."

"Why?"

"I don't know. Get dressed and come out."

"Okay, Mother."

Chandol also took an unbelievably long time to get dressed and come out to the gate with his mother. "What do you want?" he said in a displeased tone, looking up at her belligerently.

"I have something to ask you," Ollye said and then added, glancing at the boy's mother, "privately."

Chandol looked back at his mother, hoping she would stay, but she did not notice the faint plea for help in his eyes.

"Whatever business you have with my son, don't take too much time. Young boys need their sleep."

Chandol's mother went back to her room and Ollye took the boy to the alder tree grove by the road a little distance away from the house.

"Why did you fight with Mansik tonight?" she asked.

The boy glanced up at Ollye and said casually, "Fight with Mansik? What are you talking about?"

Ollye was dumbfounded by the boy's outright denial. She was speechless for a moment, wondering how to handle this boy.

"Mansik said he had fought with you."

"He did? That's very strange. I didn't fight with anyone. In fact, I never left my house after dinner. I wonder why he said that. Why would I have fought him?"

"You really didn't fight with Mansik?" said Ollye, wondering if there was any chance that this boy might be telling the truth. No, she thought, not a chance. "Mansik is badly hurt." Then she added, "His hand was injured when he shot you. He lost two fingers."

"But I haven't even talked to Mansik for three months, ever since that night when *bengkos* came to your house and, you know. . . ."

Now Ollye was appalled, a cold chill streaking through her spine; she was convinced that Chandol was deliberately lying with a well-planned scheme in mind. She suspected the boy was shrewdly leading this conversation. There was absolutely no reason for Mansik to lie to her. But this boy was so brazen that Ollye was intimidated.

While she was disconcerted, Chandol said matter-of-factly: "Well, if his hand got really busted, as you told me, Mansik might have fought with somebody. But not with me. Why don't you go ask him again?"

"This is impossible," she said, shaking her head. "I just can't believe that you're doing this. How can a boy like you be so wicked? It seems lying is easier for you than eating rice."

"This is not fair. You drag me out of bed in the middle of the night and accuse me of being the biggest liar in the world," the boy said impatiently. "You don't have any right to accuse me. It's Mansik who is telling a lie, if anybody is. Ask my mother, if you don't believe me. Ask her if she saw me leaving my room at any time tonight. How could I fight Mansik while I was asleep in my room?"

"Why on earth do you think Mansik would lie?"

"How do I know? Maybe he fought some other boy and got hurt but decided to tell everybody that he was fighting me."

"Why? Why should he lie?"

"Don't you see? He must have felt ashamed when he was beaten by someone who is considered one of the weaker boys in the village. That's the reason he named me. I'm always the scapegoat because I'm the strongest boy around. Nobody laughs if a boy says he was beaten by me in a fight. Kids kind of respect a boy who has enough guts to challenge *me* even if I beat him up. It's an honor rather than a shame for them to be beaten by me, see?"

"Stop it. I've had enough. I find you're perfect in inventing lies, perfect down to the tiniest details. Maybe what we need now is—"

"If you don't believe me, that's still okay with me. I told you the truth."

"*I* know what is the real truth. I know what you two—you and Jun— were doing at . . . over there. Mansik told me everything. He also told me why he shot you. He even told me that he once had permitted you to come and watch the room."

"Watch the room?" Chandol asked innocently. "Watch what room? I don't want to hear any more. I'm going back to sleep."

"No, Chandol boy, you're not going home until I'm finished. I won't let you go home until you tell me the whole truth."

"You won't *let* me go? Who do you think you are, anyway, to stop me? I can go any time I want to."

"Come here," Ollye said, gripping Chandol's arm.

"Take your hands off me, you dirty slut," the boy said viciously. "I don't like to have a whore touch me."

Stunned, she let his arm go. The boy turned to go home. Then she clutched his arm again.

"All right, you said it," she screeched. "Sure, I am a dirty whore. And what are you? What kind of a boy crawls to a whore's room in the dark of night to peep in?"

"You let me go," the boy growled, trying to wrench his arm free of her angry grip.

"Come! I want to show everybody what a horrible little monster you are."

"I'm not going anywhere with a whore!"

"Oh, yes, you will," she said, pulling him with both her hands.

"Where the hell are you taking me?"

"We will go to Jun's house. That boy certainly has something to tell the villagers about you."

"Let me go!"

They struggled, pulling and twisting and tugging.

"We will see who really is the dirty one," she said. "It's no use for you to try to play innocent. Kijun will tell us everything and we will hear what he has got to say about you in the presence of the whole village."

"You won't get anything out of Toad," Chandol spat hysterically. "You're a stupid fool if you expect him to tell you what you want to hear."

Ollye was struck by a suspicion that it would not help her a bit if she took Chandol to Jun. The two boys must have got together, she thought, and conspired against her while she was in town with Mansik. Chandol turned silent, realizing his tongue had slipped, but something irrevocable was already in progress. Now neither of them could turn back.

"You will come with me, anyway," she said resolutely, pulling him forward. "You will come with me and tell the village what has been going on."

The boy resisted. "Let me go, I said!" Chandol wrested his arm out of her grip but she deftly clutched his left wrist and collar at the same moment. He writhed, jerking his head this way and that, but she clung to him desperately.

"Come!"

"I'll kick you if you don't let me go."

"Go on," she rasped. "Kick, if you want to."

Chandol tried to butt her nose, shaking his head violently in all directions. Holding him from behind, she knew he was too wild for her to hang onto for long. But she kept on grappling with him, thinking of the two missing fingers on Mansik's hand, thinking of all the shame she had suffered while this little monster had been peeping at her through the window night after night, thinking she would rather die than let him go unpunished.

"Let me go!"

"Not until you tell the villagers what you have done," she said, dragging the boy out to the open road.

Chandol kept trying to butt her in the face. Her lower lip began to bleed. When she realized she was losing her strength and could no longer hold him down, she started to scream at the top of her voice so that everybody in the village could hear her.

"Listen, villagers! Wake up!"

The boy stopped fighting, astonished by her unexpected shriek. "What the hell are you doing?" he said. "Quiet. You're going to wake up the whole village."

"That is the idea," she said. "Wake up, villagers!"

"You're going to raise hell, you crazy bitch."

"Sure. You just watch. I'm going to show the whole world what kind of a bitch I am and what an ugly monster you are. Come on out! Come on out, everybody of Kumsan!"

The boy, frightened, looked around the houses where windows glowed as people turned on their lamps.

"Come on out and take a look at me! A whore is calling you! A crazy bitch is calling you all! I've got something here to show you. Come on out! Come on out!"

The first one who appeared outside was Chandol's mother, immediately followed by her husband. One after another the rest of the villagers trickled out of the huts and hovels.

"Come over here, villagers, over here! I have a cute little animal here with me to show you! Come, come this way."

Chandol's parents, surprised to see their child drooping guiltily from Ollye's hand like a chicken thief, rushed to Ollye to find out what was going on before any one else got there.

"What is this fuss all about?" Chandol's mother asked. "What are you doing to my son, Mansik's mother?"

"Step back," Ollye told her. "That's right. You stay away from us. You stay there until the other villagers come to hear what I've got to tell them."

"She's gone crazy, Mom. She's gone crazy and you must not believe what she is raving about."

"Raving?" Ollye said. "I am raving? All right, raving or not, listen to what I've got to tell you, villagers."

More farmers, some of them carrying kerosene lamps with tall glass chimneys, joined the spectators and formed a circle around the howling woman and the captive boy, asking one another in whispers and mutters what had caused this commotion.

"Everybody in Kumsan village knows that I am a whore. I became a whore a couple of months ago as you all know. Everybody despised me because I am a dirty woman and I found many scribblings on the walls describing me as a Yankee whore. I was too ashamed even to use the same boat with other decent West County people. I've become a shameless woman. And now I will behave like one. I've undergone all sorts of insults and humiliations, but were *you* all really so estimable that you could treat me that way?"

Old Click Beetle, stooping, drew his lamp to the boy's face, covering the top of the lamp chimney with his hand to keep the flame from flickering. The boy turned away, covering his forehead with his arm. The old man stepped back, nodding his head. "Yes, you were right," he said to the wizened farmer next to him. "It is Chandol."

"Of course it is Chandol," Ollye said, perspiring, her voice choking with fury. "And you want to know what this boy did to deserve this treatment? Do you know what this boy and Kijun . . . Is Kijun here by any chance? He and this boy have been prowling around the Club night after night peeping through the window at me while I was in bed with the soldiers. That's what Chandol and Kijun were up to."

Chandol, keeping his head low, stole a furtive glance at the crowd, some twenty of them by now, and then decided to act like an innocent child.

"What are these tears for, Chandol?" Ollye said with an almost bemused sarcasm. "Do you think you can buy me and these people with a few drops of water? Tell them the truth." She turned to Kangho's family. "They came to the riverside house again tonight to watch me and my friend play with the foreign soldiers. My son Mansik found them peeping in the rooms and tried to stop them. A fight started and Mansik had to fire his pistol at them."

The farmers began to murmur.

"What is she talking about?"

"Does she mean that the village boys went to watch her whoring with the *bengkos* every night?"

"What is this village becoming?"

"She said foul things to Rich Hwang last time, remember? And now she is after a young boy."

"She said Mansik shot Chandol with a pistol."

"Heavens! A village boy shooting another village boy!"

"You can expect anything when you have whores in your village. You just wait and see what will happen to us next. When the Communists come back, they'll kill everybody in West County because we didn't do anything to stop these women from offering themselves to the Yankees."

Ollye heard what they said about her and knew that nobody was on her side but she found herself unable to stop. She had to continue. She was not sure of the exact reason why she had to, but she had to. "Oh, you're wondering what I am talking about? I will tell you what I'm talking about if you want to know," she said. "Yes, the boys came to peep into our bedrooms every night. Whether you *want* to believe it or not, that is what has been happening." She kept screaming but she was not sure any more what the point was. "All right, some of you are wondering what this village is turning into. You really don't know what this village is turning into, do you? Well, *I* know. I've known all along what this village has been turning into. Do you want to know what I think about your village? I would tell you, but there are no words for what I would say." She was unable to use logic now. In fact she did not do much rational thinking as she talked; something other than consciousness, a more basic and instinctive voice in her mind compelled her to spit out her accumulated anger and resentment. She screamed on and on, hysterical, shedding torrential tears, not from her eyes, but from her heart. "And do you know what he, what that boy told me? He said he had never done such a thing. This liar not only denied his own lie, but tried to make a liar out of me, too!"

Chandol was crying harder.

"This boy was confident that I would find it impossible to prove to you or anybody what he had done. And he called me a crazy woman. He said no one would believe me if I accused him. He said I should keep my hands off him. He called me a bitch, a whore, and a crazy woman!"

"He seems to have said all the right things," said Chandol's mother. "What else can you call a whore but a whore?"

She stepped out and jerked Chandol toward her by the wrist. Ollye did not try to keep Chandol beside her. Chandol, hugging his mother by the waist, burst into the loudest cry he could give.

"Is it true?" Chandol's mother asked, her voice trembling with indignation. "Did you really go to the Imugi House every night to watch the whores?"

Chandol wept, stalling.

"What this woman is telling the villagers—is it true, my boy?" the mother said.

Chandol wept, thinking.

"It is not true, is it?" the mother said.

Ollye turned speechless at this woman's blatant prompting of her son to deny the truth. The villagers looked on curiously to see how Ollye would react to the question, rather than to find out the answer.

Chandol's mother repeated, "Tell me, Chandol, it is not true that you went to the Imugi House to watch the whores, is it? I don't believe you or Kijun did such a thing."

Chandol stopped crying.

"Tell these neighbors that Mansik's mother has been lying about you," Chandol's mother said.

Chandol said finally, "I've never gone near that house ever since *bengkos* started coming there. We used to go there often before the war to watch the snakes, but I've never been there since."

Ollye felt her knees might give way any moment. You cannot trap a liar with truth, she thought.

"Did you hear that, Mansik's mother? Did you hear what my son said?" Chandol's mother repeated. "My son says he's never been near that house, much less peeped in the rooms. What were you trying to do to my family? Why did you wake up the whole village and accuse my innocent child in front of them? What terrible wrong did anybody in my family do to you to deserve this public humiliation?"

The onlookers, who had accepted the boy's denial with silence, began to murmur again, a few of them openly sympathetic to Chandol's family. Ollye was tongue-tied. Then a shout rang out from the outer circle of the crowd:

"What a great show you folks are putting on!"

It was Yonghi who had been watching the whole thing for quite some time.

The crowd turned their faces to her and several of them stepped aside as Sister Serpent approached Chandol's mother menacingly. Yonghi stood firmly before her, bristling up like a rooster in a cockpit.

"So you think Ollye is wrong for calling your innocent boy a criminal, ha?" Yonghi said. "You claim that she is humiliating a nice innocent family for no reason at all. I've been watching what's been going on in this village and you really made me puke. Sure, we—Ollye and me—are dirty whoring bitches as you and your angelic child said, but I see a lot more stinking characters around here who are worse—much worse—than Mansik's mother or any other whore."

She looked Chandol's mother in the eyes. "You're trying to convince these hypocrites that this filthy scum, your son, is an innocent victim of a whore's lies, aren't you? You want to tell the whole world that nothing like what your son did ever happened. But I was there when the shooting started, I was there to see the two boys running away. We caught one of them, a fat boy, and the other boy managed to escape. And I heard what that fat boy said about the other boy who got away—about this innocent child, this Chandol. Yes, I know what the two boys had been doing there. Tell me, why do you think the Yankees opened fire? Do you think they were hunting ducks in the winter night? What do you think they shot at? At your innocent cunt?"

"Listen to that!" Chandol's mother screamed. "Did you hear that, villagers? A whore speaks like a whore. Please somebody do something to shut that bitch up!"

"Bitch? Do you think I am a bitch?" Yonghi's voice became shrill. "All right, I will show you what a real bitch behaves like."

Yonghi attacked Chandol's mother, her ten sharp enamelled fingernails, like cat's claws, raking across that snub-nosed face. The startled villagers pulled the two grappling women apart, but the damage had been done already; Chandol's mother had several scratches across her face. The two women charged each other again, floundering amid the snatching hands and loud voices. Everybody shouted to everybody else to calm down but nobody calmed down. While the farmers and the village women and the two prostitutes were attacking, pulling, pushing, howling, shrieking, swearing, brandishing their fingernails, raising dust, waving their lamps and tumbling one upon another, someone in the rear said that Old Hwang was coming.

The commotion abruptly subsided. Nobody wanted the old man to see them involved in such an incident. Yonghi and Chandol's mother let each other go and stood aside; Yonghi's hair was in a tangle while

Chandol's mother was bleeding from several more new scratches on her dusty face. Groaning painfully, Ollye staggered up from the ground, her whole body trampled by the villagers during the riot.

Old Hwang and his son stood by themselves in the road, a few steps off from the guilty crowd. Sokku checked their faces one by one with his military flashlight.

"What is the meaning of this untimely row?" Old Hwang asked.

But the old man's attitude did not show an intention to pass judgment as to who was in the wrong or who should be punished. Strangely, he no longer sounded like the leader of the community; rather, his reproach sounded like a casual remark, as if he was inquiring about the situation as a mere traveler passing through the village. In response to the detached attitude of the old man, the villagers kept silent. Yonghi, who still hoped to sell the house back to the old man, also became silent. Ollye remained in the center of the crowd, lost, as if she had forgotten her next line and could not think of anything to say instead.

Chandol's mother finally ventured to explain her position. "That—" she said, pointing to Ollye, "that woman came to my house at this late hour and dragged my son out of bed to make a preposterous—"

"I do not want to hear your explanation," the old man interrupted her. "Go back home, Ollye. If you speak more in anger now, it will only breed resentment and regret in your heart and in others' too. What is the use of all this anger and hatred when every one of us knows only too well that we will soon leave home to take refuge and be scattered. Don't you think this war has brought enough hate and fighting among us? We have had enough of ill feelings for one generation. Now everybody go home. The day will break soon."

But Ollye was not willing to leave. Her accusation had been stopped short and she wanted to finish what she had intended to say to the villagers. She began, "But Mansik lost two fingers. Chandol is a liar, Kijun is a sneak and a liar. They are both cowards. Worst of all, their parents encourage this, encourage them to bully the weak and scorn the unfortunate. Because of me . . . because of what happened to me. . . ." She looked at old Hwang, then at the throng of villagers. "Now you will see, all of you, who will help *you* in your time of need. You will see, soon enough."

"No more, Ollye, no more. Do not put this burden upon me," Old Hwang said.

Ollye skipped a breath. Since the unfortunate accident, she had not heard Old Hwang speak her name in such a gentle voice. Was it some sort of new beginning? Might he have decided to permit her to return to what she had been? This thought brought her sadness rather than relief. She knew no return was possible now.

NINE

Ollye and her two children joined the procession of refugees streaming south carrying everything they could load on their heads and backs and shoulders, parents holding their young children's hands. Most of them traveled on foot with only a few bundles and packages, but some others, the wealthier countryside landowners, could take along with them much more family property such as sewing machines and chests of drawers on their farming carts and ox-wagons and the backs of their cattle. Abandoning their houses, hometowns, neighbors, some older members of their families and all the things they had cherished but could not take with them, they ran for their lives, not knowing where they would go or how they would survive. They left their homes hoping the war would pass and they could come back soon, but nobody was sure when the war might end—or if it would ever end.

Ollye glanced back over her shoulder at the northern sky whenever she heard the occasional muffled booms of artillery somewhere not too far behind the refugees. The sounds of war chased them, and came closer and closer as the days passed. Now and then she sat down with her children on the roadside on clumps of dead grass to rest her tired legs and watched the countless men and women, children and old people— all strangers—who were going the same way she went with the single purpose of fleeing from the war. Babies traveled on their mothers' backs, sometimes two babies on one mother, but most boys and girls older than five had not only to walk on their little legs but to carry their own small share of the load, a bag of rice or a roll of quilt. They trudged on and on, night and day, to the south, everything needed for their survival packed into various sizes and shapes of bulging bundles, strapped onto human bodies like giant warts.

Again in her farming clothes of loose pants and *chogori* vest with sagging sleeves, Ollye looked like any other countryside housewife, although she had her hair permanented like a modern city woman. Nanhi, completely covered with cotton-stuffed clothes and wrapped in a baby quilt, traveled most of the way on her mother's back. Mansik plodded on behind Ollye, a large bundle of clothes on his back, holding in his arms the rooster that he once had tried to train to attack.

Ollye had joined the procession of refugees on an icy morning four days earlier. The previous night she packed some clean clothes, cooking utensils, the few valuable things Mansik's father had left her, the Zenith radio and the camera and some other Yankee PX goods left over from black market trading. Ollye knew those *bengko* goods, along with the handful of bank-bills neatly folded into small squares and hidden deep in her bosom, would be of a great help to her in surviving. When she crossed the frozen river the next morning to join the refugees, the war nomads, milling around on the road, she had some consolation in thinking that her family would survive a lot longer than most of these people.

When Ollye left Kumsan, only a few families remained in the village. Old Click Beetle had decided not to leave home because "Nobody on either the Communist or the Yankee side would bother to waste a bullet to kill a worthless old man like me." Pae, the village chief, and his family were busy packing at the last moment; the Paes did not want to go away leaving their aged parents behind alone, but their decision was prompted by the fearful rumor that the Communists had killed all the families of South Korean policemen and soldiers during the last invasion and that this time even the petty officials like village chiefs would be executed. "We have lived long enough," Pae's father said. "But you must stay alive to lead the family." Other families had not yet decided whether they should leave, risking the hard refugee life in a strange place or stay home, risking the possible atrocities of the Communists.

Most families had not thought or argued much as to whether they should go or not. As soon as the word got around that the Hans of the rice mill had left the county secretly at dawn without saying goodbye to anybody, the other families immediately started packing. Soon the village was virtually deserted. Ollye found nothing suspicious about the secret flight of the miller and his family; it was natural for them to be ashamed, for they were the first family to run away, after all. But she could never understand why the Hwangs had also fled secretly like criminals the next night.

Ollye left the village later than most because she had to wait for Mansik's injured hand to heal. Leaving the desolate village behind, she crossed Cucumber Island for the last time. The skeletons of Texas Town and Camp Omaha were dead and buried under white snow. Looking around the ruins of Camp Omaha, looted by the townspeople and the West County farmers after the departure of the Yankees, she had a strange illusion that she was facing her own grave. One whole phase of her life was buried there in the snow and she was leaving for a new beginning, for better or for worse, in a place she did not know.

In the town she mingled with the countless refugees surging south like a human river. A young boy wiping tears from wet eyes with the soiled back of his frozen hand, a stooped old man carrying six apple crates stuffed with clothes on his A-shaped wooden back-carrier, a woman in her fifties leading five children in a row like a mother duck swimming in a pond with her ducklings, a little girl playing alone with dirt on the road and the grownups hurrying by without even glancing at the lost child, a boy with white scabs on his head, an ancient woman cooking rice in a military mess-tin in a roadside vegetable patch, a baby with a cardboard canopy hooding her face like a box mask to protect her tender skin from cold winds, a boy limping with frost-bitten feet, children with shaven heads, a weeping old woman . . . Swept along by these people, Ollye walked south day and night with her two children.

"Mother, where are we going, anyway?" Mansik asked her when they were one day away from Chunchon.

"Well, I don't know exactly." This was the best answer she could give. "Everybody is going south, so I guess we have to go south too, if we want to save our lives."

Although she was not sure where they were heading, Ollye had an odd premonition that her family would eventually find themselves in Pusan, the port city at the southeastern tip of the peninsula, the only big city that had not been taken by the People's Army during the initial Communist offensive. Leaving for the south with Sundok and two other U.N. ladies of Texas Town before the *bengko* unit moved to Osan, Sister Serpent had asked once more, for the last time, if Ollye would like to join her later in Pusan. "Just come to Bichuku and they'll tell you right away where you can find me. We cannot do any more whoring business together because I understand you're determined not to continue this kind of life, but you surely will need Imugi's help if you want to settle down and get started in Pusan. So, be sure to look for me if you ever set foot in Pusan, okay?" she had said.

White breath steaming out of her mouth like puffs of smoke, one morning Ollye asked her son abruptly, "You hated me because I was a U.N. lady, didn't you?"

Mansik nodded his head yes. He did not need to think because his answer had been ready in his mind for a long time. Mansik had hated not only his mother but the *bengkos*, the neighbors, the Kumsan boys and virtually everything related to that village. That was why he did not hesitate to admit that he had hated his mother. But he realized instantly that something was different now and that he should have thought for a moment or two before giving that spontaneous nod. Plodding in the stream of refugees with the rooster in his arms, Mansik looked back over shoulder in the direction of his home, several days away over so many hills. Mother had not told him definitely where they were going, but he was sure they would never go back to Kumsan. "We cannot return home even if we want to," Mother had said while crossing the Soyang River. Her voice made him suspect that she still retained some attachment for the land of her birth and young womanhood. Mansik was different. He was happy to be free from the cursed place, and he would never, never go back, even after the war was over. But his feelings had been changing without his knowledge. He had come to believe that all the hatred which had consumed him belonged to Kumsan. Out here in the cold, Mansik did not need his hatred. What was the use of hatred, after all?

His resentments no longer burned in his heart, for Kumsan itself had ceased to exist. The Chestnut House, Dragon Lady Club, Aunt Imugi, Chandol and Toad, Kangho and Bong, the gravekeeper's hearse shed, and General's Hill had vanished from his world. The past was gone. He would never meet his friends again, and he would never fight in another Autumn War with the Castle village boys. Recalling the young boys of the two villages roaring and cheering and throwing stones in the autumn field, Mansik had a queer feeling that he had become a grownup overnight. The Autumn Wars of West County were over for good and he was now in the grownups' war, a war that went on too long because the grownups wanted to fight in all seasons.

If the legendary general had come galloping on his silver stallion in time, there would have been no need for the *bengkos* to come to liberate them. If the *bengkos* had not come to West County, he would have had no reason to hate his mother. . . .

Mansik finally opened his mouth to say, "But not any more."

"Not any more what?" said Ollye, who had forgotten what she had asked her son.

Mansik did not explain. He did not feel any need to tell her about his feelings.

"Oh, that," said Ollye, understanding belatedly. And she did not say anything further. She gazed for a moment at Mansik's hand, the hand that had only three fingers left to hold the rooster. Then she turned her eyes to the south again.

They walked and walked, but there was no end to the procession of the refugees. Sleeping uneasily crammed in with strangers in the dirty rooms of abandoned houses, following the flow of the strange faces along the roads and through the villages with unknown names, sometimes mingling with the retreating military vehicles, passing through the ruined towns and streets, listening to the howitzers that sounded closer and closer, glancing at the bodies of those who had starved or frozen to death on the road, watching the dreadful landscape of war, Ollye and her two children trudged farther and farther away from home.

Mr. Ahn was born in Seoul in 1941. He studied literature at Sogang Jesuit University, then worked as reporter, columnist and editor at the English-language *Korea Times* and *Korea Herald*. He has published three novels and has translated nearly a hundred books into his native language. His first work to appear in English was *White Badge* published by Soho Press in 1989 in the author's own translation, as is *Silver Stallion*.